Two Moons of Merth

Ruth Mitchell

Reviews for
Two Moons of Merth

Ruth Mitchell stunned her readers with her previous paranormal adventure, *Beyond*. Ruth's latest adventure, *Two Moons of Merth*, will keep you glued to an exciting quest story of a young peasant woman, Aadya, as she seeks and earns the respect and dignity of the men of Merth. And when Aadya is faced with her greatest challenge, will she succeed or meet with calamitous ruin? – Charles Templeton, author of *Boot: A Sorta Novel of Vietnam*

Two Moons of Merth is a compelling story. There are elements of Margaret Atwood in the storyline but I was also reminded of a bit of Haruki Murakami's work – Daniel Krotz, author of *Not Dead Yet*

Mitchell's *Two Moons* takes us to a parallel galaxy where abundant action and a dramatic love story are peppered with names of animals and objects as imaginative and humorous as those of Lewis Carroll. It is a very entertaining adventure for fantasy readers. – Dan Morris, author of *Beef and Peaches*

Ruth Mitchell delivers another intriguing and quick-paced read, this time in the fantasy genre. In *Two Moons of Merth*, readers meet the royal Karda family, Aadya and

Poma, and their valiant children, Ali, Galen, and Roark, and are captivated by the discoveries of kinetic sight, and the prophecies of an omniscient and magical orb. We follow these beloved characters through their many travails and celebrations in this multi-generational tale about destiny, family loyalty, tribal conflicts, and female empowerment – Deirdre Fagan, author of *Find a Place for Me*

Acknowledgements

This book is dedicated to every strong woman who has touched my life, especially my mother and my eldest sister, Elly, both of whom are now gone. They have been pivotal in my development as a human being; and to Cecelia, Erin, and Stephanie, who are the light of my life. My Granddaughters Allison and Riley, who are about to embark on their own adventures into the world, are my eyes to the future.

I would like to thank outspoken women like Gloria Steinem, Susan B Anthony and all the women who demonstrated peacefully on the grounds of the White House, to secure the vote for women. Where would we be without the female giants, Ruth Bader Ginsberg, or Eleanor Roosevelt?

Literature has always been a huge part of my life. I learned from the best— the Austen sisters, Mary Shelley, Maya Angelou, Margaret Atwood, Toni Morrison, Eudora Welty and countless other women who brought voices to the voiceless, freedom to the enslaved, and redemption to the victimized. Of particular assistance in making this book what it is, I would like to thank Dierdre Fagan, Charles Templeton, Wendy Taylor Carlisle and Sarah Jennings.

Foreword

When I first set out to write *Two Moons of Merth*, I wanted to portray women on a completely different backdrop than what we call reality. This made a fantasy novel located on another planet just the right venue.

Two Moons of Merth is an enchanted, mythic tale of the royal Karda family with feminism undertones. It has the high adventure of the *Tales of Robin Hood* with the underlying themes one might find in a Margaret Atwood novel. It is a new mythology for a feminist age. All the colorful characters are intended to draw you into their story and perhaps leave you asking yourself questions.

Literature has always had the capacity for us to explore topics in a non-threatening way, and that is the intent of *Two Moons of Merth*.

I hope you enjoy meeting Aadya, Poma; their children Galen, Ali, and Roark. Even their enchanted horses have a part to play in this story of women and men struggling to advance their people toward a better way of life.

Book I

1-Beyond this Point

I look out across the verdant gap and see below me an aquaphor set into the undulating hills, like a dark blue gemstone, in the deep cut of the valley. I am here to let go of my angst and become joyful again. The source of my pain, which has left me sleepless for several rotations, is a comment my uncle made in front of the tribal committee, shaming me for my bold behavior.

I watch as my companion dogs Jefa and Moh sniff and wander back and forth on an elusive scent. They were my father's warrior dogs, the only thing I have left of him. They serve as a constant reminder of when he was still alive, and are a deep comfort to me this day with my task at hand.

As I have been taught, I take my hands and mold the air in front of me symbolically gathering my troubles, into a small ball, as if they are clay. I mash, and press, and roll my palms together until I have pressed the imaginary burden into my fist, which I then open and flatten. This is my symbolic pain which I blow with great force into the wind. With my difficulties cast, they are buffeted like the floater seeds on the lion's breath weed.

I exhale heavily, letting out more breath than I take in. Another healing breath and I commend myself for my wisdom. But not all the work is done, I must face my uncle, and not defend my actions, but stand tall in light of them. In times past, my mother would comfort me, but she's no longer with us. I must guide myself now even though I'm *not of age to legally be on my own. My thoughts are stolen as my dogs, still heavy with matted winter coats, pick up the scent of an impressive buck running through the woods.*

The earth trembles as this massive animal drives toward me, his hooves pound deep into the soft earth. I hear his breath rasping through his powerful nostrils as I dive out of his way or be trampled! Picking myself up off the forest floor and brushing off the leaves, I wonder. Was this an omen from the One True God? My leggings are damp with mud I scrape off with a stick.

I must leave the solace of this sacred place. The surrounding woods comfort me as I walk the long trail home. Tonight, I have another chance to prove myself before the council. I want them to look at me, not as a breeder, but as someone worthy to carry the staff of guidance once I have reached the age of maturity, which is in less than a half of a revolution away now. My inner voice continues to push for and to seek the power appropriate for my intelligence. Perhaps this is what has threatened my uncle.

I can barely remember my father who was lost in the war zone nearly eight revolutions ago. Even back then he sensed something special about me and spoke of my responsibilities to become a leader. "Aadya, you are born to show others the way," he would often say.

It would be more comforting if we knew my father had died for certain. His body was never recovered, leaving us, his family, without closure. He was last sighted fighting with vengeance at the battle of Watongga.

Life has been difficult for us since then. Mother held on for a few years, but it was as if the torch in her soul had been unmercifully smothered. Once my mother left us for the one and only heaven, my brother Jubal, as if following her into unknown territory, shifted, becoming a shadow himself. Under normal circumstances he would follow in my father's footsteps and become a tribal leader, but that would never happen now, the way Jubal spends his days gathering the abundant toku leaves. Smoking them gives him daydreams and he stays in his own enclosed world. It causes me great sadness to see him this way.

Grandmother Woku, my mother's mother, is now my only trusted guide. She helps me to see and understand how I must seek purpose and joy. She is resolute I should live each day without considering the past, unless it is to be aware of dangers which affect my survival. It's easier to talk about living and accepting the joy, but my mind wanders to greater times yet unlived.

For now, I have my dogs and my friends, mostly boys, whom I choose carefully. I do not know where this intense desire to lead comes from, but it is like a thunderous fire burning inside me. My name is a clue to my future. My warrior father named me Aadya, which means beyond this point.

2-Hunger

The dogs bark, bringing Aadya's focus back. She stops in her tracks to observe and notice the leaves along the path rustling. She raises her bow. If the dogs stir up another beast, she is ready this time. While her main objective is not to bring home food, it is always a present need.

"Do not shoot. Please do not shoot me." Out of the woods walks her friend Poma. Jefa growls and Moh approaches him cautiously his tail slightly wagging as if to say, 'you are not accepted until you prove yourself.'

"What are you doing here friend?"

"They said you headed out this way."

"Who did? I didn't tell anyone where I was going."

"Your grandmother thought you might be out here. Anyway, I have brought you lunch, and then I thought we could go swimming."

Aadya smiles hesitantly. Since she met Poma, at a gathering of several villages a few moons back, he has made numerous excuses to see her.

"What are you doing way out here anyway?"

His question makes her chest tighten. *That is none of his business. I do not wish to concoct a false story.*

"I..."

"Okay you do not have to explain yourself," he tells her raising his hand in a peace-making gesture.

"I should ask the same, why are you here?"

"Looking for you," Poma's smile spreads across his youthful face like a beam of light.

She relaxes a bit when he says this. "What have you brought to eat?"

"Hmm, I have several delicacies," he says peering into the leather pouch hanging over his shoulder. "A tart fruit pie, some cheese, and fresh berries I picked on the way."

"What, no meat?"

He stops abruptly and peers curiously at her. "I believe it is I who have brought the provisions; share only if you like, and no complaints please."

"I am sorry. It was not my intent to be rude. But how can you stay strong without protein?"

"Oh, I stay strong," he says flexing his arm muscle to show her. "I am not comfortable killing another animal, but I will eat it if it is properly prepared by someone else."

Her frown resurfaces. "That is laughable, how can you not eat meat?"

His shoulders droop slightly, and she decides to drop the topic as he turns and points the way up the path. "Come this way," he says pushing back some branches. "I will show you a place to swim you might not know about."

When they arrive at the bank of the water, it is difficult not to be hypnotized by the sunlight dancing on the surface, like some omniscient being has cast sparkling sand upon it, but more dramatic is the nearby waterfall, pouring off a precipice of rock in a solid sheet. Poma does not hesitate to strip off his clothes and jumps in with a joyful "whoop de doop!"

Aadya's eyes are as big as friendship stones as she witnesses the stark-naked Poma flying through the air. The only male in her house is her brother Jubal and she has never seen him without his clothes.

"I did not know we were going bare!"

"Come on in, do not be shy," he beckons with a wave of his arm.

A warrior should not be shy. I am more than a breeder! There is no shame in my female body. Taking a big gulp of air, she strips off her clothes fearlessly. She is too innocent to understand the impact of the sight of her perfectly proportioned body on her swimming mate. She jumps in quickly where the cool waters at once provide cover from her nakedness.

"Aye missle frap!" She curses.

Poma dances in the water as gracefully as if he were half sea mammal hoping to entertain her, but he cannot avert his eyes from Aayda, who now has his full attention. He pauses and heads in her direction as if propelled by some powerful undercurrent. He cannot stop himself from pulling her close, careful only to touch her arms. Even this is enough to cause Aadya to shiver with the intensity of a blue movil moth's fluttering wings.

"What are you doing?" Her weak protest baffles her, and once she catches the scent of his breath, she is triggered to move in closer. Their bodies connect buoyantly in other places gently at first, and then with a growing velocity. Aadya instinctively pulls back. "What is happening here?"

"I do not know for certain," he says with a perplexed smile on his face. "What do you want to happen?"

She is not ready for this close encounter and sees regret leach into his face.

"So, let us eat," she says. "I'm famished." When Aayda reaches the bank, she grabs her soft leather tunic and puts it on first, holding it close to her chest. Poma, now transfixed, is helpless to divert his eyes, knowing all the while he should.

Drying off and dressing, Poma pulls out the provisions from his knapsack.

Aadya aches with hunger.

"Where did you find such rich cream to make this cheese?" She feels insatiable as she puts each bite carefully into her mouth.

"I did not make the cheese myself; it is just something I got out of our kitchen," he explains.

Puzzled she decides to accept his words for now, and to learn more about this foolish but intriguing boy.

3-The Kill

Having devoured their lunch, Aadya and Poma laze in the sun together along the mossy bank not saying a word. The piercing light, from the nearest star, Philotus, filters through the trees overhead and dances upon their nubile bodies. Finally, Poma fidgets and sits up. "Did you hear that?"

"No, what is it?" Aadya looks around with the eyes of a predator.

"Over there in the meadow, I see something moving."

What keen hearing and sight this boy has for someone who does not hunt. She carefully picks up her bow to ready herself for the unexpected, but still does not see or hear what Poma has noticed. She whistles, signaling the dogs to chase and circle; bringing the prey back around to where she crouches in tall weeds. The mud-soaked dogs, with their tongues dripping, abide her command happily, springing up, and challenging the stillness of the afternoon with their morbid howls of alarm.

Aadya searches the horizon, and then she sees it, an enormous buck pounding toward them, moving fast. She will only have one chance to strike. She looks over at Poma who has come to the woods without a weapon, *strange boy.*

She stands erect and pulls her bow taut, letting it go before she has a chance to second-guess her aim. Her hours of practice serve her well because the arrow lands firmly in the animal's chest, possibly making it to the heart for a quick kill. As she watches the noble beast tumble, she lets out her breath, held captive to steady her aim.

"Whooo!" Poma leaps to his feet. His enthusiasm charges her with self-confidence, which she channels by delivering instructions.

"We will have to make a sledge to carry the meat back to the village. Can you help me?"

"Of course," he says giving her a slight bow of respect. "I am at your service."

He may not be a hunter, but he must understand the importance of a kill for many people who would eat of this meat for the next week.

The hike back, with the heavy burden of the animal, would be exhausting. Aadya decides to field dress the meat and pack it with the cool, moist moss prevalent on the bank of the swimming hole. She considers, if they do not tarry, they might make it back before nightfall, and if so, they would have more helpers to get the meat strung up for drying.

With Poma's help, Aadya lays the massive buck on its back. *Could this be the same beast which almost ran me over earlier?*

She pulls out her massive knife, forged by her father, which she always wears in a scabbard at her waist. Starting at the point above the genitals, Aadya makes a shallow incision pulling back the soft, cream-colored belly hair. She then cuts through to the internal organs and pulls them out in handfuls of bloody globs. The slithery intestines wriggle in her hands. She tosses the entrails to the dogs, who wait patiently, saving the heart, which she will wrap carefully in moss. Aayda looks up at Poma whose handsome face teeters between horror and fascination.

"I have never heard of a warrior who did not eat meat," she admits, hoping her inquiry will pull more information out of her companion.

"And, I have never seen a breeder kill and dress an animal before." Horrified by his words, Aadya tries to suffocate the heat of her anger rushing to her temples, neck, and face. "What did you say? What an ass you are, I am not a breeder!"

As equally surprised as Aadya is angry, Poma is startled by her language. "I apologize did I offend you?"

"You most certainly did!" She tries not to lash out, but cannot contain her anger. "What if I were to refer to you as a buck?"

Poma cannot suppress the grin now spreading across his face. "I should assume most males, of our species, would be thrilled by such a moniker." Realizing his error, he stumbles with a comeback to ease the tension. "But I do see what you are saying."

At the point where Aadya senses he has done his best to hear her, she does her best to shake off her anger. "Here, bring the sledge and help me load him. We need to take him to the water and rinse him out." Poma complies, but a blanket of silence, like a low-lying fog, has settled in around them.

Using her heavy blade, Aadya creates a sturdy pole on which to hang the massive animal for carrying, but as they hoist it onto their shoulders, it is evident the difference in their heights will be an issue.

"Okay, little one. Are you ready?" he says playfully.

Aadya frowns begrudgingly. It happens to be the same pet name her father had once called her. She cannot think clearly as long forgotten emotions swamp her focus.

Poma lowers his end of the staff to his waist, not waiting for her verbal confirmation, and curls his arm around the staff, grasping the leather belt at his waist for reinforcement. This makes the carcass hang much lower, so they will have to frequently adjust on uneven ground. With Aadrya carrying her end on her shoulder, it balances the burden of the beast slightly more toward Poma's end.

Poma's attempts to bring levity back into play, goes unrewarded until he finally shares an admission with Aadya.

"I apologize. I must admit, I have not disclosed my station to you in my tribe." He does not completely turn around but keeps his eye on the path. "I am of the Karda family. Others in my tribe serve my family, doing everything for us, and in return we lead them using our kinetic vision, which through the generations has grown stronger. Like an animal of the forest, we see things others cannot."

This explains a lot. Whereas before she had thought he was a bit of a dufus, Poma now appears taller, smarter, and more interesting.

"Do not ever refer to me as a breeder again. Do you understand? I, too, am born to a destiny beyond what others envision for themselves."

Keeping his stride going, Poma turns and smiles at her momentarily, awkwardly, balancing the weight of the carcass. He is looking a little confused but eager to please. When he turns back to watch where he is going, delight boils up inside of Aadya, and fills her face with pride she is grateful he cannot see.

4-Much to Learn

As they near Aayda's little village of Acuna, Poma and Aadya are greeted by a handful of children, from knee high to half-grown who have nothing better to do for entertainment than follow them, watching every move they make. Aadya herself is barely older than some of their entourage.

"What were you doing with the prince?" One of Aayda's friends asks her the following day.

"Prince? He's no prince, he's actually kind of useless."

Tayo giggles. She is one of the few female friends Aayda has. "No, my friend, he is prince, of all the realms, and will one day be crowned king."

Aayda winces. *What he told her was only a half-truth then.* "Are you sure?"

"Yes, I'm sure. You of all people should know, with your desires to be a tribal leader."

How the warriors leave me in the dark about many things. I will have to listen harder and build stronger bonds with those who can help me achieve my goals. I will have to approach uncle outside of the council and let him know how earnest I am.

"Aadya, the only reason we allow you into the council is because your father is gone, and Jubal is not suitable to represent your family. Just be glad we allow you to attend at all."

"But uncle, this is not acceptable, I was born to lead, and you know it!" He looks at her sympathetically, but she knows instinctively he does not take her seriously.

"Aadya, someday you will have a family, and then your husband can represent your part of the family. Until then be patient. You may continue to attend the council, but you must not be outspoken."

"But uncle…" He looks at her long and hard struggling internally with how to pacify her. Finally, he shrugs his shoulders.

"Okay, I will allow you to attend learning walks with Heshe, who will pass on many more bits of wisdom. I will speak to her about your education."

Her eyes brighten.

"You must be patient. I am allowing you more than any other female in our tribe."

At least he does not call me a breeder.

"I tell you what, if you can have the discipline to do as I say, I will meet with you occasionally, and we can discuss happenings like what is going on in the council behind the scenes. But I'm not sure if you are schooled enough to understand." He gives her a tender pat on the shoulder as he says this, but the gesture, meant to soothe her, only inflames her frustration.

I know uncle loves me, but he needs to understand I am serious about my position on the council. I will continue to find ways to prove myself.

"Go along now, I will have Heshe come to your shelter and speak with you."

Aadya walks back through tall grass, which tickles her arms in the slight breeze. She lifts her right hand and lets it glide across the tops of the sheaths as she heads to the simply crafted wood shelter which is home to her, Jubal, and her grandmother. It is on the edge of the forest and not far from the stream which speaks when the rains are numerous.

"Grandmother, I have news," she says as she bursts into the common area of the small lodge. "Uncle is going to expand my education, allowing Heshe to school me." Aadya's grandmother, still quite erect and strong, but not even as tall as Aadya, smiles with delight. "That is excellent news my dear. You have much to learn from Heshe. I have known her many years and she is incredibly wise."

5-He Is So Beautiful

Poma is now a frequent visitor, and Aadya does not shy from sharing her dreams and many of her ambitions with him, as well as her frustrations with the council. He does not say so, but she is not sure he is completely able to appreciate her goals or the obstacles she faces. She has also learned much about his position as a prince and more about what he calls "Kinetic Sight."

"I am wondering how this intuition power of yours works," she says to him one day. They are sharing a meal alongside the creek close to her house. He gives her a look of distasteful annoyance. "Everyone asks me that. Can't you wonder anything else about me like what it is to be one with me?"

Aadya's cheeks burn hot, and she looks away. It is not that she does not want to taste the pleasures he has to offer, but she is unsure of how it all fits in with her plans for the future. *I will speak to Heshe about this or maybe even grandmother.*

"I'm teasing you, Aadya." He tussles her hair as if she were a small boy. This greatly offends her, but she forgives him instantly.

"So, what do you see for us in the future?" *Oh, I wish I had not said that. He might get the wrong idea.*

A smile creeps across Poma's face. "We are not supposed to prophesy our own future. Our ego bias tends to make our own lives murky to our visions. It is called Kinetic Sight by the way and is much more than intuition. It is fueled by our contact with the Matong.

"Can I tell you what you are going to eat for lunch tomorrow?" He teases her. "Of course not, but when I go into a vision, I see notable events for the whole kingdom. It is not a power to be used lightly or for one's own gain."

"Of course not." Aayda agrees. *He is strikingly handsome* she notices for the first time. *I must get some answers from Heshe before I do something foolish.*

And then, almost as if he can read her mind, he leans over and kisses her. Although surprised, she does not turn away. A myriad bolts of energy surge into her brain, and she is helpless to resist. He pulls her close and her breath escapes in short bursts between his kisses. She is immobilized by his grasp as he pulls her closer, his hot breath unmistakable with her own as it curls inside of her.

They are suspended in time as their bodies pull together seeking satisfaction. He reaches around her legs to pull her even closer. She becomes lightheaded and hopelessly limp within his embrace.

Suddenly, with a burst of noise and slobber, the dogs have returned from their adventures. Jefa intervenes licking the two of them with his own hot breath. They pull away and laugh.

As if rising from a dream Aadya stands and collects herself. "Poma..."

The disappointment is etched into his face as she stares down at him. "I'm not..."

"Do not say another word," he says as he stands, towering above her, and placing his finger in front of her cherry moist lips.

"It is not my intention to take advantage of you."

She shrugs and looks away and laughs awkwardly. "In every other way, I am sure of myself, but not here, not now.

"Will you still be my friend?" His beautiful eyes pierce her with sincerity.

"I will always be your friend, but I want much more."

Visibly shivering, Aadya sinks into his chest and allows herself the pleasure of his engulfing embrace. Jefa jumps up on her and whines.

"Down, you must get down." She tells her powerful dog.

6-Questions and Answers

Grandmother's answer to Aadya's question is simple and to the point. "You are too young for sex," but Heshe's answer is much more complex.

They were studying down by the stream after a heavy rain and the rush of the water was almost too loud for an intimate conversation, but Aadya lets her curiosity prevail.

"Heshe, I look to you for advice in my personal life as well as your educational tutoring."

Heshe looks at her curiously. Her eyes probing as if to see into Aadya's mind.

"Have your slept with him yet?"

"What are you talking about? I have not asked my question?"

"It is no secret Prince Poma has taken a liking to you. He is here almost every day now."

Aadya swallows hard. "So, yes, that is my question. What do I do about becoming one with him? The topic has come up and he has respected my decline thus far, but I'm afraid I do not have the wisdom I need for such a decision."

"That is precisely true, Aadya." Heshe lets her piercing gray eyes glower into Aadya's as if she can see inside the girl's mind. "Let me put it this way. You have goals of leadership in the clan although you were born a breeder."

"Yes, that is true, and I hate that term, as if there is no value to me except for that of birthing."

Heshe allows her expression to soften. "Let me explain your options. Traditionally a prince weds a virgin, which protects dilution of the royal gene pool. You could be most powerful as a princess, and your council to the prince would be highly esteemed should you wait, and have your physical relationship sanctioned.

"Or you could allow your passions to dictate your will and become his lover now, which he will undoubtedly accept. You could possibly struggle and make your way into the council as you continue to do, or you could take a more direct path. You might look at his affections as a gift where a great opportunity has been bestowed upon you. Once you are in a place of power as a princess or eventually a queen, you can use that power to advance all breeders."

Aadya's confusion is like a school of fish loose in her head. "But you are not really giving me an answer?

"And you are one that likes to be told what to do?" Heshe's smile is snide bordering on cruel.

"Of course not, but there is no easy solution here. I do not understand what difference it makes, who I am, or if I marry or not? If I contribute equally and become a warrior, even though I am female, I should be given equal privilege and prestige as warriors are."

"Let me put it in these terms, Aadya. You are but a child yourself, but eventually even you may want to have children. No matter what route you take, you will want those children to have the most advantages you can possibly give them. Do you do this as a renegade female warrior, or as a princess? What will be your legacy?"

Heshe has not given me the counsel I was hoping for. In many ways she is free with her ideas, but today her words are not what I expected. "So, you are not going to give me an answer?"

Bowing her head in a dramatic gesture, Heshe responds. "Correct, but I do encourage you to use your head and not your heart in these matters."

It is another a few days before Aadya will see Poma again, and while it will be difficult, she wants to approach the subject of their relationship again. After all, *isn't that what two comrades would do? Be open and honest?* But the next time Aadya sees Poma it is because he has come to her village to tell her he will be escorting a group of warriors, on a discovery trip to the northern borders.

"When will you be back?"

"They are saying we will be gone for many moons."

"I want to go with you."

"Out of the question."

She looks at him and feels a strangeness to being in her own body. *He has never been this cold and distant with me. Perhaps he will not return.*

He shrugs his shoulders as if he has been privy to her thoughts. "Do not trouble yourself with worry; I will return before you know it."

I have been stupid. I have taken him for granted and now he is leaving. I should have become one with him, and not given it another thought. Without thinking, Aadya grabs Poma, and holds onto him tightly squeezing and hoping, with all her physical strength, she might prevent him from going if she holds on tight enough. She is like a child clinging to a parent in desperation as the parent tries to depart. They are standing in plain view of the village, and yet when he leans over to face her and his breath is upon her face, her arms become paralyzed as he leans over to kiss her.

You could have had me at any moment, but you were protecting me.

YES! She hears his thoughts in her head as if he is speaking. YES, AND I WILL WHEN I RETURN.

7-Now Is Not the Time

The days spill one on top of the other melding into one long stream of forever, before news of Poma's scouting expedition makes its way back to Aayda's tiny village of Acuna. By then Aadya has traversed many times back and forth to Poma's city, Valtar, to get the earliest word of his return first-hand.

It was somewhat tricky to get into the massive stone structure of the royal family known as Katara, but she befriended a maid and got a job occasionally working in the kitchen. No one in Valtar knew of her, enabling her to slip in and out rather easily.

Heshe had warned her against these activities, but Aadya reasoned she had done nothing wrong. She was merely looking out for her own interests. Through her voyeurism, Aadya learned of Poma's brothers, Parsa and Bonder, but they were also on the expedition. She once nearly ran into his mother, Queen Mesa, in the hallway when she had gone to explore parts of Katara she was unfamiliar with. Rumors of the fiercely protected royal Matong, a giant orb, said to be a conduit to the royal family's Kinetic Sight, had piqued her interest.

This was probably the one foolish thing she had done, and she had vowed not to take more risks like that. In all the weeks she spent time at Valtar, she never once imagined herself as worthy to walk the halls of Katara legitimately, but that upon his return she and Poma would unite as one. He could come visit her in Acuna and perhaps they would be warriors together. When he returned, she would allow his advances, and not push him away anymore.

Unfortunately, Aadya was not in Valtar on the day the expedition party returned, but instead was practicing her warrior skills with another of Heshe's elite students, Kelbar, a strapping youth who made a challenging opponent. So, it was quite a surprise to her when Poma showed up at her door the following day.

"Oh Poma! Thank the one above you are home again. I have been miserable without you!" Poma looks tired and road weary, as if he had not even bathed. His whiskers have grown into a full beard and are much duskier than his dark red hair, he now wears long and pulled behind his head.

Filled with erupting emotions, Aadya squeezes him fiercely. For the first time since he left, she feels like herself, and not some foolish girl spying on the house of Katara.

"Let me look at you," he says pulling away from her to arm's length. "You have grown even more beautiful than when I left. But I see you still wear warrior's attire."

His disapproval fell on her like a damp rag thrown on an open fire. "Of course, what else would I wear?"

"If I am to take you home to meet my mother, then you will have to dress in female fashion, now, won't you?"

Panic pushes at her chest with the intensity of a trapped bird. "What are you talking about?"

"I'm saying my mother has met you already when you were working in the kitchen at Katara while I was gone. But now I want to formally introduce you to the queen."

The flush of shame fills Aadya's body to the point where a maverick breeze might blow her over. "She knew I was there all along?"

"Do not be concerned. She admires your pluck."

"But how? I was careful."

"Have I not explained a thousand times my people have kinetic vision?"

"But she never said a word to me."

His disarming smile ransacks her resolve. It is as if he holds a secret she does not yet know about, and now he is back, she wants him all to herself. She does not want him to have a mother, or father, or brothers, or even a horse. She wants to command his every thought and be at the center of his entire world. She wants him to become lost in his desire for her. And most of all she will not ever allow him out of her sight again. But Aadya's greedy thoughts are short lived. As she begins to realize loving a handsome prince might come at a serious price.

He holds her hands in his, hesitating, but his face bears out the determination his mouth has yet to utter. "Aadya, we need to talk of the future. I need to know where I stand with you."

"Poma what could be your concern? You know I am devoted to you." She turns away shyly after saying this, trying to hide the giddiness rumbling inside her, like a spring gushing from many rains.

When he pulls her close and looks her square in the eyes, he pushes his thoughts into her mind as he had done once before on the day he left.

"I'M CRAZY ABOUT YOU TOO. WILL YOU COMMIT TO ME?"

"How do you do that?" She recoils from his grasp not able to hide her alarm.

"Does it frighten you? That is my gift, my Kinetic Sight."

She shudders. *It is alarming. How am I going to deal with this?*

"I am sorry. Can you read my thoughts?"

"It is complicated and difficult to explain. Your thoughts are not as clear to me as mine are to you when I deliberately put my words into your mind. There is privacy, you need not worry I can't hear your every thought, although it is no secret you are crazy about me." His boldness makes him even more appealing, but as he exhales deeply, she can sense his frustration.

Aadya diverts his attention. "You haven't spoken of your adventures."

"I shall share it all with you, but now I must return to Katara. I stopped there briefly this morning, and they are waiting for me to return."

"Can I come with you?"

"No, now is not the time. Please bear with me. I will return tomorrow, and we can talk more." But instead of mounting his horse, Poma hesitates and pulls her close, not able to wrench himself from her side. With his body pressed up against her and his hot breath on her face,

Aadya is sapped of all her resolve. She lets her breathe loose as if blowing out a candle.

"As you wish, I will go meet your mother. I will put on female clothing. But only for you, I would not do this for anyone else."

His face, filled with happiness, is like the music of the wind in the trees and her heart is stilled. *Why am I helpless when I am in his presence, like a newborn lolbo.*

"Fortunately, I went to a wedding last summer. I do have one dress," she tells him as he mounts his steed, a massive black creature whose hot breath comes out of his nostrils in puffs of soft steam. Aadya hugs the horse's silky broad chest making it difficult for Poma to withdraw. She finally pulls away and watches the prancing feet of the majestic animal turn and race away.

8-Royal Treatment

Sitting at the intimate round table in one of Katara's elaborately decorated, outside covered verandas with Poma and his mother, Mesa, Aadya is painfully aware she is out of kilter. While his mother is polite to her, she feels like a fish stranded and flopping on the side of a riverbank. Poma has instructed her the proper way to address his mother is as "Queen Mesa," and he has shared some other pointers, but she still feels completely unprepared for this encounter. *He must have planned the short notice so, I wouldn't have time to wriggle my way out.*

"Mother, Aadya and I are committed to each other. I can't trust myself to wait another minute to be with her as one."

A rush of heat floods Aadya's cheeks, and her heart pounds within her rib cage. *Really this is how you speak to your mother?*

"Poma, watch yourself with the poor girl," she says giving Aadya a sympathetic look.

Poor girl? Is that how she sees me?

"Have you gone over with her what becoming part of our family entails?"

"Uh, not really."

"Then you are being unfair to her."

Grinning, Poma looks over at Aadya, "It is not my purpose to frighten her."

Queen Mesa takes a deep breath swiping with her hand the rich texture of her dress and shares matter-of-factly with Aadya. "In order to become Poma's wife, you will have to make many sacrifices.

"First of all, your main purpose will to be to provide him with children."

The queen's words pierce Aadya like sharp knives. *I am not a breeder!*

"Most importantly, this union will not happen at all if you have already slept with him." Aadya instinctively lowers her head in shame to protect herself from the vicious words coming from Queen Mesa who was convivial moments before.

"Mother! Please, you have it all wrong."

"I'm not trying to be cruel, but these are important matters."

"I told you we have not been together."

Mesa looks at Aadya and touches her lowered chin gently to bring her gaze up. "Is this true my dear?"

Every fiber in Aadya's body wants to leap up and curse at the queen, but Poma has grasped her hand, and his determined gaze assures her to be strong.

"Forgive me Aadya, I can now see into your heart, and it is true you are chaste." Queen Mesa takes a sip of her honey nectar tea and resumes her explanation of the events that will have to take place.

"If the king agrees to this alliance, which is most unlikely, you will be expected to bond with the Matong on the day of your wedding before the marriage is consummated. That is the most important part of marriage to my son. You will receive the gift of Kinetic Sight, so you see this is not just about friendship, or lust, or companionship, it is about all those things, but mostly it is about your inner strength and how you will assimilate with the Matong."

But what if I do not want the gift of Kinetic Sight?

"This is a serious commitment, Aadya…" Queen Mesa gives her a compassionate smile.

"You will not regret it." Exasperated, Poma breaks in, meeting his mother's gaze with an avowed determination.

Mesa returns the annoyed look and proceeds. "Following tradition, Poma would wed someone his father and I helped select, but I can see we are too far in for that to be helpful. I am concerned for you," she says directly addressing Aadya. "You have had a vastly different upbringing than my son and you have unusual… ah ambitions. You are also quite young, but that is not necessarily bad in this situation."

Aadya squirms in her chair, poking absently at the meal she would have ordinarily devoured quickly. *I wonder what she means?*

"After this meal, I will take the two of you to the Matong. You will not be allowed to touch it, Aadya, but this will give us insight. If I am directed, we will proceed, and then present this betrothal to the king." Queen Mesa folds her arms uncharacteristically.

"I can't stress this enough. You two must not be tempted to have each other as lovers. You do and this is over. Do you understand me?" She looks directly at her son. "Poma I am going to suggest to your father that he send you on another scouting trip."

Aadya can see the disappointment in Poma's face while she is dealing with her own numbness. *My brain has abandoned me! I have wandered too far into unfamiliar woods.*

9-Matong Magnificence

The heavily guarded room where the Matong stands, appears unusually confined to house such an omniscient power. Now that she has been invited in, it is hard to imagine how she could have gotten a sneak peek of the orb through the cracked door weeks before when she was working at Katara as a kitchen maid. Aadya's skin crawls as she now wonders if such exposure was divine intervention.

The Matong looms above the three of them, a huge pearly white, luminescent orb perched on a polished white, shimmering alabaster stone pillar wider than five or six men gathered might be able to reach around. At the top of the orb is a richly detailed gold crest that Aadya can barely see standing close to it. The orb looks top-heavy at such close range.

Emanating from it is a radiant warmth, which engulfs them softly like a caress, Queen Mesa walks around Aadya and Poma, searching their faces for answers to the unspoken questions she has. She then takes her son's hand and places it on the orb and puts her hand beside his. With their eyes closed, Aadya cannot sense their presence in the room, as if they have departed, although she can still see them. She waits in this suspended state until the queen finally lets go, or perhaps it is the orb that has released her.

Breaking the silence, Queen Mesa works to control the emotion in her voice. "It has been a long afternoon for us all. Aadya you must return to Acuna, but Poma you will stay here. We will send her home with an escort," she says to Poma as if Aadya is not present.

"Aadya, I would like to have some clothing made up for you. We will have my seamstress take your measurements to create your wardrobe for you. I know it is not your practice, but you absolutely must start dressing like a woman, if we are to get the king behind this union. We will meet with him when he is able in the next day or two."

What is going on? What did this strange, mystical power say to them? Poma gives Aadya an apologetic look as if to say, 'it is all out of my hands.'

"As you wish mother. Aadya, I will escort you to your carriage."

"Take her to the antechamber of my quarters first, where she can be fitted for the necessary garments."

"But what is happening here? What did the Matong say to you?" She looks first at Poma then at the queen. Poma is grinning ear to ear; the queen is only mildly scowling.

"It has been ordained," the queen says lifting her arms to, straighten the heavy jewels around her neck.

Poma takes Aadya's hand and pulls at her to come with him. The two of them break away from Queen Mesa, first reverently and then, unable to contain their joy, rush down the hall allowing giddy laughter to erupt as soon as they are out of earshot of the queen. Poma stops and pulls her aside. Looking directly into her eyes, he grows serious.

"Aadya. I know this is all overwhelming. But this is the best way I believe, sharing the gift of Kinetic Sight will bring us closer than we can possibly experience without it." He pulls her closer to press his point. "Please, say yes to all of this and be my wife."

Despite the misgivings she has been entertaining all afternoon the one word that comes out of her mouth, like an air bubble rushing to the surface, is "Yes."

10-Summoned

In three days' time, a carriage shows up at Aadya's door. She stares wide-eyed through the thin curtain of a small window and watches as a woman, with voluminous skirts like Aadya has never seen before, pulls herself out of the carriage. Her spindly feet, bedecked in impractical footwear, barely hit the ground when she begins snapping her fingers at two valets who tug at a massive trunk, so large they barely manage to get it to the door of Aadya's humble abode.

Aadya has discussed her situation with all the wise ones she could find who would sit still and listen. And the consensus is, she would be a fool not to marry Prince Poma. *I am both drowning and swimming in good fortune. I will have Poma as my own, but I have to leave my life behind. My memories of my mother are here in this small place.*

The entourage enters the house like an unexpected gust of wind. Aadya watches as the smartly dressed woman clucks and whistles more than speaks to two attendants who apparently are unable to think for themselves. They pull out several incredibly ornate gowns to Aadya's astonishment. *They are works of art meant for someone other than myself.*

"My name is Bodalena, but most everyone calls me Bodie. I have been assigned to you, as you join the royal family, and I am here should you have any questions," she says with arched eyebrows decorated with sparkling powder.

"Where is Poma?"

"He awaits you at Katara. You two will meet with the king and queen this afternoon and you shall stay for dinner in the great dining hall." As Bodie looks around the room her head tends to bob as she warns Aadya to notify her family and let them know where she has gone. Grandmother is at the market, giving Aadya no one to share this curious solicitation with.

Then something remarkable happens. One of the attendants, per his swiftly articulated instructions, goes out to the carriage to "fetch the looking glass." Aadya's astonishment causes her to gasp.

The only reflection I've ever seen of myself was in a still pool of water. What kind of magic is this? Who am I! she wonders as she steps into the first dress, and indeed, she is as pretty as any of the young women in the Capitol city of Valtar where she will soon live.

"Why you are absolutely transformed," bobbing Bodie declares. A faint smile springs forth grudgingly on the woman's judgmentally sculpted face. "Here, try these on." She dangles a pair of silky slippers off her right index finger.

"I can't walk in those. The skirt is long," Aadya says lifting it to expose her feet. "I can wear my own boots. No one will see."

"Aach poor girl. I will see it in my nightmares. No! You cannot wear those tattered, foul boots into Katara. No, that is out of the question."

Grimacing, Bodie scans Aadya from head to toe and lightly touches the girl's wispy blond tresses, twisted unceremoniously into a knot on the back of her head. *She looks at me as if I am a piece of fruit at the market.* "I should have brought the hairdresser. I want to deliver you ready to go."

Really, you should speak like that to me? After all, and the realization hits her with the force of a rogue sea wave. *I will be married to the prince soon and you will work for me.*

But instead of protesting, Aadya allows Bodie to comb her honey-colored hair and bind it in the back of her head, using clever twists with her hands and an ornate clasp to secure it. She also does as she is told and writes grandmother a note of explanation. Aadya, because of her persistence to be educated, is one of the few women in the village who can write or even has the materials to do so. Her grandmother, on the other hand, will have to take the note to someone who can read it for her. "When shall I tell her I will return?"

"You will be brought back tonight. We have strict orders to keep you separated from Prince Poma. And thus, we will be posting a guard at your door when we return, for your protection of course." *For my protection or theirs?*

11-His Eminence

Dinner with King Larsa and Queen Mesa is more intimidating than Aadya imagined. While it is obvious the king is trying to be gracious and charming, he cannot disguise his doubt about his son's choice, and being he had recently come to know about Aadya only in the past few days, his bitterness is fresh and undiluted.

At times he speaks to Poma directly as if she is not in the room, but finally, knowing her husband and that timing is everything, Queen Mesa speaks up.

"May I remind you dear, Aadya has been vetted by the Matong?" Smiling generously at Aadya, Queen Mesa directs her gaze first to Aadya then to her husband. "If you have doubts perhaps you should see for yourself what the Matong has to say."

"Of course, my lady. You are one step ahead of me. Let us go now and have our dessert later," he says picking up his golden goblet, still half-filled with rich dark wine. Pushing his chair away from the massive dining table, he stands up.

Aadya's heart accelerates like a stag leaping a fallen tree. *God be praised, I hope I pass this test. Even if the queen likes me, it is the king who will discard me, should he not think I'm worthy to carry his progeny to life. No matter then, I will be one with Poma anyway and enough with all this nonsense.*

At night, the pulsing flow of energy within the Matong is more distinct in the shadows of the dim flickering candlelight. Even though Poma offers his arm to steady her, Aadya waivers feeling distinctly isolated as she draws closer to the orb. "Do you sense it?" Queen Mesa asks her husband. "Do you perceive the acceptance and love toward Aadya?"

The king grunts and his demeanor softens. He places his hand on the orb and once again Aadya experiences his departure from the room, despite the fact she can still see him. When he releases, he turns to Poma and Aadya and lets a smile pierce through his scowl. "I guess it is to be."

After desert they all sit in front of a roaring fire, Aadya and Poma on a loveseat together and his parents in separate chairs, opposed on either side of them. Although the chairs are more comfortable than the ones in the dining room, the atmosphere is still charged with unspoken expectations.

"We will summon your uncle Tabathian tomorrow, Aadya. Once he is satisfied with the union, the preparations for the wedding will begin," King Larsa announces to Aadya who is biting her lip to control her trembling. "He will be rewarded handsomely for your pledge to my son. For now, you are to return to your home, for the next few days, and prepare for your relocation. We will ready your chambers here at Katara where you will stay until the wedding.

"But Poma," He turns to his son and looks him squarely in the eyes. "You will be sent off for now and won't be allowed to return until your wedding day."

"But is that really necessary? Are not these old-fashioned traditions absurd?" Poma's questions are met with a glazed stare.

"Yes, father," he says backing off with a tone of deep respect. Poma gives Aadya a look void of all objection, and she is forced to examine her own rebellious thoughts. Taking a deep breath, she slips meditatively into a thick forest to calm and protect herself.

If these powerful people can put their faith in me then I need to live up to the challenge of their expectations.

12-House Arrest

After two tedious days of being detained in her home, Aadya becomes agitated in a way which frightens her.

"They won't even let me hunt or go to market or bathe in the stream!" She bemoans her frustration to her grandmother with fists planted firmly on her waist.

Woku nods, sadly listening to Aadya express her discontent. While luxuries like food delicacies and hot baths are provided, Aadya is growing impatient. She decides to do something about the guards who now stand continuously as sentinels, outside her door, keeping her from her one true desire, to see Poma.

"I need to get a message to Poma," she tells one of the younger guards who is most likely to comply.

"Yes, mistress Aadya, we are not allowed to do that. And we do not know where he is."

"Perhaps he is still at Katara."

"It is possible," the soldier says as stiffly as he stands.

"I know you are here in shifts. You must return home at the end of the day. Please find out where he is, and tell him to meet me at the place near the lake where I felled a deer. He will know the place. Tell him to meet me there; tomorrow at noon."

But the next day, shortly after the first light crosses her doorstep, the sound of horse's hooves can be heard on the grassy pathway leading to Aadya's front door.

Bodie and her entourage are there to escort her back to Katara. She is to be wed in one week, and she would see the prince "soon enough," she is unceremoniously told. It is the first time she has a hint how her life was changing, and it stirs up a memory of when she was a little girl, which she tells to her grandmother. "I had a rabloot I caught with a snare. I named it Porsa, and kept it in a cage I made of sturdy sticks. Jubal teased me and said he was going to make rabloota pon, a stew made from my little pet.

"I loved that little rabloot, but truthfully nothing was more satisfactory than releasing her once Jubal threatened to cook her in a stew. I will never forget the way she looked back at me, and I could see the gratitude in her eyes before she bolted for the woods."

Grandmother Woku listens and then hugs her granddaughter goodbye. Aadya slumps in her arms and wipes some unexpected tears away. "Grandmother, you must come with me!"

Woku Tempa, seeing her resilient, warrior granddaughter weeping, breaks down and weeps too.

"I cannot, child, who will tend to Jubal?"

"He can come too." But as soon as the words slip out of her mouth, Aadya knows she is not sincere. Whatever has happened to her once-adored brother has transformed him into someone she no longer understands, and she is not comfortable being around him, despite her many attempts to engage him in meaningful conversation.

"Grandmother please come!" She pleads again. "Having you there would make me much more comfortable."

Grabbing her grandmother's wrists, she lowers her voice to a whisper. "I need your support."

"You know I can't child, but I will visit often. You of all people must gather your courage and pursue your dreams." She squeezes Aadya's hands tightly. "We will all be there on your wedding day."

Standing sternly nearby, Bodie clears her throat. "It is a short distance by wagon. Once the wedding has taken place, you will be able to visit frequently." She rotates her weight nervously from one foot to the other. "There is not a minute to waste. And soon you will be wed and have the prince's full attention."

Turning to the door reluctantly, Aadya complies and looks around the small, familiar room with its meager furnishings.

"I have brought more clothing for you to wear," Bodie declares waving her arm at her helpers who spring into action. "While you dress, they will pack up your other things." Bodie takes a large breath as she visually assesses what that might be in this humble dwelling. "Now my dear, we mustn't keep Queen Mesa waiting."

Aadya does as she is told but cannot stop thinking about her little Porsa. "What about my dogs?" Aadya asks of Bodie already surmising Bodie's evil look and negative nod of disapproval.

"They must stay here for now." Bodie says tersely.

13-An Empty Heart

Aadya's rooms at the castle, four of them, are opulently appointed for her comfort, but she will not stay there after the wedding when she will join Poma in his spacious quarters. Aadya peers through the tall windows of her rooms looking out at the vast wooded lands, which surround Katara, and feels more isolated than she ever has. *What have I gotten myself into?* She asks herself repeatedly.

Each day Bodie appears punctually, after Aadya is served an ample breakfast in her rooms, to school her in the machinations of the wedding festivities and royal protocol. Aadya occasionally lunches with Queen Mesa and for a short time she is allowed to roam freely around the castle in the afternoons. She is permitted once, to explore the town of Valtar, but she is heavily escorted making the tour tedious not restorative.

Not one to have many friends, who meshed with her values and interests, she does not pine for friendships lost. It is her forfeited freedom to wander the woods, hunt, and play with her dogs, which is eating a hole in her heart. She could ask Queen Mesa for her dogs, but thinks better to wait for Poma, who will defend her needs blindly.

It is at dinner that her existence is most awkward, when she must dine with the king and queen and their assorted guests. Each night is populated with gregarious visitors, she has nothing in common with. It is their perceived judgment of her, as dark and heavy as a moonless night during the weeks when the two moons are obscured by Merth's own shadow, which weighs on her.

The luxuries of wealth surround her and yet she starves for connection to her lost world. The only thing to keep her from leaping out of a window and running away is Poma, who sends her messages each day.

She asks for a visit to see her Grandmother Woku, but is told it would be better if Woku were brought to her. "Okay, then let us arrange it. I should like to have her brought to Katara tomorrow for lunch," she tells Bodie. "And I would like to have a tour of the castle arranged. I have not seen all of it myself."

Bodie squints and sucks in her lips a bit. "I'll see what I can do your grace." Aadya lets out a small smile, she hides from Bodie. *I have been elevated to 'your grace'.*

When Woku arrives wearing a clean, but worn garment, Aadya has seen her wear for many revolutions, she privately tells Bodie to do something about this. "And she will need a special garment for the wedding."

"I have already given this thought," Bodie replies, giving Aadya a curious sense of respect. *Maybe the woman is sympathetic to my cause after all.* "I will set up a fitting after the tour of the castle. As your grandmother, she must be presentable. And what of your brother?"

This question causes Aadya's stomach to knot up. "I am not sure if he will even come to the wedding. But perhaps you could send Woku home with something for him. He is close to Poma's size, but not quite as tall.

"I know what to do," Bodie winks at her. *Whoa, if this woman gets any nicer, I suspect the two moons will collide.*

When the wagon pulls up to take Woku home Aadya walks through the magnificent wooden doors of Katara's front entrance to escort her grandmother. They hug and the straw-like wisps of her grandmother's hair, now the color of shonton metal, sift into her face. "Your mother and father would be most proud of you, Aadya."

Aadya returns the loving smile, but inside she aches. "I have done nothing to be proud of yet, except to fall in love with a magnificent man."

"Oh, you are too modest, coming from where you came to be a princess in this," Woku waves her hand across the backdrop of the castle. "This, whatever it is, and to become one with a prince, and you will have Kinetic Sight, whatever that is." A winsome grin spreads across her aging cheeks.

Woku's jocularity and their time together has lifted Aadya's spirits. "I'm glad you came today, please feel comfortable to return whenever you like."

Woku smiles warmly and squeezes Aadya's hand, her bright blue eyes piercing Aadya's heart, but they both know Woku will never be at home in a place like Katara.

14-Devouring a Work of Art

The morning of the wedding, the two lovers are finally reunited for an intimate breakfast together on an open terrace, in a far corner of Katara, before they will meet in the enormous hall for their vow ceremony. There is a slight chill in the air, but a fire has been made in the pit nearby.

"In name of the one true heaven, I am glad to see you!" Adya rushes to embrace Poma who is holding a large bundle of flowers, he carefully protects by opening his arms as she melts into his chest, and clings to him taking in his smell, the warmth of his body, and the strength of his broad shoulders. The satin textured tips of the exotic blooms tickle her arms. She pulls back and takes a hard look at him. "You look different," studying him she realizes they will be wed in a few hours. *Why am I so judgmental and insecure?*

"You look older," he says, letting his surprise leak into his voice. His smile stills all her doubts which have been swimming in her brain all week like venomous snakes in a pit. *How could I be so attached to this man? He was just a boy last week, a comrade.*

"It has been a busy week. I bring your bridal flowers." He offers the opulent spray of honey clusters, gypsopana, gardenal wisps, and lilapetals to her. The heavy fragrance curls up into her head spinning seductively like a lyrical song.

"They are amazing!" She says noticing them for the first time.

"Here, let us sit, and have some nourishment, I am ravenous." Servants rush forward to pull out their chairs. Before them is their own private feast made up of a cleverly crafted wedding scene, the cooks have prepared for them, with little cakes, berries, butter, cheeses, exotic breads, and tiny little sausages. Their own likenesses face a miniature altar of white frosting and cake anointed in strong rumbar sauce.

I can't believe how beautiful this is. "What are we going to do? We cannot eat this work of art," she says sweeping her arm across the vision of the wedding scene. "But I am frightfully hungry."

Poma does not hesitate to signal the servants to serve them at once, and they quickly devour the fantasy scene of food until there is little left but some whipped crème on Poma's plate, which he playful dips his finger into and shares with Aadya.

They linger in the absence of anyone telling them what their next duties are, sipping on aromatic teas. He takes her hand in his and they sit in silence.

An unusually large crimson bird with a long curly blue tail begins to sing in a nearby Cotto tree.

Poma points toward the bird. "Look it is a gift from the Matong"

"I have never…"

"Because they do not exist anymore," he tells her finishing her sentence. "The Matong has sent it as part of our wedding blessing."

If we could only stay here in this bubble of paradise forever.

YES, MY LOVE, LET US ALWAYS STAY IN THIS SPHERE OF LOVE AND CONTENTMENT.

Oh! It always startles her when he places his thoughts into her mind.

SOON YOU WILL BE ABLE TO SHARE YOUR THOUGHTS WITH ME IN THIS MANNER.

I trust you now. I did not know you at first.

But the peaceful moment is over as the attendants come in and glide them away for ceremonial preparations. Aadya's gown itself will take hours to be fitted with last minute adornments.

15-Preparations

Surprisingly for them both, the prince is brought into Aadya's spacious chambers where they are escorted into the generous bathing room with a sunken tub square in the middle of the floor. The steaming water from the gilt faucets fills the air with a foggy mist. Small flowering trees have been brought in and butterflies, with waxen wings, flit through the air. As the servants close the heavy double doors, bright yellow butterflies drop down and transform into crouching maidens, with gossamer gowns embellished in intricate floral embroidery. They unfurl like blossoms; opening to undress the two lovers, whom they lead down the steps into the steaming waters. The transparent maidens wave brightly colored, exotic bottles of oils under Aadya's nose, and if she approves, add them to their bath laden with florid petals.

This is beyond wonderful! I know I cannot project my thoughts to you yet, but you can read mine. THAT IS A GOOD THING BECAUSE MY THOUGHTS ARE FILLED WITH LUST FOR YOU. I DID NOT KNOW THIS IS WHAT AWAITED US. MORE SURPRISES FROM THE MATONG.

The maidens scrub their backs and arms rather vigorously making Aadya giggle. Poma playfully squirts water at her. Next the maidens lead them out of the bath, and direct them to lay on small beds, brought in and covered in the softest cashmere fur of the lama dama goat. They are both massaged with more botanical oils. Aadya peeks shyly at Poma who rests his eyes on the vision of her nakedness with an obsession that fuels her own fire.

MY LOVE THIS IS SIMPLY TORTURE. MY DESIRE TO BE ONE WITH YOU CONSUMES ME.

Aadya smiles through her haze of contentment, and as she drifts off into a hypnagogic state, she floats into a realm where the magical bird is singing to her. Its lyrical tone, like a flute in a cavernous space, puts her to sleep. When she awakens, Poma is gone, and she is totally alone.

Unsure if she has been dreaming, or the bird was real, she touches her arms and marvels at the softness of her skin; after having been anointed with all the fragrant skin potions, made from crushed flowers, treasured seeds, and mother's milk from various species. The maidens appear with mirrors and start to comb her blond tresses, now longer than when she first met Poma.

I could get used to this. Still, she knows she must mentally prepare for wearing the bejeweled bridal gown with the long train, and perform for hours as her duties require. *This is far removed from where I thought I would be such a short time ago.* But being with Poma is a dream she had not imagined back then either, or the newly acquired respect from her uncle. This above all is a gift she never anticipated.

As promised, grandmother is brought to her chambers later in the day. Woku's rags have been replaced with an appropriately glistening tunic and satin leggings to cover her wobbly. wrinkled knees. "Are you nervous my child?"

"Oh grandmother of course I am, but once Poma and I are together, all will be right. Until then, I must be careful to act in a way to please all of the people. This day is not just about Poma or me, this day is about what is good for the royal family and thus our people."

Woku nods. "You have become even more wise my child. You will accomplish great things."

Will I? Is this what I have been dreaming of? Or is it just a big fancy wedding to a prince? "Oh grandmother, we shall see about all of that."

"No, Aadya, this is what you have been preparing for your whole life. You thought it was something else, but this is the leadership position you always wanted."

"Perhaps, or maybe it is all a dream, an elaborate deception."

The final step in preparation for the ceremony is to enter the back of the gown held up by the maidens. It is more like wearing armor than a dress. But Aadya, despite her diminutive size, is physically strong. With the assistance of her hand maidens, she has it on in less than a few minutes. Then the long, voluminous train is attached. Aadya has exhausted her imagination of how the events of the evening will play out, and how it will go once she is alone with Poma. They had rehearsed tirelessly what was expected of her. But her fears about gaining Kinetic Sight are the focus of her attention. *My wedding day should be about becoming one with Poma, but somehow there is much more to this than I can even imagine. At least he will be there with me at the Matong.*

"Drink a sip of this." Bodie brings a heavy golden chalice to her lips.

"What is it?"

"It is something to prepare you for the Matong."

Aadya peers curiously into the bottom of the goblet adorned with twinkling gems. It is awkwardly heavy requiring both her hands to hold it up to her pursed lips. Inside the cup, is a small serving of a pearly liqueur, which, when she squints, appears to swim and stir on its own accord. Aadya dutifully does as she is instructed. The liquid makes her mouth tingle like an exceptionally strong minted mash, and once it starts making its way down her throat it is as if she is swallowing tiny fluid stars. Soon her whole body is prickly with sensations of light points, and it is as if her feet are not touching the ground. Her oppressively heavy dress, which had at first glistened with gemstones of many colors, now absolutely glows as she becomes more and more weightless.

"The drink makes me feel strange, Bodie"

"Yes dear, that is what is supposed to happen you will experience a lightness throughout the ceremony, but you need it for the bonding with the Matong, and of course for wearing the dress."

"Will Poma have this too?"

"No, Aadya, he has already bonded with the Matong, but he will have his own bridal elixir to enhance his performance as a groom."

"And what does that mean?"

"I have already said too much. We must go, it is a small journey to the great hall, and walking with your train will be most tedious."

16-Aadya's Long Walk

Entering the hallway, Aadya can hear the music reverberating throughout the expanse of Katara. There are stringed instruments, and drums, and a magnificent machine that creates musical vibrations with pipes and clashing metal disks. When the guards open the gargantuan doors to the Cathedral, she is shocked to see how many people are present and waiting for the ceremony to begin. A blast from musical horns above her startles her, and she almost drops her bouquet that cascades from her waist to the floor. The heady fragrance of the flowers, now enhanced by the elixir she was given, swirls up around her with its own mesmerizing spell.

The only thing keeping her from floating off up into the rafters of the great hall is the magnificent gown that lies across her chest. Her small bronze shoulders are bare, and at her throat, encrusted with shimmering jewels, is the symbolic chamra, the same spellcaster Queen Mesa wore on her wedding day. The tingling sensation from the strange potion still flows through her veins and her mood is emboldened. As if to remind her, she is protected, her breath is sometimes visible in traces of swirly vapor, but mostly she has the sensation she is outside her body; she herself is a spectator in this grand parade.

Her first glimpse of Poma sets her heart to pounding and she gulps in air. He is waiting for her at the end of the aisle, with his brothers at his side. His gaze is firmly focused on the vision of her in the astonishing gown. *I want this feeling to last forever!*

And the walk, as tedious and filled with drama as it is, is like an infinite journey as each step she takes is a deliberate passage of time. So, that when she arrives at Poma's side, she has evolved. She has metamorphosed into something greater than she was at the beginning of her journey down the long hall.

He extends his arm to her and when she touches him, she experiences a peculiar sensation, a warm tingling bolt travels up her arm and then gently strikes into her heart. He leans in to steady her. "My heart is filled with love, you are such an incredible creature," he whispers.

She wants to respond but it is as if her vocal cords have been frozen. She merely nods to him, with a slight and respectful bow of her head. *In what plausible world am I an incredible creature? I belong in the woods with my fearless and muddy dogs.*

Later she would not be able to recall the words they spoke, only that a white silk scarf had been symbolically tied around their wrists. Once she and the dress, with its long train, are turned, she and Poma walk triumphantly down the aisle as cheers by the crowd resonate across the chasm of the enormous room. Waiting attendants escort them to the Matong chamber where they are met by the king and queen.

The four of them are glowing with the emotion the bridal vows have imprinted on their minds, but not a word is said. They have rehearsed this part, so Aadya knows what to do, though the volume of the dress, with its long train, sends a sudden burst of panic through her body. The gossamer attendants appear from nowhere and lift up the length of the gown, folding it delicately to accommodate the small chamber. She kneels on a stool placed before her and faces the prince who kisses her hand and beckons her to rise. This is symbolic of her respect and humility for the powers of the Matong.

The bride and groom then face King Larsa and Queen Mesa together who return their motions of bows and lowered heads, gestures of humility and respect. Poma leads Aadya over to the shimmering Matong and places her hands onto the glowing orb. She is met with a surge of energy filling her with a thousand thoughts rushing into her mind like a stream bursting from the obstruction of a jammed log in an early Spring snow melt. Her mind, already influenced by the contents she consumed from the golden chalice earlier in the day, is afire with sensations. She hears herself say, "I will." But she is not certain to what or to whom she is saying this. Feeling strangely depleted and renewed at the same time, she looks weakly toward Poma for guidance. *He is absolutely tantalizing.* It is then he begins to stream his thoughts into her mind.

SOON WE WILL BE TOGETHER. WE WILL TOUCH AND BECOME ONE AND THE ECSTASY WILL BE ALL.

YES. I AM YOURS. It is the first time she is aware of her thoughts being projected to Poma. And also, the first time it does not alarm her when he responds inside her head.

Poma bends over with his steel gray eyes focused on hers and kisses Aadya's hand. WE ARE ENCOURAGED TO BE ALONE NOW BEFORE THE GREAT FEAST. IT

SHOWS WE ARE HUNGRY FOR EACH OTHER. OUR CHAMBERS HAVE BEEN PREPARED FOR US.

Aadya lets a drowsy giggle escape from her pursed lips. LET US GO THEN. All apprehension about being with him is gone. *I can't wait!*

17-Together at Last

The bride and groom walk to their freshly appointed chambers in silence, arm in arm, with the anticipation growing between them like electric bolts of charged energy bouncing back and forth between their two bodies. The dress weighs them down as Aadya can only move precariously slow in it, the long train dragging behind her like a sea anchor.

She giggles sensing his frustration. PATIENCE POMA. WE WILL GET THERE.

He stops her there in the hall and reaches for her chin with his open hand pressing his mouth into hers. *I love how he tastes. I love him.* I AM SO HAPPY!

He does not answer her thoughts, but his face, tells the same story.

When they finally reach the bedroom chamber, they both balk. There are the handmaidens languishing on their intricately carved four-poster bed. YOU HAVE GOT TO BE KIDDING ME! Poma's thoughts are hers.

"What are they doing here? They've got to go!" Aadya suddenly panics. *Are the maidens going be part of our bridal union?* Poma lets out a deflated sigh, but once the maidens begin to flutter around and help her out of the gown, Aadya understands.

They dress her in a sheer shimmering tunic that floats on her skin, tantalizing her body with wispy erotic sensations. Two of the translucent maidens help Poma out of his clothes but they leave him naked. The bed chamber has been transformed with flowering trees, potted flowers, and a shower of white translucent butterflies swirling in erratic patterns. The mythical bird, perched by the window, sings to them with liquid notes, briefly hypnotizing them both, then flies out the open window with a raucous caw. The maidens follow, floating out the window like billowing tufts of moist air.

Then they are all alone.

Beaming with anticipation, Poma pulls his bride into the sumptuous bridal bed where fragrant petals from the most aromatic flowers have been strewn. Aadya has been thinking of this moment ever since this morning's sensuous bath. There are no dancing maidens now to distract them from their union. She looks at Poma unreservedly taking in his broad, strong shoulders, his muscular chest, and legs. Startling sensations now pump through her veins, and she experiences full-throttled passion. She lets her hands peruse his muscular body. While she knows what the anatomy of a man is like, this is the first time she has seen Poma hard with lust. She suppresses a desire to giggle, instead channeling her delight into a smile she cannot escape.

Poma cautiously approaches his virgin bride, but there is no hiding his desire. He pulls off her gown slowly, carefully, judging her willingness. As they embrace Aadya softens with the intimate touches her husband makes, and without reservation, opens herself fully to him. Their bodies press together as they inhale each other's breath and rush together as two streams, heavy with rain, colliding together into one flow.

Consumed, they do not stop until their youthful bodies are exhausted. Laying with her head on his chest, Aadya listens to his pounding heart, experiencing a connection she had not thought possible.

He begins to let his hands wander the terrain of her svelte body again.

"Stop it!"

"What?" he looks innocently about.

"Stop! I cannot resist you."

He shrugs, "I do not understand your resistance then," he says grinning at her.

"The guards have been knocking on the door to call us to dinner, haven't you noticed?"

"So?"

"Poma, we must go now," she insists, but he ignores her feeble attempts to stop his hands from their pursuit. *The wedding party must wait.*

18-Sustenance and Frivolity

The massive crowd cheers as they enter the great hall. Aadya, now wearing a rich cerulean gown designed specifically for this moment, is a little unnerved by all the attention focused on the two of them. The warm glowing sensation, still full blown in her body as it was in bed with Poma, continues to make her head swim. The freshly imprinted hours alone with him are circulating through her veins; as the pulse of life bonds her with her husband in unspeakable ways. *Could this all be real?*

YES, IT IS

"No!"

Poma is visibly surprised at her response. She gives him a shrewd, lascivious smile to taunt him. "I will not have you reading my mind unless we are in the bed and my thoughts are only of the way I wish to be pleased."

He takes her hand in his, laughs and kisses it ceremoniously. "Aadya, you are full of surprises."

"I mean it." She gives him the sternest glare she can muster and then sucks in her breath. *I can't believe I spoke to him like that, but he does not mind. Going to bed with him has already changed the way we are together.* YES, MY LOVE YOU ARE RIGHT.

The realization that Poma could now be easily in her mind causes her to hold her breath close. *There will never be secrets between us.* Squeezing her hand tightly, Poma leads her through the throng in the great hall. The swath of people parts in sporadic waves before them until they reach the head table where King Larsa stands and salutes his son. The crowd, having cleared a sizable circle around them, roars as he returns his father's salute by raising his arm while still grasping hers in a tight clutch.

Aadya is mortified as she realizes the meaning of this dramatic exchange and her cheeks flush hot with the shame of it. But no one notices. They are all too busy having a good time.

Hunger claws at her resilience, and she folds into her chair when she finally reaches it. To her delight, succulent meats buttery tender, and falling off the bone are served to her. She still does not quite understand what Poma's relationship is with meat. *He still eats small amounts.* She encourages the server to keep coming with the slices of delicately seasoned meats and plunges into the feast. *No one has told me not to eat meat.*

There are also fruits, candied bitter and salty, berries, breads and cheeses both sweet and tart, nuts of distinctively sodden tastes, dishes of creamy roots and tendrils of forest vegetation, wine of many colors and sweetness, and tiny cakes, fermented, sweet and savory. Of particular interest to Aadya, are the sugar crystalized flowers still aromatic from the ground they sprouted from, which are delicate but crunchy when you bite into them. Aadya looks over to Poma to guide her through this maze of delicacies, but he is busy toasting with his family and friends. There is a ring of tables on the outside of the crowd filled with the same delicious fare the royal table is being served, but people are mostly snacking and roaming, rather than sitting. The few tables where guests are sitting are filled with elders and children who pop up sporadically to ramble.

Aadya's uncle makes his way to her table with a ludicrous grin on his face, making her acutely aware of how drunk he is.

"So, little one, you are a princess now!" He raises his glass to toast her. Your father would be immensely proud."

"Thank you, uncle but I have accomplished nothing. I have only followed my heart."

"It must be a good heart to follow." He says with more kindness than she has ever evidenced. "You have found your path and it is favorable." Aadya cannot contain her sour expression. *Favorable to fill your own coffers.*

With wobbling knees, her uncle wavers, and his wine teeters on the edge of his goblet. Aadya is afraid he might collapse there in front of her, but suddenly a hush falls over the boisterous crowd as a man and a woman enter, and the crowd again parts ways.

The man, bearded, dark, and naked from the waist up wears golden serpent bracelets twisting up his muscular arms. The woman's body is mostly bare except for a few strategically placed pieces of gold cloth secured with cords of gold and gems. She is both buxom and petite, with defined body features men notice, and women envy. A small corps of muscular men, naked from the waist up also, appear pounding on drums as the two begin to dance. Their movements flow like liquid grace, and all eyes are riveted on their performance. As the drum sounds soar, the din of the jovial diners dies down and the dancers began to leap into the air in a captivating, erotic display. Aadya, who had just hours before been introduced to the fine art of physical expression with a man, is overwhelmed by the beauty and eroticism of the performance, and despite how hungry she is, succumbs to the rapture of their dance, only occasionally dabbing some tasty morsel clumsily to her mouth.

Poma grasps her hand and with the look of desire, slides their two clasped hands down between her thighs. Compelled by intense pleasure she momentarily fades between the present and the immediate past of their time together in their bedchambers. Shaking it off, she gives Poma a modest smile and continues to watch the dancers who spin and leap with pure grace and synchronicity. The dancers finish with a deep throated kiss and a dramatic fusion pose, making the crowd roar and stomp their feet.

Poma jumps to his feet clapping vigorously. The dancers approach and bow dramatically to the matrimonial couple. Poma hands the woman one of the flowers placed nearby for such a gesture. The female dancer smiles and bows even deeper, her plump breasts nearly cascading out of her costume. Her actions make Aadya feel uneasy, but Poma quickly takes Aadya's hand and lifts, helping her to her feet. He gives her a peremptory nod, indicating she should honor the male performer, which she does rather awkwardly. *Yet another unrehearsed moment.* She hands the performer his flower, startled at the lustful look he gives her. Poma laughs when he sees his bride falter from the gaze of another man. MASTER BRUTUS KNOWS WHEN HE SEES BEAUTY. She shakes her head.

NO, IT IS NOT WHAT YOU THINK. I ONLY DESIRE YOU.

Poma's smile blossoms as his pride soars.

The crowd begins to chant and stomp their feet. "We want Princess Aadya, we want Princess Aadya!" This is the part she is sure they are supposed to dance. Because Poma had been in exile before the wedding, Aadya had been trained with a surrogate, while Bodie chanted the measure of the steps to music with all the passion of a bored animal trainer.

I can't do this. I'm going to disappoint everyone! Her stomach roils and her knees grow weak. Then Poma lifts the ceremonial cup, sitting on the table before them, drinks and then puts it to her lips. It is the same pearly white tincture given to her before the ceremony, and again, as soon as it touches her lips, she is instilled with all the confidence she needs. They begin to dance before the crowd effortlessly. Sometimes when Poma spins her, it feels as if she becomes airborne.

Their perfunctory performance is brief, and the couple sits down to listen to hours of endless enunciations of blessings and toasts, from everyone in the room of social significance, until at last the king and queen speak.

Queen Mesa stands and lifts her goblet toward the nearby couple. "My dearest son, we partake in the fulfillment of prophecy tonight and bless this union which shall commence a new era. It is your first born who will lead this world of ours into a brighter day."

What? No one has mentioned prophesies about the future. Aadya lifts her heavy goblet unsteadily toward her new mother-in-law and smiles with enthusiasm. She is genuinely appreciative for the acceptance the queen has generously bestowed upon her, but she remains leery. *And what will the king say?*

King Larsa, looking like an older version of his son, stands to speak. "My dear son and his bride, we lift our cups in celebration of the years ahead and welcome our new daughter, Aadya, into our hearts." *Short and sweet. No apparent negativity. No spilled secrets.*

This night is almost over. I am exhausted. Aadya turns to Poma and with her eyes pleads to leave. He takes her hand and escorts her to their chambers where a roaring fire awaits them.

19-A Secret Awaits

It takes several days for the effects of the enchanted elixirs and the excitement of the wedding to wear off. Not surprisingly, the newly married couple decide to sneak off to the hunting lodge for some time alone together. The journey requires them to travel on horseback and Aadya, as experienced as she is in hunting and hand to hand combat, has had no experience with horses. The only horses she had seen before meeting Poma, were wild horses, and these extraordinary creatures rarely came close to her village. In fact, there were some people in her village who thought horses were magic and claimed they could fly when needed.

When she told Poma this he had laughed and explained. "Many years ago, there were Matong warriors who were allowed to expose their steeds to the Matong, and perhaps this is where the village stories come from. With progress, access to the Matong has become more limited," he explained.

Having had enough of the dresses for a while and learning they would not be required at the hunting lodge; Aadya insists Poma should teach her to ride a horse because she did not want to ride in the carriage while he rode.

They were standing in the royal stable when she reminded him. "I am your equal." And to this he gives her a good-natured smile, with the neutrality of a seasoned diplomat.

"We will stay for two weeks, and then I promised Mother we would return and resume our education."

"Education? What kind of education?"

"You must be instructed in the ways of becoming a queen and, I must resume my studies also. Education always continues for those of royal lineage."

Great more duties. She takes this moment to once again remind him her role would not be as a breeder. "I want to be involved in leadership, and not just be a figurehead."

Poma laughs, "My dear Aadya, I think there is no doubt all who have encountered you are aware of that. All the more reason for your thorough education."

She gives him a meaningful look. "This week you must finish teaching me to ride," she says with much innuendo and thinking herself clever for the layered meaning of her words.

"Is that so? If that is the case, then I think you are going to love my gift to you." Poma gives the stable lad a nod, who returns leading a most extraordinary opalescent horse.

"Oh, Poma she is mine?" Her heart is racing, and her breath is short.

"Yes, my love, she is yours."

"Poma, you walk the bridge!" she says, referring to the popular folk legend that those brave enough, could walk from one moon of Merth to the other on an invisible bridge defying death. This was described as 'passing over the bridge.' It is the highest compliment she could give him. Aadya's emotions are surging, and she is confident she has made the right decision to marry Poma. *Perhaps all this pomp and circumstance is worth it if I am to have my own horse.*

Poma laughs heartily as he hears her thoughts. Still a novice at thought projection Aadya is insecure that her inner voice might leak out to Poma when she did not mean to share. As she practices more, she would have more privacy, but Poma does not need to remind her. She has been instructed, now she must figure it out for herself.

Aadya rests her forehead against the horse's muzzle and allows the hot stream of the mare's ephemeral breath warm her face. Running her hand down the horse's flank, she marvels at the softness of the animal's silvery coat.

"What is her name?" she asks, peering into his eyes.

"She is called Chelsea, and she comes from the ancient bloodline of the Matong soldiers. If there are magical horses, then she is one of them."

Poma's pride is visible in his intensifying grin. Aadya, who is much smaller than Poma, squeezes him hard around the torso like a joyful child. *I have not made a mistake. I will do my best to live up to this. Woku was correct this is my true destiny!*

"Here let me demonstrate. You grab the reins and the horn of the saddle, put your left foot in the stirrup and then swing up like this."

From Chelsea's back he looks down on her.

"Okay, I'm ready to try."

Poma dismounts and stands behind her to assist. He puts the reins in her hands. "Keep your heels down, grip with your knees and do not try anything fancy. We will only walk at first. Just follow behind me until you get used to riding."

Leaving most of the adornment of her new royal status behind, it is a comfort to be wearing soft leather pants and tunics designed expressly for her. The designers had even come up with a long-split tunic, buckled at the waist she could ride in with more ceremonial situations. It was comforting to know her desires were being acknowledged despite the fact she was progressively bucking cultural norms.

The exquisite mare turns her head sharply and sniffs of Aadya's leg as if to welcome her. Then stomps her foot as if to say, 'I am at your command!' Aadya leans over to hug the silken neck of the magical steed and inhales her horse's scent, musky and sweet.

All their provisions have been loaded onto a cart that has already left Katara. So, they have nothing to worry about except getting to their destination.

After a couple of miles, Aadya becomes more confident with her riding skills. "Chelsea and I are tired of looking at your horse's butt," she says urging her mare to catch up by his side. They are following a road on the edge of a golden field of tall hay that has not yet been cut for harvest.

"Great, I was tired of turning around to talk to you. This is much better."

"So, what is your horse's name?"

"This my beloved Hunter. I have had him for several years. He has proven to be as loyal as he is strong," Poma remarks with satisfaction stroking the obsidian-dark coat of his horse's neck.

"Yes, why did you name him Hunter when you yourself do not hunt?"

"He was given to be by the Yarrow tribe as a treaty gift. The name came with him."

"I think I will teach you how to shoot the hand crossbow," she tells him out of nowhere. For several days, like a premonition Aadya has been haunted by a vision of Poma using the treacherous weapon that could sling arrows with the flick of a wrist.

"Now why would I want to do something like that?"

"Because you never know when you might have to defend yourself?"

"From what exactly?"

"You should not rely totally on the gifts of the Matong. You might become vulnerable some time when you do not expect it. Like now, we are headed to the outlying lodge, I should have my bow and arrow with me. Besides now you have me to look after, and what if we have a child?"

"I suppose with you as such a sharpshooter, you will look after me."

Really? She recognized he was teasing, but still she thought it would be more becoming of a prince to act more like a warrior.

"Do not worry Aadya, we are always protected. You may not see our royal entourage, but they are always nearby. They are trained to protect us at all costs. Under the reign of my father there is peace on all sides of our country. War is something he has tried to eliminate."

The rocking motion of Chelsea's gait beneath her has now become second nature to Aadya, leaving her free to relax and process some of the more recent events.

"So, what is this prophesy about our child changing everything?"

"You know that is a closely guarded secret I have not been privy to," he tells her, but she is not convinced. "I mean I have heard of it, but it has been unexplained to me until now," he shrugs. "I suppose my parents withheld certain things from me, with good reason. You may not believe this, but at times I have been a rebellious youth."

"Really?" She turns her head to meet his gaze. "I would not have thought so."

"I imagine as soon as you are with child, more will be revealed concerning the legend."

"So, what if I am unable to conceive?

Poma stops his horse abruptly and she in turn pulls back Chelsea. "That my love, is not a possibility. When my mother first consulted the Matong about our marriage, you were approved."

Approved?

"You will grow to be more intuitive as time goes by and you are exposed to the Matong. And you will come to understand. He turns and looks at her, resting his palm on Hunter's broad rear.

"Are you ready for the next step?"

"What do you mean?" she says, suddenly anxious he was proposing they should immediately have a child.

He looks across the horizon. "The sun is getting low in the sky, and we should pick up the pace a little. Chelsea is a specially gaited horse, so her next stride will be faster but smooth. Should she break into a canter, you need to pull her back, you will not have the grip down yet."

"Of course," Aadya breathes more freely as her chest loosens realizing the prince only has getting to their destination on his mind.

Poma clucks at the horses who immediately quicken the pace. Chelsea arches her neck in a showy gesture.

"Wow! I love this!" The swift, but smooth gait is exhilarating. And for the first time in her life, Aadya is at peace inside, a feeling that will only continue to grow.

Approaching a hillside, Poma points. "We will cut through the woods over there toward the clearing."

As the two of them approach the lodge Aadya hears something which sends her heart soaring as if it has left her body and is floating on a string above her. It is the sound of Jefa and Moh who race to greet them nervously pacing close to the horses, because they have never seen such creatures. Moh growls menacingly and Aadya whistles softly to signal to him all is well.

20-My Home Is with You

The two weeks of their marital retreat pass quickly and Aadya has become so in love with Poma, it scares her. *I never knew I could feel this way. Just watching him cross the room makes me giddy. He adores me too! Our connection has such intensity it could be set to music, strummed on a lucre, and my heart could be played in harmony with his. How did this come to pass?*

Every luxury is taken care of for the two of them including extravagantly prepared meals by a staff, staying in a lodge on the other side of the woods, who come and go discreetly without disturbing the newlyweds. Fresh flowers are placed about the lodge daily, and each morning, after their night spent together in each other's arms, they wake to the smell of freshly baked breads and sweets.

Each evening they sit by the fire and rest on soft blankets, made from the silky fur of the lama dama goats, after an active day of riding, or swimming. The dogs have become accustomed to join them, and they all puddle up together snacking on wine and fresh cheeses and fruits.

"Every time I ride Chelsea, I am in awe she is mine," she tells Poma on more than one occasion. The two of them spend a good deal of time riding, and Aadya is becoming more skilled every day.

"I know, I'm not sure who you love more, Chelsea or me," Poma teases her.

Aadya grins. "Well… she is a horse. You understand you're up against some tough competition."

"I want you to teach me those moves you were doing on your horse today. You know how you made him bow to me, and how he hopped on his two hind feet."

Poma grins "That is not terribly difficult. I will show you."

By the time their respite comes to an end, Aadya is riding her horse like an expert. "You are a natural on a horse. I have to admit," Poma tells her. "I'm dissappointed we must pack up and leave in the morning."

"I know but I do not want to. Couldn't we stay a few more days?"

He squeezes her and pulls her close enough she feels the pulse of his breathing.

"It is time. I promise we will do this often. I have never been so happy, so relaxed."

"Do we always have to live at Katara, under your parent's close watch?"

"It's not something I've given much thought to," Poma's posture becomes more rigid as he mentally prepares for what sounds like an uncomfortable conversation coming. "Katara is where we live."

"But I have not always lived there. It is not my home. I'm not used to living in the city, and we deserve to have our own home." *I shouldn't be so demanding when every luxury has been bestowed upon me, but I must speak my mind.*

Poma's smile fades as he looks into her eyes and says, "My home is with you now. Where would you have us live?"

"I do not know…perhaps we could live beside a stream where the magic horses roam," she says half seriously.

He laughs, "you are always full of surprises, little one."

"Poma," She looks at him with all the seriousness she can muster. "You may call me that in private, but do not ever say it in public." Her words spill out like a knife to a grinding stone.

The confusion Poma experiences crosses his face like an errant cloud on a bright day as he considers how little he understands her. IT IS AS YOU WISH MY BEAUTIFUL BRIDE.

21-Return to Katara

The returning newlyweds take their time on their journey home and are startled to be met by the king and queen with a small entourage on the road entering Katara. "We wanted to surprise you and welcome you two home," Queen Mesa explains. "So, I had a scout sent to discover your whereabouts."

The welcome party and Aadya's regret about returning, spark a peculiar reaction in her. She has a sudden urge to impress the welcoming party with her newly acquired riding skills. Buoyed by her recent elevation to princess, she impulsively clucks to Chelsea, precision trained in dressage, and sets her through her paces performing balletic feats. Rearing up on her hind legs Chelsea performs a careful turn with Aadya holding tight. They end the brief performance with Chelsea bowing on one bent knee while Aadya also takes a bow astride the lustrous white mare. The small crowd applauds. "Oh, I'm not sure where that came from," she whispers to Poma. He has already become more distant now they are no longer in seclusion.

Later when they are alone, he tells her, "It was okay today, to honor my parents with your skills, but when we are in the presence of either the king or queen, we must not take the focus off them."

"There are too many rules! You shame me."

NO, I DID NOT MEAN TO he speaks inside her head.

"The performance was fine."

"It's all so confusing."

"I know, but your classes in royal etiquette will clear all this up."

"You mean there's more?"

Poma looks away and she lets her chest collapse in frustration.

At the feast for their return, Aadya finds herself seated by her mother-in-law who is bubbling over with inappropriate questions for the newlyweds.

"Mother, please do not press my bride," Poma tries to intervene while putting his arm around her as if to protect her.

"We had a lovely time, let us leave it there, Mother. All is well in the bridal chamber."

But Aadya, simmering with joy and a little inebriated, from the obscene selection of extravagant wines the servants keep pouring for her, whispers to Queen Mesa, "I am intensely smitten with your son. We are very happy."

Queen Mesa uncharacteristically giggles, obviously buoyed by her new daughter-in-law's revelation.

It takes a good deal of time before Aadya eases into the expectations of her role; she spends as much time with Poma as his schedule allows, which dwindles with each passing day. Her free time, when she is not expected to be studying how to be a proper princess, she spends on the back of Chelsea exploring and hunting in the near-by countryside with Moh and Jeffa. With time, even this pleasurable distraction leaves an emptiness of purpose, to spin deep within her, as she has no reason to hunt, to put food on the table, for her family. Sometimes she has the meat packed up and sent to her family, but it has the quality of an empty gesture as they now have a stipend, due to their relationship with her, and want for nothing.

It is Aadya's introduction to numbers, in one of her endless tutoring sessions, where she finally finds purpose.

"Numbers. Do you know the nature of numbers?" Aadya asks Poma one day. He gives her an awkward look.

"Of course, I know of numbers. Where does this come from?"

"I didn't know such things existed. I am learning much now we have gotten past all the etiquette nonsense."

"Protocol is not nonsense, Aadya, it is about respect for the leaders of the land."

Ignoring his change in subject, she pursues her purpose. "Why do we not teach everyone about numbers?"

Poma gives her an even more confused look. "Why would we do that? The farmers in the field have no need to understand calculation."

"Sure, they do. Knowledge of numbers would help them when planting the crops. They could keep records and know how much seed to plant. It would help them improve their production."

"We already have agrarian advisers."

"I should think there are people out there who need to be able to evaluate numbers, including women. There has to be a better way to organize and educate everyone. The only way I became exposed to knowledge was through my questions to the elders. I really had to make a pest of myself to get the limited knowledge I did. I've learned more in the past few weeks than I did my entire life."

"Perhaps you are ready to experience the Matong more often."

"What for?"

The Matong will give you clarity about the things you are searching for like this education idea. Why not go together now and ask for guidance?

"You will come with me then? I have not been in there alone."

"Of course, and you should be comfortable to go there by yourself anytime you want to."

Really? I could go in there alone. I am not worthy.

Poma takes her hand and leads her to the Matong chamber.

"Do not be timid," he reassures her. "You are a princess now. Place your hand on the orb and think about whatever is on your mind."

Poma turns and closes the door behind them, giving them complete privacy with the Matong.

She looks at him, he nods, and she cautiously places her hand on the warm, glowing sphere. She can feel the Matong's power surge into her body, flowing up through her arm where the warmth radiates across her body, circling around her heart with the power to squeeze the life out of her if it chose. There are no words spoken as the Matong explores her thoughts.

The release is startling. She opens her eyes, and it is as if she has traveled to another place.

"What happened?"

It takes a minute for her to reassemble her worldly thoughts.

"I am to send for Heshe. She is the first one to be educated." She smiles as her own words start sinking in. "Poma, this is joyous news. And I am to teach you weaponry with the help of the soldiers."

"What? The Matong told you?"

"No," she laughs, but you need to learn."

"Maybe so," he shrugs, "it will be enjoyable if you are my teacher." Changing the subject, he reassures her. "You may visit the Matong any time, but for safety, I request you let me or someone in the family know when you do. Too many visits too often, will leave you drained. So, watch yourself."

"Yes, master," she curtsies to mock him.

"I tell you this from experience," he says lowering his eyes in a mysteriously humble manner.

22-Your Child Shall Heal All

The day comes when Aadya realizes she is with child. She has many questions. For some reason it is more important for her to reach out to Queen Mesa, than her husband.

Heshe has never had a child what could she know? And then there was the Matong to consult, but first she must seek out the queen.

"I must speak to you confidentially," Aadya tells her at their next private moment together.

"What is it dear? Queen Mesa leans over the small table to draw closer.

"It is the news you have been waiting for. I believe I am with child." She whispers manically as if the walls might reveal her powerful secret.

Watching the great Queen Mesa succumb to unexpected emotions startles Aadya while at the same she realizes she is delivering news her mother-in-law has been waiting for ever since Poma has grown into a man. Aadya is less afraid of Queen Mesa than she had been in the earlier days of her marriage. She has come to understand they are simply two women in similar circumstances.

"Have you told Poma?" The queen tugs at her heavy bejeweled bodice, trying to maintain a dignified presence.

"Not yet, you must not breathe a word of this until I do. Not even the king must know until I have told Poma."

"Are you absolutely sure?"

"No,"

"Have your hands been itching? And does the air smell salty?"

"How did you know?

"Those are sure signs!" the queen says, clearly excited.

"The only way to know with certainty is when you feel life, but this is your first time, and you will not experience this miracle until you are starting to show anyway." The queen purses her lips as her thoughts spiral.

"Let us go to the Matong together and get counsel."

Aadya looks around. "I was on my way to ride with Poma."

"It will only take a moment; we are not far from the hallowed chamber."

Heat radiates from the Matong and Aadya detects a slight humming sound she has not noticed before.

"I will also touch when you do. Together we will be nourished with the Matong's power."

Aadya nods. With a strong magnetic pull the orb sucks her closer. Her thoughts are instantly pushed out of her mind. When the orb lets go of its grip on the women seconds later, the two spontaneously have knowledge of the life Aadya now carries. They have been given permission to announce it to the king and all the people of the land.

YOUR CHILD SHALL HEAL ALL. The message reverberates through Aadya's mind.

"What does this mean?" she asks the queen.

"It is a prediction the king and I have been blessed to know for many years now, but this time I was merely told to prepare for the birth and be ready."

"Ready for what?"

"I am not sure," Queen Mesa tells her looking somewhat puzzled.

As the reality sinks in, Aadya experiences a slippery gush of emotions. "It is a relief to know this is going to happen. Poma will be beside himself."

Suddenly Aadya remembers Poma is waiting for her at the stables. She jumps up and races down the hallway before Queen Mesa has the inclination to detain her.

"I am grateful we have this time together," she tells Poma. He has been busy with official duties lately, and she has seen little of him.

But as soon as they embark, Aadya urges Chelsea into a fierce gallop, eager to show Poma her growing horsemanship.

Grinning, he spurs his stunning black mount, Hunter, of a breed known for its speed and characteristic feathery fetlocks. He quickly catches up.

Giddy and feeling a surge of joyous energy Aadya pulls up on Chelsea and comes to an abrupt stop. Pulling sharply on Hunter's reins, Poma also spins around wildly to a halt. "Remember where we stopped by the stream last time? Let us go there. I have something to tell you."

Aadya takes off again leaving him to follow. Hurrying ahead she throws down the napping hide she has brought made from the soft plush coats of Yeshan goats. Plopping down and eyeing him with a willful invitation she tells him to hurry. Unable to contain herself, she blurts out, "I am with child!" before he even has a chance to fully dismount.

He drops to his knees beside her. Their mutual joy surrounds them as he takes her into his powerful arms and squeezes her. It is a moment they would long remember even after the years of pestilence and strife are behind them.

23-You Really Do Not Know

Pregnancy is not how Aadya assumed it would be. Her brother, Jubal was three years older than her, and their father had disappeared in battle when she was a small child, leaving no other children to come behind her in her family. The women in her country village, known most vocally by the men as 'breeders,' quietly and dutifully carried out their gestation time working as hard as usual without consideration of their condition. Children were sometimes still born or not carried to full term.

Aadya, on the other hand, now so blessed with all comforts imaginable, continues her studies, and is encouraged to take recreational walks in the woods under heavy guard. She is also urged to eat only the healthiest foods. Poma, who rarely eats meat himself does not like her eating meat at all while she is with child. But Aadya has friends in the Katara kitchen who sneak her a few morsels whenever the opportunity comes along.

Heshe, who has taken to wearing flamboyant green sparkly fabrics, and dying her hair iridescent green on the top layers of her still jet-black hair, often accompanies Aadya on her walks when Poma is unavailable. Riding Chelsea is strictly off limits. This is the most unbearable part of pregnancy. She is, however, allowed to lead her horse along on her walks.

Work has begun on a nearby residence, at Aadya's insistence, which will be their home. It will have a protective wall, mostly for keeping out wild animals. With the prolonged stability of the kingdom, marauders are not of much concern. Curiously, at the queen's insistence, there is to be a subterranean tunnel to facilitate the safe return to the embrace of Katara's stalwart protection should it be needed.

"We will have a magnificent garden at our estate," she tells Heshe as they walk one afternoon. "We will plant vegetables and fruit trees, but we will also have a perfectly frivolous garden with woodland trees, within the walls, and a small lake. I can't really believe how fabulous it will be."

"And yet the people starve."

"No, Heshe, the people are not starving."

"I speak with embellishment. Let me say, in comparison to life at Katara, they are not equally endowed."

And yet you wear extravagant clothing now. Aadya glares at Heshe but says nothing of Heshe's indulgences since coming to Katara.

"We are working on these matters Heshe, Poma and I want to make changes. We have spoken to the king, and he has agreed. Now peace has taken root in the land, there needs to be prosperity for all. Besides, you are learning the skill of the numbers, and soon will take such knowledge to the people. How is your progress?"

Heshe snorts. "I think there are more important things to teach our people."

"What would you suggest?" The baby grinds its legs against Aadya's ribs causing her to wince.

"We need to hone hunting skills and food preservation. We need to replace the people's silly superstitions with appropriate knowledge."

"Yes, go on."

"Well, and you know this, we must learn to value our women."

"You have hit a note with me. Our women have much to offer our world beyond their bodies used as incubators for our progeny."

"This is one of my main concerns, when we venture forward with our teaching; how will the men react as we educate our women?"

"First we must educate our educators, make them strong, and prepared." Chelsea dips her head and pulls at her lead to chew on a few select and tender morsels of grass.

"Tomorrow, I would like to join with your group of educators and see what directions they are taking," Aadya tells Heshe grabbing her round stomach as she feels the baby roll within.

"Of course, my princess." *I will never get used to her calling me that, and yet it is the proper way for Heshe to address me.*

Later the same evening, Aadya and Poma stare out the tall open window of their bedroom as they lie in bed with a bone-warming fire popping and cracking in the fireplace. Aadya is too big and full of baby to do much else. They watch the twin crescent moons Ava and Duna—oddly given feminine names—as they rise together in the sky, a rare occurrence. A tangle of stars lays scattered across the night sky except for one curious blank patch known as the 'Immense.' It is the season of the wild creatures rebirthing. Everywhere you look flowers and plants are popping up with rejuvenated growth. The birds sing indiscriminately at all hours both day and night and colorful winged lizards and moths take to the air in spherical mating dances.

"We are immensely lucky to live on such a beautiful planet," Poma says squeezing Aadya playfully. The contentment in his voice is like fresh wine to her. *Ever since he received the word he is to be a father, an aura of still waters has settled around him. I, on the other hand, I am more industrious than ever.* For her everything has sped up, as if her life will end when her child's life begins.

"I spoke with Heshe today and she has concerns about our education programs."

"Oh," he says rhetorically knowing there is a flood of information about to break loose from Aadya, and the peaceful moment will be over.

"I'm going to become more involved with the educators, and how they are going to go about instructing the people. I think they need to travel with, a few at least, of the sacred books to share with the people."

"Aadya, we've been over this, the sacred books are not leaving Katara."

"But we need to bring the people here and let them see them."

"You are about to give birth to our child, who is supposed to be the savior of our kind. Isn't this enough?"

Aadya bolts up. "Why will the Matong not tell us if we are to have a boy or girl?"

Laughing nervously Poma is once again taken aback by her distracted thinking.

"Aadya, we've been over this too. We will have a boy."

"But you do not really know," she chastises him.

24-For All to See

"**B**reathe!"

"Can you not get her out of here?" Queen Mesa whispers to her son as a room full of people dutifully watch Aadya struggling to give birth. They are gathered in a spacious public bedroom often used for this purpose through the decades. The elegant bed with its intricately carved headboard is the same bed where Poma himself, his brothers, and even his father had been publicly born.

"No, I cannot!" He whispers back brusquely. "Aadya would kill me. Besides the royal physician is here. Not only does she trust Heshe, but she is also of the people in a way the citizens of Valtar are not."

"The crone is in the way, and it is setting an example I am uncomfortable with."

"At least Aadya has allowed witnesses to the birth. It took me forever to convince her it was vital to the people."

"I know," mumbles Queen Mesa, "we had to build her a castle all her own."

"Mother, if you do not check your ill temper... I'll... I will have to ask you to leave. My child is being born."

Looking offended, Queen Mesa stands up from the lavish chair they have brought her to sit in during the lengthy labor of her daughter-in-law. Poma flashes her a beseeching look, and she sits back down in a halfhearted huff.

"Bonder," Poma says softly to his brother, "Over here." Bonder who is slightly taller than his brother Poma, reluctantly comes to his side, uncomfortably close to where Aadya lies on the bed discreetly covered, but still in the most compromising of positions.

"Can you please stand here with mother. I've got to help Aadya." Suddenly a thunderous wail comes from Aadya making Poma shudder, and the whole roomful of people shuffle uncomfortably; some women themselves gasping in remembrance of their own birthing experiences.

"Breathe!" Heshe commands, " and do NOT push yet." The physician looks crossly at her, but is too focused, or afraid to challenge the green-haired crone. He backs down.

Heshe whispers into Aadya's ear. "Do not be alarmed but I need to check how far along you are."

"What does that mean?" She says through gritted teeth as serving maidens anxiously wipe her sweaty brow.

" I need to see if the baby is crowning."

Another pain wrenches Aadya speechless as she tries to restrain herself from screaming, but it is no use. Another scream, primal and demanding, forces its way up and out her throat, and once released Aadya is ashamed by her lack of control especially *in front of this ridiculous audience!*

And with the experience of someone who has assisted with hundreds of births, Heshe inconspicuously slips her finger inside of Aadya's birth canal to check on the status of enlargement.

"It is time," she tells Aayda softly into her ear. "You are ready to push." Heshe gets behind the princess, and, with her hands, braces her back, while nodding to the physician to ready himself to deliver the baby.

At this point, several women hold up a tapestry to provide for privacy, and all the physician has to do is grasp the baby and pull. Several other women step in quickly to swaddle and wipe the baby down as the physician pulls out the afterbirth and cuts the cord.

Aadya, who has been in labor for close to eight hours, fades in and out of consciousness as Poma steps to her side to welcome his child. One of the nurses places the swaddled newborn into his hands. Poma's body responds with echoes of emotion as he holds the miracle of the magical tiny person in his arms for the first time. He kneels beside Aadya who smiles with pride as they both embrace their newborn with the infinite love only a child can induce.

Heshe beams with pride, and the doctor makes his way to the parents. Without saying a word, he opens the royal baby blanket, made especially for this birthing with its sateen softness and royal insignia, to show them the sex of their baby girl. Aadya grins while Poma's face pales to the same pearly color of the blanket his baby is swaddled in.

"But how can this be?"

"See, I told you, you did not know," Aadya whispers to him.

"Mother, Father!"

The crowd parts for King Larsa who is standing toward the back of the room trying to show support without being obtrusive. Queen Mesa, still in her nearby chair peers in behind the blanket. They too look bewildered when they see their son holding a girl, and not the boy everyone expected.

"I do not understand why the Matong did not warn us. Is this really the child who is supposed to save our kind?" she asks the king. Misgivings scurry down Mesa's spine like tiny spider legs. "I am going to consult the Matong," Mesa whispers into her husband's ear. "For now, let us keep this to ourselves." Then she looks pointedly into the eyes of all who stand in the small circle and says softly "No one is to announce details of this until I consult the Matong."

"No!" King Larsa commands. "This is not a mistake but the will of the mighty above. More will be revealed. We must have faith."

The king takes the baby from Poma's hands, nods for the tapestry to be dropped, and holds his swaddled granddaughter up victoriously. "We have a beautiful new girl to join our family!" Cheers and clapping saturate the room. King Larsa's pride can be seen in his face as he turns in a half circle from the raised floor of the royal bedroom, and lifts the infant higher allowing all to see and admire his progeny. Taking the child back, Poma huddles with Aadya, and holds her until the crowd is vacated from the room.

25-Healing Spirit of Love

For several weeks all Aadya does is nurse her baby and stare at her incandescent purple eyes. No one has ever seen such color in a child's eyes before, which is reminiscent of the tõramalli gemstone, rarely encountered on Merth. There are only five known stones, and all are in the possession of the royal family. This, combined with the fact the infant never cries, only serves to validate the Matong's prophecy. What warms Aadya's heart most, is the acceptance of the child almost immediately by King Larsa, even before the baby had opened her eyes.

In order to not cause a stir, the family has been keeping the newborn's presence protected, but gossip soon spreads despite their best efforts. "This child is a miracle, but she will forever be a challenge to protect," the king confided to his son one day.

"Yes, I have given it much thought," Poma agrees feeling a twinge in his mouth as if he had eaten a bitter seed.

Aadya secretly wants to name her baby after her mother, Mayalina, but knows it will not be allowed. The Matong will ultimately be consulted for naming this most important child of the kingdom.

On the fifth day after her birth, Aadya and Poma, accompanied by the king and queen, go into the Matong chamber, after an elaborate private ritual ceremony in the queen's chambers. First, they feast on petite white crystal sugar cakes and rich, dark red fruit juice which tingles as it is swallowed; they are guided in meditation by the queen's favorite spiritual guide, Hoya, who then leads them down the hall chanting until they reach the Matong chamber.

Hoya bows her head and nods to Poma who raises the baby, wrapped in an intricately embroidered quilt made of a shimmering fabric and delicate lace, as high as he can. Even so, his precious cargo is only one-third as high as the orb. The king and queen also put their hands together and place them on the orb. When Poma lowers the infant to Aadya's reach, she touches the baby with one hand and places her other hand on the orb. The light in the room dims. Struggling to see, Aadya watches as the name forms in dancing light circling around them spelling Galen Kama, later translated by Hoya from the ancient language as 'Healing Sprit of Love.'

After a few weeks Aadya tries to pull on her buttery soft Saffron leather leggings to go riding, but they are even now too tight, and she has to let out the drawstring as far as it will go. Alarmed by her body's inability to snap back to its prior condition, Aadya consults with Queen Mesa to ask if she will ever return to her previous physique.

"Yes, of course. As active as you are it will take no time at all. Do not despair."

The first trip outside of her quarters, is to ride with Poma and Galen, who is carried by Poma in a pack on his stomach, to their home still under construction. Chelsea prances and side steps with joy to be ridden again. Aadya is giddy with her own freedom and sense of belonging to this incredible little family of three.

Once she is assured Galen is snugly secured on her Daddy's stomach, Aadya takes off into a controlled canter, then releases to an all out gallop letting the wind rush through her loose hair and across her face. The emotional release is short lived as she pulls back on the reins to turn around and check on father and baby.

Poma smiles and waves from a distance behind her, not entrusting his cherished bundle with anything faster than a gentle walk.

Aadya races back to their side enjoying the release of the wild flame of her spirit as it soars with joy. Her mothering instincts smother further outbursts, and she pulls Chelsea up tight, snugly against Poma's horse.

"You pass the test. You are officially a good father."

Enjoying the full blast of her praise, Poma beams. "Of course, I am."

"Stop, let me check on her." Aadya leans over and lifts a corner of Galen's blanket only to see the cherished one is asleep.

"Good I do not want to feed her again until we get there."

"We're close."

"I know too close," she says cynically with reference to the proximity of their new estate to Katara. "At least we have the forest to buffer us."

Their residence, Compana, is completed enough they can enjoy a picnic and a fire in the fireplace, but not yet comfortable, or secure enough to spend the night. As they walk the grounds and view the work being done, Aadya is pleased to see the great hall will be as grand as Katara's. She envisions public festivals of merry making, but also the massive wooden tables and tapestry covered chairs will be used for lectures and demonstrations for educating the people. The kitchen will also be functional for large groups. It is lit with natural light and possesses expansive open spaces, with what appear to be acres of wood counters, for preparing meals for hundreds if needed. Their sleeping quarters will take advantage of views of stone outcroppings, the valley beyond the precipice with its vivid hues of layered stone, eroded over centuries, and the silver ribbon of river at the base. There is a wall of course for security, but many rooms in the royal residence have views because of its positioning on a knoll.

What is most appealing for both Poma and Aadya, are the gardens. Every outdoor space inside the wall and beyond the wall for miles, is to be carefully planted with ornate design to augment connection to the spiritual world of Merth.

26-Breaking Away

By the time Galen begins to walk, Aadya and Poma are still living at Katara, and Aadya has become increasingly frustrated they have not moved into Compana. Even worse, Queen Mesa has been putting pressure on Aadya to let others help her with the care of Galen.

"This will give you more time, to do all the things, you've been wanting to get done," the queen argues. "You have not been able to get educational programs started with all the running after your child you are doing now."

"She has found a way to pull at my heart," Aadya tells Poma later in the evening.

"I think she is right; you are struggling to keep up with our child." He flashes her a charming smile to win her over. "Besides, you would have more time to spend with me."

"When our two moons collide!" she raises her voice to Poma. "I will not hear of it."

It is the first time since they married, Aadya and Poma are at odds with each other. As much as he loves Galen, Poma understands he is not the vortex of Aadya's affections anymore, but enough is enough.

After several days of tension building between them like murky shadows at dusk, Aadya proclaims she will allow a dedicated servant to "assist," but not take over the child rearing duties of cleanliness, and supervision. *It is for our marriage* she tells herself. *Perhaps this will allow me time to get us moved out of here!*

"I know your mother is not happy about us leaving, but they will never finish the construction if we just do not go ahead and move in." She tells Poma defiantly one morning. "We wear ourselves out going back and forth, and we have some furniture in place finally. We need to sit down with your mother and map out a plan."

"Oh, she is not going to like this!"

"I know, but it is time. We have much to do. Please ask her to meet with us and we will set the date, the sooner the better."

After several days of waiting on Poma to do something, Aadya takes the matter into her own hands, inviting the queen to lunch. It is too risky to involve the king in their announcement at this point until they get the support of the queen, or at least her resignation to the idea the move was going to happen sooner than later.

"You must comply!" Aadya realizes her voice is rising above the level one speaks to a queen, especially if you were essentially asking for her permission. "Queen Mesa, truthfully, I am smothering here. We are not trying to take your granddaughter away. You can see her every day if necessary. It is time for us to begin our own lives. You want that surely?" Aadya has compassion for the strong woman she has learned to love but hates the hold she has on her son.

"I do not think it is safe there yet for Galen, there is still construction being completed. How will you keep her safe?"

Oh please! Aadya struggles to keep her thoughts from being projected to the queen.

"Your highness, I have done as you asked and now allow special servants to assist with her. We will take a heavy guard with us to Compana and create stringent protocols for Galen's protection." As Aadya says these things to her mother-in-law, she realizes her education has influenced her and how she communicates with more authority now. This fact makes her hum inside with satisfaction.

Oddly, it is the king who intervenes and bestows his approval for the young couple to make their exodus after Queen Mesa complains to him concerning her unsatisfactory meeting.

"Come now woman, you are clinging to them. Let our son and his wife begin their own adventures! We have built a citadel for them to protect our precious Galen. We must give them some breathing room to come into their own."

27-A Third Voice

As Galen grows, Poma and Aadya also grow in their roles as leaders. There have been disturbances in the outer reaches of the kingdom causing Poma and his brothers to spend more time traversing to the far corners of the land. While they have had success at handling conflicts with diplomacy, it is Aadya's educational programs which inspire the people to work together to prosper.

Galen now four, despite the prophecies surrounding her, is living a rather normal childhood at Aadya's insistence. She plays with other children and is learning to ride her own pony.

With increased exposure to the Matong, Aadya's Kinetic Sight has been strengthened and helps her to keep a close watch on Galen when she is out of earshot. While Poma and Aadya have dreamed of having more children, much to their disappointment, there have been no more preganacies.

What felt like a grandiose idea at first, Compana, and its surrounding village, has become a diverse community of thinkers, and a lively, productive hub of the kingdom. The prosperity has spread throughout the central region of the kingdom, considered to be as far out as can be ridden on horseback in five days. Aadya and Poma know most of the people in the village personally and Aadya intentionally avoids being cloistered with only royals.

"You have to admit, Poma, while commoners might be limited in their thinking, they are keen to learn once they are exposed to opportunities for knowledge. There is nothing more rewarding than watching a child become absorbed with ideas once they are engaged."

"This is true Aadya, but leaders must lead. We risk losing our people's respect if we are too familiar with them."

She rolls her eyes at him when he brings up this argument. "You are too old-fashioned."

But time has not been gracious to all. Grandmother Woku is now confined to her bed. Aadya visits her almost daily in her little house just beyond the stream and woodland garden. "Come with me to visit Grandmother Woku," Aadya says to her daughter one day knowing Woku's days are limited. "We can take her some soup to cheer her."

"Yes, mother, I will pick some flowers on the way. She loves it when I bring her flowers."

When they enter the small bedroom, Woku has not left in weeks, her eyes are closed, but a small smile creeps across her face when she hears their voices nearby. Her breathing is erratic and rattles from her lips.

Sunlight filters through the window falling on Galen's soft cheeks and luminous bronze hair making the space around her glow. "Mother something is wrong with Grandmother Woku."

"Yes, dear she is ill."

Galen pulls on her mother's sleeve. "No, mother she is leaving her body. I can't stop her."

Aadya bends down beside the bed. "She is extremely ill Galen, but she is still breathing."

"No, mother she is leaving. I can see her leaving her body."

Aadya takes a closer look, and it is true, she no longer can see or hear the tortured breathing of the woman who had raised her.

"Mother her time is now, we must say goodbye."

Startled, Aadya looks at her beloved daughter and feels chill bumps sprinkle across her arm and spread up the back of her neck.

"Woku can you hear us?" Aadya asks.

Her slight smile creeps a little wider on Woku's chiseled face. Galen puts her small hands on her grandmother's deeply wrinkled cheeks and looks up at her mother. "We must say goodbye now, it is her time. She is ready." Woku's eyes pop open briefly, startling Aadya and causing her to lurch slightly backward. Galen places her hands over Woku's eyes and Aadya now senses Woku has passed.

Aadya chokes and coughs, and struggles for breath. *Is this possible? What has just happened?*

"She had a good life," Galen says. "She is healed now."

When Aadya hears her daughter's strange proclamation she is stunned. *She used the word healed. Is this what is meant for her to be a healer? Rather than heal people back to life, was Galen going to be the one who guides them to their deaths?*

"Come we must go!"

"Where are we going mother?"

"To the Matong."

Aadya snatchs the four-year-old, too heavy and awkward to be carried anymore, up into her arms and races to the door. "Tell Heshe to find Poma and meet me at Katara, at the Matong," she shrieks at the nurse standing by the door.

While Aadya often rides to Katara with Galen riding her pony, she is too concerned to tarry.

"Fetch my horse please!" she shouts at the closest royal attendant she can find.

"Have you seen the prince?"

The attendant boy looks confused, but he now has Chelsea at the ready. "Please find him for me and tell him to meet me at the Matong." She suddenly realizes in her haste she has not explained to Woku's nurse she has passed, and preparations for her funeral should be made. "And go tell Woku's nurse to ready her for burial."

"Yes, Your Majesty, I am terribly sorry to hear this."

Aadya leans over for Galen to be handed up to her.

They tear out in a whirl of dust and straw with hooves pounding the familiar road, and Galen holding on for dear life as they race to the Matong for understanding. When they get to the gates of Katara, they are held up temporarily as the overzealous guards do not take riders racing to the gates lightly, no matter who they are. Chelsea rears up impatient with their demands as a guard grab her reins. "Is the prince here at Katara?

"Yes, Your Majesty, he rode in about an hour ago."

"Find him and have him meet me at the Matong."

Aadya does not stop to get off Chelsea until she climbs a loading ramp to the kitchen entrance. There she drops Galen down first and dismounts grabbing Galen by the hand and racing her to the Matong chamber. It is toward the direction of the moons rising almost a thousand steps.

The guards break away from the door to let her enter. Still holding Galen's hand, she touches the orb. As it grabs her up into its magnetic field, she realizes she is still holding onto Galen.

Electricity arcs through her body and into Galen. There is no releasing her now. Aadya looks down at Galen who is timidly smiling. *What have I done? She appears to be okay.*

Then Poma walks in looking somewhat alarmed but joins them by placing his hand on the giant orb now pulsing with light like a gigantic opalet stone.

As usual the orb releases them when the wisdom has been passed on.

WHAT IS GOING ON? Poma pushes through to her thoughts to discuss with her without including Galen.

Aadya responds with her Kinetic Sight by sending him her mind's replay of the events with Woku.

THIS IS MOST DISTURBING. BUT THE MATONG DELIVERED TO ME 'ALL IS WELL.'

ME TOO. MY DOUBTS ARE DROWNING.

AS USUAL WE ARE NOT TO KNOW EVERYTHING ALL AT ONCE. I AM CONFIDENT GALEN IS TO TRULY BE A HEALER AND NOT SOME DEATH REAPER.

I HOPE YOU ARE CORRECT.

ALL IS WELL. A third voice joins them. Startled, they look down at their angelic daughter with the haunting purple eyes who is smiling as if to reassure them.

THIS IS HIGHLY UNUSUAL. WE MUST CONSULT THE PRIEST!

28-The Gift

Galen's gift is further revealed the next day when she picks up a sparrow with a broken wing. As it flies away Aadya is taken over by a burst of joy at the miracle she witnesses. *My child is a healer! Thanks to you merciful One True God.*

Before they have even buried Grandmother Woku, there are two more incidents where Galen inadvertently heals a stunned green Tempar lizard and a baby Barl owl, knocked out of its nest.

"I saw it with my own eyes."Aadya tells Poma later in the evening. "It was on the ground screeching. It was awful. It almost sounded like a human baby, and it was really quite frightened. Once Galen stroked its head to comfort it, it became calm. The nest was too high for us to return the little owl, but it sat there for a minute then flew away. I do not know if it was its first flight or not, but it was gone."

But once the four-year-old's powers have been unleashed, Aadya becomes filled with angst. Her hypervigilance surfaces unexpectedly, like a storm about to purge, making everyone around her wonder why she is irritable. The normal activities she enjoys, like riding and target practice, listening to the musicians play, and sitting with her family in the evening before a roaring fire are now distracted by worries of how to protect her precious child.

"We are going to have a meeting in the morning with mother and father and Hoya," Poma promises her. Aadya practically hisses back at him,

"I do not want her used! She is only a child."

"And neither do I. We both want what is best for Galen," he tells her pacing the floor as he speaks. "She needs to be protected at all costs. But the weight of this responsibility does not rest entirely on your shoulders."

"Yes, it does, I am her mother, you are her father. You of all people should carry this burden with me."

"I think this talk with the elders will help ease your concerns. We will develop a plan to secure her safety."

But leaving the king's voluminous chambers the next morning leaves Aadya unimpressed with the solutions offered. In her paranoia, she had insisted the royal guard be dismissed from the room for security reasons, while several ideas were bandied about.

All they can agree on, is Galen will be more heavily guarded going forward. She will be sheltered from sick and injured people in the hopes she will not be tempted to heal, and thus expose her gift to any undesirable, who might be tempted to abduct her for their own pursuits.

Hoya is against this, "The child has a gift, and we are not to allow her to use it?"

"She is only four revolutions old and our only child, not to mention heir to the throne. There will be time enough for her to be a healer when she gets older," Aadya snaps. "If I catch wind of you violating our trust, I will have you punished to the full extent of the law!"

"I have to agree," the king takes Aadya's side. "We must protect her at all costs. We will continue to seek an answer to this," he says, drumming his fingers on the richly oiled surface of his carved wooden desk. "The Matong has been silent on the issue. Perhaps this is a test."

Always respectful, Hoya bows to the king and asks him to keep her apprised of any developments.

"Of course. This is my granddaughter we seek to protect."

29-Her Triumph Is Palpable

It was just after the big fanfare of Galen's fifth birthday, when Aadya realizes she might be pregnant again. She had almost given up hope.

They were on a diplomatic council in the far reaches of the kingdom. Poma convinced Aadya to join him by encouraging her to bring a staff of teachers to leave behind for further educating the people of the Dupong region of Merth.

He even convinced her to leave Galen at home with Queen Mesa and a hefty guard detail as they were only planning to be gone for seven moonrises. "She will be safer there rather than with us on the road." Aadya had to agree, and she was curious to know what was going on in the outskirts of Merth.

The Dupes, as the people were known, had been most welcoming, and extended every hospitality to the royal entourage. Lacking a castle in which to entertain, a group of dignitaries from the Dupes small village had created a celebratory campground for the visiting envoy to commingle with the locals.

"They have made a more gracious welcome with you joining me than they ever did for me or my brothers before. Unless of course the king was present." Poma complains to her the first chance they are alone in their luxurious tent.

Aadya smiles pleasingly at Poma, touching her slightly bulging stomach.

"My clothes have become tight," she hints hoping he will catch on.

But as Poma unleashes his waist from a too-tight pair of breeches himself, he is in his own world, mentally preparing for the diplomatic talks coming up, the drunken dinners he will be obliged to attend and the games of physical competence which will be played.

"Mine are too," he laughs.

She sashays over to him seductively and plants herself in front of him to get his full attention. "I do not want to get your hopes up beautiful prince, but there is a possibility there is another child on its way."

"What? Could this be true?" The promise of her words awakens in his face.

"I hope so. I will not know for sure until we return and consult with the Matong. I should have told you before we left, but with all the excitement for Galen's party and our journey here. I forgot to consult the Matong."

"I am pleased!" He pulls her close and showers her with tiny kisses.

"Just to make sure, perhaps we should test the softness of our bedding before we dine."

"Just to make sure the bed is comfortable or if I am with child?"

"Both." He gleefully picks her up and carefully lays her on the bed.

Word of the prosperity in other regions of the kingdom, and the overall success of the educational programs have already reached the Dupong region before the arrival of the royal envoy. The Dupes are satisfied with the staff of mentors brought to them and are eager to begin the process of educating their people. The region, being on the fringes of society, is still biased unfavorably toward their women. This causes Aadya to take every opportunity to be an advocate for her gender, and she makes a point to personally extend, to the leaders of the community, her advice on bringing women into more active participation in their destiny. To demonstrate her point she proposes an archery competition for women.

When this idea is met with confusion, it is because there are not any women in surrounding villages who hunt. This causes her to suggest adding to the games an archery demonstration to show women are capable of hunting skills. She even considers briefly participating in hand to hand combat but decides she might be somewhat rusty at this, and it might be too radical for the people, not to mention a danger to her possible pregnancy.

"You should demonstrate your skill with the wrist-crossbow," she tells Poma.

He laughs, "As long as you promise not to make me look too bad." With her encouragement he has become a formidable predator with the wrist-thrown arrows, but has not mastered the standard bow and arrow, which puzzles Aadya as the wrist-thrown weapons are considerably tricker than their larger counterparts.

The crowd is in a garrulous mood with all the festivities, music, and food in abundance.

The drum and trumpet corps fire up the enthusiasm of the throng with their signature calls to action. As the people gather, Prince Poma practices with the weapons. *Whoooosh* the arrows leave his crossbow landing in the center of the target. He receives cheers, calls, and applause, causing several of the best marksmen from the Dupe tribe to challenge him, and only one bests his score landing an exact bull's eye.

"Now it is your turn dear wife," Poma announces to the crowd. There is a bubbling murmur as curiosity spreads through the throng like a rock-scattered stream. Aadya takes her place on the same mark where the men have drawn as the drum and trumpet corps begins its thunderous introduction. *Whoooosh.* She too hits the center with her bow and arrow. The crowd roars with approval and she bows, her deerskin breeches scandalous enough in the wearing, but the fact a woman is a marksman is beyond what the Dupes have ever imagined. After her performance, the local warriors compete against the best team the visitors have brought with them.

"Would it be too much if I were to demonstrate Chelsea's moves?" She asks Poma. "I do not want to overdo the… I do not want to come off as arrogant… be too pushy." *Change is best delivered in small doses*, Heshe's words echo in her brain. "But I'd love the women to see what an amazing horse she is. This tribe in particular because they do herd horses and ride."

Poma considers her suggestion thoughtfully and agrees. "We have had such a comfortable gathering up until this point, I think it would be the icing on the cake," he tells her.

Chelsea is brought, out and Poma whispers to the announcer who signals the drummers, and Aadya mounts. She runs Chelsea through her acrobatic moves and leaps, as the crowd collectively oohs and aahs, confirming she has made a dazzling effect with her magnificent horse. The women's faces light up, while the men fold their arms and shake their heads. Change is slow but her triumph is palpable.

It is later, when the crowd has convened to the dinner tables, set up outside in a corral of flags and torches, when Aadya is approached by a young woman. "Excuse me Princess Aadya," the woman bows deeply, almost touching the ground. "I wanted to ask you if you would support me," she says boldly.

"Yes," Aadya takes in the strange looking woman. She is tall and sleek like a well-bred racing horse. Her deep-set golden eyes are augmented by full arching eyebrows the color of sapphrite. *Very exotic.* "How can I help you?"

"I would like to learn the marksman skills you demonstrated."

"Yes, of course."

"But you do not understand they punish women here for doing such things. I would be cast out."

Anger welds Aadya's expression. "This is undeniably wrong, but typical I find."

"Get me Poma!" she commands one of the nearest guards.

"He has retired to the magistrate's tent to discuss trade programs."

"Then we must go to him this minute. Show me the way." Despite the fact the girl looms over her when standing, Aadya takes the girl's hand in hers as if she were Galen. "What is your name?"

"Magdala."

"Magdala, we will address this now."

The magistrate's tent is on the edge of the field nestled between two other tents of high-ranking officials of Dupes. They have to cross through a muddy area and horses can be heard neighing and stomping as they approach. It is growing dark, but the escort tries to light the way for them, although he struggles to keep up with Aadya.

"Wait here," she tells the girl. "Announce me, please." The soldier dutifully mutters to the sentries. They frown but do as they are told, and Aadya is admitted to the tent.

"Forgive me for the intrusion, but I have just been delivered some disturbing news."

"What is it my dear?" Poma questions her.

"There is a young woman outside who wants to hone her skills as a marksman, but tells me this is not allowed. She tells me it is even possible she could be shunned for such practices. Is this true magistrate?" She asks the dignitary, whom they have come to know on a first-name basis as Kwatar, putting an emphasis on her indignation.

The magistrate's eyes visibly dilate at this unexpected development. "Princess," he stumbles for words. "Your highness, with due respect," he bows his head. "In our culture we do not engage breeders in hunting."

Idiot! she wants to shout but does not. "Magistrate have you not been paying attention? We must begin now! And most of all we must stop referring to our precious women as breeders!"

"Aadya" Poma appeals with his eyes and then with his thoughts. WE MUST NOT DO THIS NOW. WE HAVE AGREED CHANGE MUST COME SLOWLY. Aadya glowers at him as if he is personally responsible for the magistrate's offensive reaction.

I AM SORRY POMA, BUT THIS NEEDS TO BE ADDRESSED BEFORE WE LEAVE. I WILL APPROACH THE MATTER CALMLY, IF YOU WILL SUPPORT ME.

Poma lets go of his breath and his shoulders lower slightly.

Taking a stand Poma looks directly into the eyes of the magistrate. "Kwatar, let us discuss this now before we leave. We have been dancing on the edges of the topic, but our culture must be altered, and if we do not address it openly, we will not experience change."

"I'd like to bring in the girl in question," Aadya demands. Kwatar looks alarmed and Poma nods his head subtly to say no.

Aadya ignores both of them, and motions for the girl to be brought in.

"This is Magdala, if you allow her to follow her heart and train with the soldiers, she might save your life someday." She glares at the official.

Kwatar looks down at his feet, not knowing how to respond.

Poma chuckles, "As you can see my dear wife, princess of the realm, is even more passionate about this than I am."

The magistrate looks to the prince for guidance on what to say, but a war is going on inside of him with the teachings of everything he has ever known now battling with the words of the prince of all the land, second only the king himself. "Is this what the king has decreed?"

"Yes, we have full authority to educate your people in ways of thinking. This is part of the promise of knowledge we bring to you."

"Magdala, I know your parents. Are these your wishes? Do you really want to be a marksman?"

"Yes," she says demurely, but does not lower her eyes. "My parents have sworn me to secrecy for fear I would be cast out."

Aadya feels an ominous chill spread across her face and down her arms. She knows if they do not press their point, this poor girl, who at least has the desire for change, will never be able to access her dreams or her skills.

30-Homeward Bound

It is on the second night of their journey home when the envoy is invaded by a herd of wild hogs. A perimeter had been set by the guards as usual, but late at night and smelling the tangy leftovers from the camp's evening meal, the feral hogs, somewhere around twenty of them, overrun the camp. It is dark and difficult to see them, most of the fires and torches have been extinguished for the night. A handful of men, playing dice games late into the pre-dawn hours, are the last to retire, but even they have gone to bed. The raucous squealing, of the pigs as they forage for tangy morsels cast off by careless diners, awakens Aadya. It is an eerie sound of savage beasts rooting into the ground she has not heard since before moving into Katara.

"Holy prate!" she giggles punching Poma awake. "We are being overrun by hogs! "Grab my bow!" Poma foggy with sleep is unclear what is happening.

"Guards!" he shouts reflexively pulling on his robe. Aadya reaches for her bow which is always nearby when they travel. She enjoys helping to feed their crew with fresh game whenever possible, but tonight's intrusion is exceptionally critical because of the damage the boar's can commit.

"Guards check the horse's tent!" she shouts hoping there is someone to hear her.

Hastily tying her night robes, she pushes open the tent door and pulls an arrow out of her quilven. She can hear the horse's brisk neighing and snorting. Without shoes she races toward them in the darkness. Aadya glances up at Ava, the lesser moon of two, but being in a in a singular phase without the luminescence of her sister moon, Duna, there is not enough light to secure a shot. Aadya hears the massive pigs bullying the horses, which does not make sense *unless they are trying to break into the grain bins. They must really be hungry. They can easily injure the horses with their tusks.* She closes her eyes. '*Give me sight, oh righteous one.*'

As if in a dream Aadya's spirit leaves her body as the pull of the Matong positions her to guide her arrow, lifting her slightly off the ground. She has nothing more than shadows and grunts to take aim at, but her hearing is enhanced to such a degree she is amazed. She has not experienced such a strong pull of her Kinetic Sight. Aadya sucks in a huge breath, lifts her heart, and with her eyes still closed lets loose her arrow. It runs true, straight into the heart of a ferocious boar.

Crazy with rage and not dead yet, the wild boar turns and charges at her. She reaches to pull out a second arrow but before she can draw it, another arrow goes singing past her, not one handsbreadth beyond her own hand. Ducking reflexively, Aadya flattens herself on the cold, wet ground trying to minimize the attack of the charging boar when she hears the horrific squeal of the boar dying.

Poma rushes to her side. "Aadya are you all right?" She looks up. He has felled the grotesque boar now close enough they can smell its stench mixed with fresh blood.

She laughs nervously, "I think so. I am all wet. I hit him. He just kept coming at me."

"I know."

Several of the royal guards come running up with torches. "Sheer mayhem. I apologize sir." The vicious herd appears to be retreating, most likely frightened by the scent of fresh blood from their own pack.

"Please! Have this meat dressed," Aadya barks as she bats at her soaked clothing. "See to the horses and for heaven's sake make sure the garbage is buried better!"

"Let us get you back to bed and warmed up," Poma tells her lifting at her elbow to assist her.

"I need some hot tea. Let us build a fire at our tent and sit outside for a while. I have not seen our radiant morning star rise since Galen was a baby. I can't sleep, can you?

YES, I SHALL GET US TWO CHAIRS AND SIT WITH YOU, MY LOVE.

Her smile, not seen in the dark by Poma, is one of deep satisfaction. Aadya, knowing they would have a few moments together before she would begin hearing snoring sounds of the weary, coming from his chair, sits gratefully beside him. She has been rescued by her prince.

31-The Travelers Return

The travelers arrive home late. They have journeyed hours by the shadowy light of the single moon, Ava, in order to avoid setting up camp one last time. When they get to the house,

Galen is already in bed, but neither Poma nor Aadya can resist going into her room to check on her.

"Maybe we should have taken her with us. It is such a lengthy time to be away from her," Aadya whispers to Poma.

"I agree, but we are home now."

"Shh, I think she is waking."

Poma grins and makes his way toward her bed sitting heavily beside his sleeping daughter with just enough contrived commotion to awaken her. Galen stirs. "Father you are home!" She sits up sleepily and hugs him.

Aadya rushes over and joins the two of them. "Yes, little one, we are here. We missed you!"

"Mommy!" Galen rubs her eyes and smiles. *She is such a little angel. How could I have left her here without me?* Aadya squeezes her child, soaking in the physical warmth of her child's body as their genetic bond flows and circulates around them.

"There is something unusual about you." Galen notices, then her childish face brightens. "Do you carry another child?"

Poma looks at his daughter and his wife in disbelief. "How could she know?"

Aadya shrugs. "That is Galen for you." The fatigue of their journey washes over her, and she kisses Galen on the forehead. "We will see you in the morning and catch up then, we are all going to bed now."

"I am supposed to go to Katara in the morning for breakfast. I do this every day and then I spend the day together with Grandmother Mesa."

"What? You have not been having your lessons with the other children?"

Galen lets a wry little smile creep out, bows her head innocently and says, "No, we've been too busy."

"Yes," Aadya takes a deep breath, "we will send someone to let her know we are home. Now go to sleep."

"I can't believe how she has grown," Poma says softly.

"Yes, it is too much, too fast. How will we even know how to deal with a babe in arms again?"

"I have a feeling it will all come back to us," he says as he drops a cumbersome satchel on the wooden-plank floor of their bedroom and falls headlong first onto their big bed. Despite how tired she is, Aadya awakens him, and fusses until he takes off his clothes and gets under the covers. *It is good to be home. And our bed large and comfortable with its billowing pillows, luxurious blankets, and laveaux-scented sheets is a dream! Time on the road has been hard on my back because I am with child.*

The two full moons are starting to wane since returning home, but their twilight radiance, known as 'asunder,' will be with them a few more nights before their gradual depletion. The first few days after their return are filled with many duties to recapture time lost while they have been gone. Rediscovering her house is a marvel of sensual details she has grown to take for granted, like the sound of the stream outside her bedroom window, the view of the waterfall just beyond the nearby woods, and the gardens now in full bloom filling the air with their aromatic scents of ravelin, jamasine, and dorcascilly.

It is the food though she has missed the most. Fresh stalks of charter, shoup, and rutahard are part of every meal as they are in season. The cooks bake up full, hot meats at every meal and while she had plenty of cheese during the trip, *there is nothing better than when it is served fresh from the cave with just-out-of-the oven breads and recently picked fruits.*

32-Tragedies and Miracles

"Run Galen, Run!" Aadya shouts to her child, who is at twice the distance from her if she were to have thrown a stone. She is reacting to what looks like an enormous burning fluorite crystal, the size of a small house, which appeared in the sky only moments before. The sound it makes screeching through the atmosphere, pierces her consciousness. It blazes blue and orange and wicked white, and suddenly, not two hundred paces from where the children are playing, slams into the ground with a thunderous explosion which makes the ground tremble.

Despite the intense heat emanating from the fireball, and being heavy with child, Aadya runs toward the children scrambling to get Galen out of harm's way. The dire screams of the children are excruciating, as some of them falter and drop to the ground, even as the small group of guards and attendants nearby race to their aid.

Responding to her mother's shrieks, Galen runs toward her mother, but stops abruptly to look around for her classmates.

"No, Galen Run!" The second blood curdling scream, erupting from Aadya's panic, is heard all the way past the trees and as far as the stable where Poma is consulting with the blacksmith. Without thinking, he jumps on Hunter, who has nothing more than a field halter to hang onto. But sensing the urgency his horse holds steady and true directly to the sound. The rampaging white flames can now be seen high above the trees.

At last Galen reaches her mother, and falls into Aadya's arms, just before a second horrific explosion occurs. Fiery debris scatters everywhere crashing indiscriminately across the meadow, where moments before wildflowers grew and waved in the wind. Aadya pulls Galen to the ground and tries clumsily to shelter her from the explosion. Something sharp and scalding slices into her flesh as she shrieks in horror.

Aadya wakes up hours later on a cot, in a room she does not recognize.

"Where's Galen?" are the first words to surface from her muddled mind.

"Sshh… Do not struggle," she hears the familiar voice of Heshe. "She's safe. We have sent for the royal physician, but you must remain still or risk losing the baby."

"What's happening to me. I feel strange."

"I'm right here Aadya. Please resist moving." She hears Poma say in the background as he bends over to reach her hand and grasp it. "You've been hurt."

"But where is Galen? I must see her."

"She is fine, you saved her life. We are keeping her outside for now. Until we can determine the depth of your wound," Poma explains. "A shard has hit you and embedded itself into your lower back." His face is pinched with worry. "It is extremely close to your core. We must proceed cautiously and wait for the doctor."

Still in a state of confusion, Aadya cannot understand why she is being held on her side, but when she makes the slightest movement, a savage pain engulfs her, causing her to shriek.

"My darling, you must lie completely still as if you are about to let your arrow go." Poma whispers and squeezes her hand. "I need you to follow our instructions, be brave, and most of all be still. Galen is fine, you sheltered her with your body."

"But she must be terribly frightened."

"Mother is with her in the other room."

"Where are we?"

"We are in the house of Gorgan Holeu. It was the closest place to where you were hurt."

"What caused my injury?"

"Nobody knows. The fires still burn, but the people are working hard to put out the flames."

"What about the other children?"

"Aadya, I need you to be still and concentrate on your own life."

A searing stab of pain flows through her body and pauses with vehemence on her lower back. "Are the other children out of danger?"

"Some of them have burns, and one is unconscious."

"By the Grace of the One True God. Why did this happen?" her voice comes out squeaky and intermittently broken.

"Luckily Galen's guard detail was there."

"I must see Galen!"

"Shh, the physician has arrived."

Still on her side, Aadya is turned away from the door, and she cannot see the physician enter. Behind him are Queen Mesa and Galen, who has slipped unnoticed behind her grandmother. Stealthily she inches her way in through the small, crowded room. Poma nods negatively to her and scowls but does not want to alarm his pregnant wife who has a heinous looking, shiny metallic shard sticking in her back. The image is surreal, and he breathes consciously to try and dissipate his fear.

Because the fragment had been white hot when it hit her, Aadya's bleeding is minimal. The physician quietly approaches, and winces at the sight of the jagged projectile despite his training to always remain neutral. "Princess Aadya, this may hurt some when I pull it out, but you've been particularly lucky," the doctor tells her. "I believe your wound was cauterized by the intense heat of the object. If your organs are not damaged you should fare well."

Pushing forward, Galen reaches her mother's side. "Mother I am here."

"Oh, thank the One True God, Galen I have been anxious and worried about you." Galen takes her small hand and places it flat on her mother's side before anyone can protest. The pain suddenly disappears, and Aadya can feel the doctor tugging at the jagged shard until it releases. The sensation is like pulling a knife out of a thawing block of ice, resistant, but coming out clean. The wound starts spewing blood the minute the fragment is removed. What happens next startles everyone in the close quarters of the modest bedroom of a farmer.

Galen moves her hand gently from her mother's side to where the wound is. And closing her eyes Galen lets the blood flow over her hand until it stops. When she removes her hand, the wound is healed.

The doctor, stunned by the miracle, wipes the blood off Galen's hands with a clean cloth.

The tiny room, holding a handful of people, is charged with wonder. The only noise to break the silence is a few short raspy breaths from Heshe.

"It is true then, she can really heal," the physician mutters under his breath. He, like others had known of the prophecy, but he would not have believed it if he had not witnessed for himself. He turns and faces the others. "I do not understand what has happened here, but we must consider it a miracle."

The king stirs and clears his throat. "Everyone in this room is sworn to silence. We must protect this child; mindful she is heir-apparent to the throne. The prophecy of the Matong has informed us of this child's coming. And now it is our privilege to see her fulfill her destiny."

Concerned for Galen, Aadya sits up with the help of Poma, and squeezes Galen tightly to her chest. Choosing her words carefully, she speaks. "We must remember Galen is a child. We must protect her from those who would take advantage of her gift."

Galen squirms, like any child her age would have done in similar circumstances, uncomfortable as the center of attention. "Mother," she whispers. "I must see to the other children. But first you must put this around your neck."

"What is it?" Aadya asks her daughter.

Galen presses a small rock with a hole in it and a tiny round luminescent bead with a soft leather tie.

"This will help protect you from harm. It is a glowing stone I found in the nearby firth."

A feeling envelopes Aadya, newly rescued from the disastrous accident, which came close to killing her, her child, and her unborn baby. It is the warmth of the miracle which floods her with joy. She has been the recipient of her daughter's sanctifying gift.

"I will wear it always." She presses the milky river stone to her heart and raises her voice.

"We need to make room for the injured children to be brought in here at once."

One by one the children are brought in to be healed by Galen. Their parents are not permitted to accompany them, protecting the knowledge of Galen's gift. Most of the children are badly burned and in pain. Galen places her hands on them and, miraculously restores them to health. The last child to be brought in is Tantu, an unconscious seven-year-old boy, covered in cinders. Galen bows her head and whispers to her mother. "I cannot help him. It was his time."

Aadya nods discretely to Poma who looks bewildered. Aadya nods again, this time she closes her eyes. THIS CHILD CANNOT BE HEALED

He approaches softly to pick up the small boy. Limp in his arms he carries little Tantu out to his parents. It is the sound of their wailing which curdles through the room, dampening the spirits of everyone despite the seven children saved.

Still concerned for her baby, Aadya feels movement, and is bolstered by this fortuitous sign.

33-Nothing Could Prepare Them

When the second royal child is born, on the eve of the two moons of Merth crossing paths, the timing provides plenty of fodder for rumors, innuendo, superstitions interwoven, and angst. The fact Aadya has given birth to another girl, puts King Larsa in a fit of temper he tries, but fails miserably, to conceal. And while the direct line to lineage to the crown is through Poma, Prince Parsa too has married, and his wife has produced two boys in quick succession.

Aadya could not care less about the politics of birth as she cuddles her baby while Poma and Galen look on mesmerized.

"It will be a few days before the naming sacrament with the Matong so, I am calling her Cherry because her face is still bright red."

Poma scowls. "That is not flattering,"

"I know but she does look like a little round cherry, you have to admit."

Poma takes the baby gently out of her arms. "You my dear, must rest." Poma nods to the doormen to signal it is time to get the birthing gallery emptied. King Larsa puts out his hand to guide the queen to leave. "Let us give them some privacy," he whispers.

"But I have not yet held the baby!"

Realizing what he is up against, the king releases her hand and urges his wife to proceed with a dramatic wave of his hand.

"What a sweet blessing this child is," she tells her son and Aadya, taking the baby from Poma's arms. "What do you think Galen, of your new sister?"

"She's tiny," Galen says innocently, not yet understanding how she will have to share the devotion of her parents from now on with one more family member.

The swaddled newborn rests peacefully in the arms of Queen Mesa, until she becomes aware of the king behind her, shifting his weight restlessly from foot to foot. "Get over here and hold your granddaughter," the queen scolds.

"Ah, yes, of course." He surrenders to his wife's remonstrations and holds the swaddled bundle like a tiny loaf of bread in his arms. Feeling the warmth of his granddaughter, so peaceful, and exhausted after many hours of birthing, melts the king's indignant temperament.

The fact being, although Aadya would give birth to a son in a few short rotations, this baby to be named Aella Anemone, meaning Fierce Wind, would be a leader of great proportions. All agreed the name was too difficult to pronounce, and Aadya decided they would call her 'Ali.'

When Roark is born just one year later, there is not much fuss made over him except for the fact he is male. Some posturing is made by a few council members that even though he follows Galen and Ali in birth placement, as a male, he should be named heir-apparent. This notion is popular in some circles, but met with disdain in the growing privileged culture of the female population.

As the three children grow from infants, to toddlers, to a rowdy gang of three, Aadya remarks one day to Poma, "Roark is beginning to challenge the two girls more when they gang up on him."

"Actually, I think it is Galen who is changing. She has become more intent on mothering the two younger ones now she is getting older. I saw her instructing them on their ponies yesterday." Poma tells her. "It was really kind of cute."

Frowning, Aadya mulls this over in her mind. "Perhaps you are correct." She is disappointed with herself because Poma is more tuned into the children than she is. "They are each coming into their own personalities. I hope they always love each other and stay devoted to one another, the way they are now as simple children."

But the harmonious years of childhood pass far too quickly. As Galen grows into a young woman, it is becoming increasingly difficult to guard her from the lure of healing as her reputation reaches far and wide across the kingdom and sometimes beyond. It has become Galen's overwhelming desire to do what she was born to do.

To compromise with their renegade, not-quite-adult child, Poma and Aadya allow her to attend to the wounded, sick, and dying in the presence of a heavy guard, in the halls of Katara, only on a limited basis. They set up a system, whereby Galen is allowed to see only the worst of patients for the laying on of hands, but others, such as those with typical aging issues, are seen by Heshe and other 'wise ones,' who treat them with herbal remedies. While the overall health of the people of Merth is increasing, thanks to Galen's ability to heal, the educational programs, initiated long ago by Aadya, are creating a more enlightened population. But none of these progressive programs would prepare the people of Merth for the invasion soon to come from the sky.

Book II

34-Awakening

It happened on a night so still, not the tiniest leaf rustled. The fires had all been stoked with ashes for the long hours of peaceful rest. It began with the most wonderous display of cascading lights, brilliant blues, tangerine oranges, chartreuse, reds dark and moody, and electric whites. The colors, coiled brightly across the night sky, awakened almost everyone except those exhausted by too much work or too much drink. Many abandoned their beds and ran outside with mouths wide open. So mesmerizing was the display, people soon forgot it was the middle of the night. At Katara and Compana, the people flooded out onto the open courtyards reveling in the sheer beauty and horror of this unexpected, and terrifying aerial spectacle.

But not all share the celebratory mindset. With a cautionary escort of personal guards, Queen Mesa and King Larsa, awakened by the commotion, are discreetly ushered via the tunnel to the Matong chamber to confer with the deity. There they are met with an obvious agitation brewing inside the enormous globe.

"I have not seen this much combustion in the Matong since we were at war with the Omis years ago."

Queen Mesa shudders, "I know, it's deeply disturbing."

As was sometimes the case, the message they receive upon bonding does not immediately make sense. They are told to take to the tunnel with as much fresh provisions as possible. GUARD WITH EXTREME CARE THE HEALER. SHE WILL BE YOUR SALVATION.

"We must get word to Poma and his family immediately Larsa tells his wife."

"Yes and send a guard detail to fetch Galen."

Freakishly, Galen is awakened, by her skin, which is tingling in sporadic swirls the full breadth of her body, much like the phantasmagorical light display above her.

Before she is fully cognizant, the ever-present guards outside her door now pound on it. "Princess Galen you must awaken at once! The king and queen insist you join them in the tunnel."

At nearly twenty revolutions-aged, Galen had moved back to Katara, quite some time ago, after announcing to her family her abdication and unwillingness to continue as heir-apparent. "It is obvious Ali should be our next leader. I have other important work to do and have no inclination or skills to lead," she had told them. Moving to Katara also meant closer proximity to the Matong which she consulted frequently, but first and foremost she had been ready to get out of her parent's house.

Now in a state of surprise, she looks out the window and catches the last remnants of the heavenly light display when the guards break their promise and enter her room before she responds to their knock.

"Forgive us Princess Galen," one guard stumbles for words. "We were concerned when you did not answer." Galen jerks the silken sheets up around her nakedness. She finds sleeping in the nude is more restorative for her healing touch. Her nearly waist-long curls cover her bare shoulders, but she feels vulnerable by the intrusion, despite its intended purpose to protect her. Galen's mind wanders to a thousand places, and she fears she may not be able to meet the demands of this unforeseen catastrophe.

"I must go to the Matong."

"The king and queen have already left and are readying for shelter in the tunnel."

This news creates surprise in Galen who is focused on her need to bond with the Matong.

"Yes, but you must get me to the Matong first."

Once inside the chamber, the Matong pulls at Galen and her hand falls firmly on the globe now fluctuating with bolts of light. THE REVIVAL OF MANY IS ON YOUR SHOULDERS. HEAL AND BE ONE WITH THE ALL. *What else? Please instruct me further,* she begs of the Deity, but there is no more response.

It is at this moment a loud explosion happens, the building shakes and rumbles and the Matong itself teeters for a moment on its pedestal sending a virulent shock wave through Galen's nervous system. Outside the crowds, beginning to make their way back inside, are suddenly filled with terror as an enormous blast of fire drops straight out of what is known as the 'Immense,' the portion of the Merth sky which is peculiarly void of all starlight. Some describe it as if "a God has ripped the fabric of the sky tearing and scarring it forever." The blast makes the ground shudder for miles and lights up the countryside as if it is the middle of the day. The bright glow lasts for hours.

35-Bruta and Kilnor

Galen makes her way to the tunnel which is pulsating with activity as people ready themselves for an unknown, and possibly extended stay, in a too narrow tunnel built for passage between two points, and not as a domicile. The protection of the tunnel is only large enough for the royal family and the staff and families of both Katara and Compana. Galen, unfortunately, cannot avoid rubbing up against others in the crowded space. She knows to avoid crowds, when she can, unless of course she is healing, because unnecessary touching depletes her healing powers.

When Queen Mesa lays her eyes on her eldest granddaughter, she blurts out an uncharacteristic shriek of relief and squeezes her hard. "Thank the One True God you are safe!"

"I'm fine, but I do need to find some space."

"Over here my child, they have already brought a chair for you."

Word of the holocaust trickles in at first. It quickly becomes obvious, those who had gone out and exposed themselves to the unnatural light where falling prey to some sort of hideous infection. Galen stays for a single rotation in the tunnel, but as reports come in of the dire conditions of her people, she prepares an envoy of her healers to embark and begin the process of restoring the sick.

"You shall not leave here without me!" Prince Poma declares when he hears of her plan. "I understand your need to heal, but you must be protected. I will lead a legion of warriors to escort you and the other healers."

Aadya agrees. "I will also go," but even as she says this, she regrets the warriors are mournfully ill-prepared. While the changes she and Poma have made for allowing women into the ranks of the militia, and other positions of power, only a small percentage of the warriors are prepared for combat should the need arise to protect Galen the Healer, as she is now known.

"Our sources tell us there are many nearby who need our help," Poma explains to his daughter. "We will start with Katara and work our way outward from there."

Galen keeps silent as she prepares for departure, letting others work out the details. Her focus remains on the mental acuity of healing, nothing more.

Even with all the measures they have taken, it is probable they do not have enough resources. Those who stayed indoors, when the explosion and display of sky colors took place, are experiencing fewer symptoms. Those who spent the longest time outside, are succumbing to hideous side effects like shortness of breath, oozing wounds, and chronic cough. Perhaps worse than this, many of the grain crops have been scorched. It is apparent farmers will be facing even more hours in the fields, and many of the population may suffer from hunger in the near future.

Fortunately, stabled cattle and horses appear unscathed allowing them to be able to rely on their strength for the journey. With the abnormal light of the event dissipating, Poma signals to have the horses brought to the wide opening of the tunnel for the healing party's departure, and the carts are loaded with supplies.

As Aadya and Poma ride out of the darkness of the tunnel, she is shocked to see hordes of Merthians devastated by their ailments and lying on the ground. She blinks several times to adjust to the light and the horrific situation.

"We must get inside Katara and assess the damage," Poma leans over to Aadya. Behind them Galen has already jumped out of the wagon she was riding in. A cold reality shoots down Aadya's spine. *This will be most difficult. Perhaps the greatest challenge of my lifetime.*

"I have an idea," she says hesitantly to Poma.

"What?"

"You may think I've lost my mind. But what if we took our horses into the Matong chamber with us. I know you think it is only a legend. But we do not know what we will be up against. When people get hungry, they get dangerous."

Poma is uncertain what she has in mind, but his instincts tell him to stick with what he knows. "No. I am not in favor of this."

"We ride young horses now. We no longer have Chelsea and Hunter to see us through our dangers. Both our steeds are descendants of Chelsea's breed. They have the genetic code of warrior horses."

Contemplating how difficult it is to argue with Aadya when she has her mind set on something, Poma offers nothing but his silence which is as still and deep as a crater pond.

WE MUST CONSULT THE MATONG BEFORE OUR JOURNEY ANYWAY.

Hearing her thoughts projected into his brain, Poma is somewhat bolstered by Aadya's confidence, and gives her a subtle nod of approval. He gives the signal to his commander to pause the expedition, for the opportunity to administer to those in the sea of bodies around them. Everyone, absorbed with their duties, fails to notice the two of them climbing the steep rear loading ramp astride their horses. This ramp puts them directly to the level of the Matong.

Clad in her now famously emulated attire of leather breeches, Aadya pushes open the huge double doors of the kitchen delivery entrance and walks her horse inside. "Prince Poma is behind me, please assist him," she tells the bewildered door guards. "And please fetch Princess Galen. I saw her outside administering to the afflicted. Tell her to come at once to the Matong chamber."

There are still servants, who have not left the protection of Katara's walls, who are mostly fit, handling the day-to-day affairs of the castle. It is quickly becoming evident shelter at the time of the disastrous event is the one and only protection from the debilitating physical symptoms.

"This is eerie," Aadya says in hushed tones to Poma as if spending just one night in the tunnel had eroded her confidence in established security protocols. The sound, of both horses' hooves on the stone floor, sounds promiscuously loud and inappropriate, but they proceed down the hall to the Matong anyway. Relieved to see the guards are at their post, this one sight of normalcy lets Aadya fill her lungs in comfort as if she were inhaling a whiff of steaming cider on a cold day.

Even more reassuring, is the Matong still stands upon its pedestal despite the cataclysmic explosion.

"We will first ask the Matong, and only if allowed, will we let them bond." She turns around to let Poma know what she is thinking.

Poma proceeds cautiously with the horses, but anxious to amend their present circumstances, he is willing to try almost anything. He has learned through the years to trust Aadya's instincts.

The guards are bewildered at the sight of Bruta and Kilnor, two magnificent steeds chosen as the best in the kingdom for the prince and princess. Kilnor, Poma's horse is a white stallion dappled with black patches and Bruta is smaller and so black she shines with iridescence, their rippling muscles and arched necks with flowing manes, make them the envy of all who know of horses.

The space is tight with both horses in there with them. They place their hands on the globe as high as they can reach. While in this position they receive the insight to touch their horses, particularly important to their mission. A low humming occurs as the river of energy passes through them to Bruta and Kilnor. The horses prance in place buoyantly.

PROTECT AND DEFEND THE HEALER AT ALL COSTS. PREPARE FOR THE UNEXPECTED.

Aadys's balance is offset by the light-headedness she often experiences when the orb releases her. "I would have liked more reassurance. But still, we have our directive."

"I wish I could say I was filled with confidence," Poma admits. "But I would only be providing false bravado."

Suddenly, their daughter Galen pushes open the heavy, ornate doors to the chamber and enters. "What is it?" she asks trying to disguise her annoyance at being pulled from her task of healing. "And why in the name of the One True God are your horses in here?

"We will explain later. We have connected. You must be given your directive." Aadya tells her.

"I bonded before I entered the tunnel."

"Oh, I didn't know." Aadya says apologetically.

Prince Poma looks tenderly at his daughter and thinks how it was only a few revolutions ago he had held her in his arms, no bigger than a loaf of bread and here she was supposed to save the whole of Merth.

"Never to mind. I will take advantage of this moment to reflect," Poma and Aadya join her. With a surprising sensation Aadya turns around and sees the horses as if through water. Then she has a violent vision of a brutal battle and fire. In her vision, she can hear the sounds of the battle and the surging flames. It leaves her further weakened and defeated.

When all three are released no one speaks and Galen hurries out.

36-The Journey Begins

For three revolutions of Merth, the healing party sets up lines to organize the sick of Valtar and Compana, and other nearby villages, to be healed by Galen's touch. The lines are endless, the people hungry, and ill, but those healed now have the energy to help set up wagons and provisions for their departure to more distant lands.

Once order is reinstated at Katara, Poma allows his father and mother to return, bringing with them Ali and Roark. No one rests. For the first time in his life, Poma sees his parents digging in and getting their hands dirty.

As soon as they can build a sizable caravan with wagons of provisions, guard details, and herbs, they set out. But it is ultimately Galen's healing touch, which determines who will be healed. As they travel, they discover they are too late to save many.

As predicted, they are mobbed by the sick and the hungry, which makes them all the more determined to help. When someone comes too close to either Prince Poma or Aadya, their Matong horses become agitated rearing up and sometimes floating above the ground. The first time Bruta does this, Aadya is alarmed. She cautiously makes eye contact with Poma and without words they agree to keep this low key.

"We need to get a Matong steed for Galen," Poma tells her.

"Yes, we are not out so far we couldn't."

"I will take a couple of warriors and ride back, and get her horse, and have it bonded to the Matong. If I ride hard, I will be back before daylight."

BE CAREFUL MY LOVE.

Now they are on the road, Aadya's ever-growing concern is for her daughter's safety. A lifelong habit of worry, is now enhanced by real circumstances.

When workers begin to lay down a camp for their first night on the road, Aadya requests extra guards to protect her and Galen who will share a tent. They eat a light supper and prepare for sleep, exhausted by the day's activities, when they hear scuffling noises outside their tent.

"What is it?" Aadya protectively shields Galen who moves to open the flap of the tent. Her tight grip on Galen's arm prevents her from doing so.

One of the guards peeks in carefully. "I'm sorry princess there is a boy out here insisting on seeing you. I told him you weren't to be disturbed."

"Who is it?"

"Let him in," Galen intervenes. It is a lad from the village down the road, they would not reach until the next morning.

The ragged boy bows and pleads with his eyes and his prayerful hands. "I'm sorry princess, but my mother is dying. The healer must come at once if she is to be saved"

Aadya and Galen meet each other's gaze and there is no question Galen intends to go.

"Wait," Aadya commands. "Darkness has swallowed us, and I cannot let you go Galen. We will have the woman brought here tonight.

"Take this young man outside and have him show you the way. I want at least ten warriors to accompany you…and Derke," she motions the guard over to where she can whisper to him. "Have Bruta brought here into my tent."

The guard gives her a puzzled look, but shortly the magnificent horse is brought in. Galen is also obviously surprised about the request. "What on Merth are you doing?" Galen subdues a slight laugh.

"Sshh, do not worry I'll explain. We will tie her over in the corner where she will not soil the carpets. I need to have my eyes on her. This is not an ordinary time. We must be extra cautious."

"Seriously Mother what is going on?"

"I had Bruta brought in to keep her protected. I have not explained to you yet about the horses. That is why your father has gone back to bond your mare to the Matong. She is a bay and does not look like a magical horse, but she has the lineage, and exposing her will make her have powers like Bruta and Kilnor."

"What do you mean?"

"Our horses come from a long line of warrior horses. You saw us in the Matong chamber before we left. By bonding them with the Matong, they are given special powers like the ability to fly."

Beneath her blankets, Galen fights to quash a shudder. "But what do I need with a magic horse"

"Honey, can you not see how crazy people are getting? We do not even know where half our guard detail is. We are doing all we can to safeguard you, and an extraordinary mount might give you the edge you need to protect yourself."

The two women wait for the men to return with the sick woman, but minutes become hours, and they finally realize the men are not coming back. Rationalizing rest eventually overcomes worry, Aadya has more guards posted outside, and they finally get to sleep just before the morning star peeks above the horizon, and pierces through the creases of their tent. Aadya and Galen are brought trays of fresh fruits, soft breads, and cheeses, tastes which are enhanced by the fresh air and the danger of their precarious situation. Bruta snorts softly when she is brought fresh grain.

"Does anyone know of the prince's location?" Aadya asks the food server.

"No, your highness, but Derke made it back only a few hours ago."

"Send for him immediately…please."

Derke is dirty, bruised, and bloody, but he stumbles in to make his report.

"It was a trick. We were ambushed. We lost three good men," Derke reports.

"The boy's uncles put him up to it. All the women in their family have died because of the disease. I tried to bring the boy back for punishment, but he jumped off a cliff to escape."

"Did he perish?"

"It's very possible. I do not know how he could have survived although none of us could see his body. Fortunately, most of us lived through the attack."

The unsettling news wrenches tighter the knot of growing concerns Aadya is experiencing. "We must all head back to the safety of Katara. Galen I cannot have this. Those were trusted men and now they have been murdered. We cannot sacrifice the good for the bad."

The irony of the warrior's demise is not lost on Galen who realizes suddenly, she is not living in the Merth of her childhood, but a dangerous place now divided by good and evil.

"Please take Bruta out and let her relieve herself, the poor horse is too proud to pee in here and I'm quite thankful. Guard her with your life!" Aadya emphasizes to a guard. "Derke if you will excuse us there is much to discuss with my daughter. When do you expect the prince?"

"He should be here any time now. I will have an escort detail ride out to find him."

"Let me know what you discover."

Aadya turns to her daughter, "My dear Galen I do not know how we are going to carry out this mission safely."

Galen sighs. "If we could only consult the Matong at this moment."

"This is also another concern about taking this trek across the country," Aadya replies.

"Maybe we are going about this all wrong. Maybe I should go with a small guard and help those in need without a big assembly." Galen offers.

Aadya grasps her hands in hers. "There are too many dangers, my daughter. I cannot allow such a dangerous mission."

"But you are not the healer, and you are no longer in charge of me."

What insolence brought out by uncertainty. "We will discuss this more when you father arrives."

37-With Much Discretion

What should have been an easy return journey for Poma and his crew turns out to be a challenge at every turn.

"Getting back to Katara was not a problem." Poma tells Aadya and Galen. "We spent last night there, and intended to get an early start this morning. But King Mesa was feeling ill and therefore I brought Heshe in to look at him," Poma eyes his daughter, trying to read her face, as he shares this information. As he suspects, Galen's concern is splashed across her face like tepid water.

Aadya puts her hand up as if to stop her husband from continuing. "We have made a mistake, we should not have left Katara, it is too dangerous out here. We need to turn around this minute."

"But mother what about the others who still need me?" Galen reaches and touches her mother's arm to emphasize her point.

"Look at you my darling, even with the freshest food, you are becoming diminished. We must take care of you, or you will not be able to take care of others."

"Your grandfather needs you too, at this time," Poma adds, hoping this logic might play to the girl's sensibilities.

"We're certainly not getting anywhere with this parade going on." Galen spits out her words with clenched teeth. "I will return with you for the time being, and we will continue to allow the citizens to bring their sick to us for healing. This is not what I see as best for the people!"

Even for Aadya, who had insisted on their return, arriving at home feels like they have been defeated by the disease, now haunting their former way of life. The first thing Galen does upon arrival is to visit King Mesa. She is shocked by his decline in the few days they have been gone. Queen Mesa and several healers surround him.

"You are not well, my dear grandfather." Galen squeezes his cold, limp hand. It is nothing like the powerful grip, which had made her wince as a small child.

"Yes, I am not long for this world."

"I have done all I can do for you."

"Yes, I know." He nods peering into her eyes as if for the last time.

"We can make you comfortable, but you have not responded to my touch, and I went to the Matong before coming here."

"Send for Poma and Princess Aadya and the Chancellor. It is time I abdicate my reign to Poma," he tells Queen Mesa through lowered eyes.

Galen carries on for several days hoping she might be there when the king passed. But time is pressing her to act, and she begins brewing a plan.

"Who is the handsome warrior over there?" she asks her brother Roark when he brings her food and drink for her brief respite from the infinite lines of healing.

"Oh, I believe his name is Kandar. He is one of our best warriors."

"I've noticed." A demure smile creeps over her face as foreign to her these days as wind in the hollows.

Roark grins, "Why my sister? Are you interested?"

She looks up at him with her most convincing look of sincerity. "I believe I am. Can you arrange a meeting? It must be of utmost secrecy."

"I do not know him personally. What should I tell him?"

Galen looks around at the hordes of people waiting to see her. "It will be difficult for me to get away from here. Tell him I would like to meet him tonight after the dinner hour in the far courtyard where the upside-down tree grows."

"But what should I tell him it concerns."

Galen continues to mislead her brother.

"A girl has a right to keep the company of handsome men does she not?" Roark gives her a sly smile, curious about Galen's uncharacteristic request.

"I suppose you do."

"But do not give him any clue. Tell him I will explain when I see him. And this is secret Roark," she emphasizes with a dramatic lowered voice. "Tell no one." She bites her lip and adds. "Be sure to tell him to keep my confidence!" she whispers loudly to him as he leaves on his mission.

Admittedly Galen has picked the soldier for his prowess, his strength, and character visible from at least a hundred paces, but upon meeting him up close she realizes what had been a whisper of interest, has become a surge of energy she has never experienced. *Pull it together. This is about the mission,* she cautions herself.

As scheduled, Kandar appears promptly as the bright star of Merth is setting for its nightly rest. "I am Galen," she greets him, her right palm open to her chest as is the custom.

He returns her symbolic gesture. "Yes, and I am Kandar. I understand you wanted to speak to me about something."

"Are you someone who can be trusted?"

Kandar reflexively turns his open palm into a fist. "I serve our honorable King Mesa."

"Yes, but can you be trusted?"

"I have sworn an oath to the king."

"Yes, but my grandfather is close to passing."

Insecurity splits Galen's resolve like a sliced apple with seeds exposed.

"Perhaps I should not have summoned you. I do not know too many of the people personally. I have lived a sheltered life as the 'healer.'"

"They say you are peculiar, but even in this dim light I know this is not true. Your eyes are hypnotic, I cannot stop looking at you."

"You are very kind. But I am peculiar. I carry many burdens." She looks at him curiously. "What does dim light have to do with it?"

Kandar smiles softly with kind eyes she had not noticed at a distance. "I can see, even in this poor light, your spirit light shines."

Perhaps he is the best choice to take on the journey.

"As royal princess, first in line to the throne after my father Prince Poma, I am planning something criminal." *No, too strong.* "Well, let us just say I am planning to go against my parent's wishes. I need a band of sturdy warriors to make my journey possible. I will need you to swear your allegiance to me and not my grandfather. Or when he passes, my father."

"Tell me more."

"I need to travel quietly to the far reaches of our kingdom without a huge entourage.

"You were with us most recently were you not?" she asks him.

"Yes,"

"You saw all the problems?"

"I did not. We had matters well managed."

Galen shuffles the weight of her slender body from one foot to the other, still questioning herself if she has made the best choice. "There were plenty of issues. While I understand the need for security. We were too vulnerable as a massive army. We need to move in the shadows this time and with much discretion." She pauses wondering what to say next.

"I need a small, but loyal band of men, who will guard me with their lives and swear their allegiance to me. I have my personal guards, but they are too protective. I need warriors with fresh vision. Do you think you can muster such a crew?"

"How many did you have in mind?"

"At least ten, but they must be the very best soldiers."

"And how am I to do this if they have to swear allegiance to you and break their vows to the king?"

"They will all be given medals to be worn on a ribbon round their neck. This medal will carry my seal. You will be a special envoy, only we will leave in secrecy.

"Can you make this happen?"

"You are asking me to commit treason."

"And what would the king say if you failed to protect me despite knowing about my mission."

Regret crosses Kandar's face with the slow and steady progress of an eclipse. "I must think about this Princess Galen. I will speak with a few warriors who might be interested."

A soft wind blows the wispy branches of the upside-down tree brushing her cheek, and Galen knows instinctively what to say.

"You have two revolutions to gather a dozen select men, provisions which will take several wagons to haul and spare horses. Take my talisman and barter with those who I have already healed. Tell them I am requesting supplies for those unable to work yet. No one will turn you down. We will leave in the dead of night. Now go before someone should see us."

She turns to walk away then remembers to caution him about letting any of the palace guards know about her plans. "They are dreadfully protective and will go to my father immediately."

38-She is Gone

"She is gone!" Aadya roars into Poma's council chambers. "Someone has taken our daughter. I knew this would happen."

Poma looks up from the maps laid out on the table. He is surrounded by a few of his trusted advisers including his brothers, Parsa and Bonder. With the king bedridden he has taken over running the country for all intents and purposes until the king's abdication is made official.

"Are you sure?"

"Look out the window, do you see the people lined up to be healed by her? Her horse is gone and several of our warriors are unaccounted for."

"And then there is this!" Aadya thrusts an envelope into his hand. It is sealed and addressed to Crown Prince Poma. "Calm down, Aadya," he admonishes his wife as he breaks open the envelope.

Dearest Father…

I appreciate you might be angry with me right now. But we tried your way. Time is running out for the sick. With every day that goes by, and I am not able to heal them their condition worsens, and I have less ability to renew their health. I have consulted the Matong as I'm sure you have. This is my destiny now. It is safer to travel in the shadows of night and heal our people as need be. We will have the ability to move swiftly. I have procured the assistance of some of our very best soldiers who I have listed below. Please accept them for the heroes they are. I hope to return by the time our two moons meet in the sky again,

I love you and mother with all my heart! Please forgive me and those who protect me.

Kandar Zola
Edgin Twide
Polar Panta
Creek Virtue
Jazide Wilks
Chesta Wilks
Jip Tweed
Oscant Salat
Port San
Arguid Chav
Niels Jarga
Danturn Mela

Stunned, Poma looks at his livid wife. "At least she picked our best warriors. I couldn't have done better myself."

"Are you crazy? We must send an envoy at once to bring her home!" He braces himself in front of her with his arms settled on his waist and thrusts his thoughts into her head.

YOU MUST READ THIS AND FORGIVE. IT IS OUT OF OUR HANDS. I WILL GO WITH YOU NOW TO THE MATONG.

Aadya reads the note again fervently looking for clues of her daughter's whereabouts as if her handwriting might reveal her secret.

"Something must be done!" She stamps her foot like a petulant child.

"My dear wife come with me to consult with the Matong." He touches her gently on the arm and leads her toward the door.

"Gentlemen if you will excuse us, we have a personal situation to take care of."

He looks at his two brothers and nods but cannot share his thoughts as Aadya is pressing her thoughts into his consciousness.

DO YOU SUPPORT THIS?

AADYA LET US WAIT AND SEE WHAT THE MATONG TELLS US.

Galen and her team ride hard the first night to create some distance should a rescue party be sent, but scouts reveal there is no such obstacle to their mission. They set up a tent discretely hidden in the woods, and blindfold those who come to be healed from the nearby villages, keeping their location undetected. They change their site every couple of days without fail.

Poma, as directed by the Matong, does not interfere but decides to post protective forces in nearby villages disguised as civilians to keep close watch on Galen's activities should she need assistance. This practice will go on for many revolutions of the moons until the time Ga-

len's party has crisscrossed the land and she is finally able
to return home.

172

39-The King Passes Over the Bridge

King Larsa lingers on bedridden for nearly an entire revolution of Merth. Poma refuses to be crowned king while he is still alive hoping his father might miraculously awaken, get out of bed, and return to his life. Others are appalled by the prince's denial, continually urging him to go forward with his coronation.

"It is of little matter," he tells his brothers and other close advisers. "I am running the country anyway. I do not think we need to fell a man before his time." He exudes confidence, but deep inside he is in no hurry to become the king and carry the burdens of the title.

It is Ali who is the first to notice King Larsa is not breathing. She has come into his chambers to bring him some soup and to entertain him for a while. Nothing delights him more than to watch her play chakra toss. He had been his granddaughter's first serious opponent, but as of late could only watch her play the solitary version.

At first Ali thinks he is napping, but upon gently nudging him a couple of times, she gets no response.

"Someone come quickly! I do not think he is breathing." The king's nurse is in a nearby room instructing one of the day attendants how to fold the linens, so they do not irritate the king's aging skin.

"What is it, Princess Ali? What is wrong?" The nurse walks heavily with a weakened ankle she has been favoring.

"Is my grandfather dead?" she gasps.

"Sshh, hush my dear. Let us take a look," she says gently pressing her hand against his cheek. It is cold to the touch.

The once proud leader, now with mottled skin drained of all color, has a ghostly appearance. His lips have turned purple in sharp contrast to his ashen face.

"Oh, grandfather please do not go, please do not leave us," Ali begs as she grabs at him and tries to shake him awake.

"Princess Ali, please stop!" Run go get your mother or father, or both!" the nurse swipes back her hair and tucks it behind her ear. She fans her hands at the willowy teenager as if to urge her into action. Ali's long-flowing honey-colored curls, almost reaching her waist, swirl around her like a flowing skirt as she races to get her mother.

"I cannot accept this!" Ali pleads with her mother as they stand by the royal bed where the quickly cooling corpse of King Larsa has replaced the man they knew and loved. "We must get Galen to come back and save him."

"Ali, listen to me," her mother grabs both her arms and glares into her child's golden-flecked blue eyes. "People die, Galen has already tried to heal him. She would not have left if she could have saved him. You must control yourself. You are making this more difficult for everyone. We all loved him." Aadya glances at King Larsa's corpse and a shudder runs down the length of her body. *Change is coming like a thunderous deluge, and we are not mentally prepared for it.*

Poma's reaction is even worse than Ali's. He sobs as if he is a broken vessel leaking wine, while Queen Mesa sits nearby clutching her skirt unable to get close to the king's body. Hoya strokes her hair to comfort her, and Roark paces uncomfortably about the room like he is waiting to go somewhere less disturbing.

40-The Healer Returns

When Galen and her band of devoted sentinels hear the news of her grandfather's death, they waste no time to travel home to Katara. They have almost run a full circuit of the land and were close to returning anyway. As the death of her beloved grandfather weighs on her mind, Galen feels the chasm between her and her family as if the time away was a dense forest, and she must now navigate to find her way home.

The exhausted healer is unrecognizable to her family at first. Galen's bronze curls have turned pure white, and her normally peachy complexion is now pale as a Jil moth.

"My poor child!" Aadya embraces her daughter who smells of campfires and forest trees. "Thank the One True God you are home!"

"I need rest and nurture mother. Please allow me to seclude myself in my chambers for restoration," she whispers in Aadya's ear as she slumps down off her loyal steed Marcus, who lowers himself to his knees like a dromedary. Kandar lifts her and carries her to her chambers, weeding through the many halls and chambers of Katara.

Aadya follows with attendants carrying fresh water for bathing and for drinking. She snaps her fingers. "Bring broth!" she commands in hushed but forceful tones.

As Kandar lays Galen on the bed, she grasps his hand. "Do not leave me," she whispers in a voice raspy and eroded by fatigue. Her lips are as cracked as the punti fruit skin, and her eyelids languidly droop half open, obscuring the light of her soul.

"I must rest now if I am to make it to Grandfather's funeral in two revolutions," she tells her mother. "Kandar must not leave. After these many sacrificing days, he was my most trusted adviser. He cannot leave my side now," she pleads as she presses her body to rise, but the energy is not there to lift herself up off the bed.

The following day when Ali comes to visit her sister, Galen is able to sit up propped up on pillows. She is looking a little stronger and able to smile. Ali sits on her sister's bed and whispers. "Does mother know yet?"

"Know what?" Galen asks.

"You are with child."

"Sssh, I haven't the strength to tell her yet. How did you know?"

"I had to pry Kandar away from you last evening. I had a feeling…" She looks around and speaks softly. "I asked the Matong. I was as surprised as anyone when it was revealed to me. Typically, the Matong does not share personal information with others, but seeing you are so weak perhaps I am here to help."

Galen takes in a deep breath. "Perhaps." Galen looks around the room.

"Where is he now?"

"I convinced him to go get cleaned up and get some rest while you were asleep. I promised him I would guard you with my life. It was difficult to persuade him. How have you bewitched him so?"

A smile, sweet with adoration at its source, creeps across Galen's face. "He is good as a golon to me. And I am such a weary mess. Bring me a brush and help me to get presentable, sister."

As Ali begins to brush her sister's thick hair, the color begins to come back into her cheeks.

Your gentle touch does not weaken me the way others do. Thank you, Ali."

"I can't believe your hair turned white; you look most unusual now."

"Is it ugly?"

The remark surprises Ali as she has never known her sister to have the slightest inkling of vanity.

As Ali continues to comb Galen's long hair it brightens and softens into a silvery glow.

"No, actually it is merely a change I must adjust to."

"Help me to get presentable to receive mother and father I want to tell them about their grandchild."

Galen lifts her head and asks. "How is Grandmother?"

Ali nods her head slightly releasing her concern in her expression. "She has kept to herself since we lost Grandfather." Then she brightens with optimism. "Perhaps you can restore her to health."

"Ah sister, I can't do much for the elders." Her words fall out scattering aimlessly.

Ali folds Galen's abundant silver curls into loose knots and pulls a flower out of a vase to tuck in beside her right cheek.

"I appreciate your love Ali," Galen's eyes glisten as she takes in the comfort of returning to her home. "Let us get a beautiful silken robe out and call everyone in to tell them the news."

Ali admires her work. Galen now glows, and she notices how the unique lavender tint to her sister's eyes, once considered strange, now radiate and sparkle.

"Get Kandar first and we will tell them together." But Galen is still teetering unsteadily when she rises to pull on the silken wrap. Galen sits down in a nearby chair, her lips trembling. Ali's concern pushes across her face like an errant cloud.

"It's okay sister." Galen understands her sister's concern. "I am diminished. I will regain my strength."

"What about the baby?"

"He is fine. He is strong. We had to travel far and fast to make it in time for the burial. My strength was sapped." And as if Ali had asked, she adds. "You know our world has changed because of our mother. In the outlying reaches of Merth they treat women like cattle."

Ali looks at her sister, "And what might have brought this topic on?"

"If I were pregnant and living in the outer reaches. My value would be nothing more than a host for some man's baby. Women are not cherished or valued."

"Yes, but you are the healer. You are considered sacred wherever you go."

Galen's only response is a humble smile quickly transformed by doubt.

"Go now and get Kandar, please."

Ali could not help herself to unleash the question she had been harboring ever since she first felt the presence of the baby. "Are you married?"

Galen laughs for the first time since returning home. "What if we weren't?"

Ali stumbles over her words. "You know this will be a shlizstorm, and it might make it more palatable if you were married. Mother is going to kill you!"

More laughter pours out from Galen. "You forget I am the great healer."

"You're still Mother's daughter."

"This is true, do not worry I'm a big girl. I will tell you our story sometime soon when we have the time. Now please go get Kandar"

"Oh my! You look beautiful!" Kandar enters the room and glides to her side.

Ali notices how Galen beams with grace at him in a way she has witnessed between her father and mother.

"How are you feeling I have been exceedingly worried about you and the…"

"It's okay she knows."

Galen sets Kandar's hand on her barely bulging stomach. "Can you feel him?"

Kandar's face lights up like a spark on a cold night. "Yes, yes, this is the first time. I almost did not believe you when you said you could feel him kick now."

Ali looks at her sister "It is a boy for sure?"

"Yes."

"But how do you know?"

"The Matong sent us a beautiful bird which followed us on our journeys. And he would sing to me, telling me things I needed to know."

The door opens and Poma and Aadya enter quietly not wanting to disturb Galen's rest.

"Mother and father," Galen greets. "Please someone bring them chairs."

Kandar scrambles, for the chairs looking visibly distraught and grateful for the task.

"Mother and Father. "We have joyous news to tell you." Reaching for Kandar's hand she takes a deep breathe.

"We were hoping to hear of your journeys. Are you strong enough for this?"

Another uncharacteristic grin edges across Galen's face. "We will get to my journeys soon enough." She squeezes Kandar's hand who looks a little woozy despite his warrior's demeanor. "This is a lot to handle all at once, and with preparations for grandfather's burial, but" she swallows hard. "But I want you both to know I am with child."

Aadya's gasp wrenches from her lips like a minor explosion.

"How did this happen? Where you raped?" She points her rage toward Kandar. "You were supposed to protect her!"

"Mother, please, you must let me finish." Poma takes Aadya's hand and squeezes it.

"My life was in danger several times, and Kandar always protected me. He is my husband now."

There, it was laid out for the world to see, their secret, their magnificent secret now brewing in her belly.

"How could you do this to me!" As soon as she says this, Aadya regrets her impulsive outburst. "I'm sorry. I didn't mean to… well." She reels her anger back in and tries to listen without judgment.

"It was actually Kandar who insisted we have a local holy man anoint our betrothal and union," She smiles at the father of her baby, who absent-mindedly squeezes her hand tight enough it hurts.

Finally, Poma speaks up. "But you are the actual heir to the throne."

"Please I abdicated years ago and do not carry the title princess. Ali will serve as heir-apparent; she is much more qualified than I am."

"But it was not ever made official. We must make it official before we announce the birth of the child."

IT IS ALWAYS ABOUT PROTOCOL WITH YOU. Aadya glares at Poma. OUR CHILD IS GOING TO HAVE OUR FIRST GRANDCHILD AND YOU ARE THINKING ABOUT PROTOCOL!"

"Sir I," Kandar fidgets.

"No, Kandar, this is my doing. Let me explain to them."

41-Galen's Story

"Do you have time for this?" she asks her parents.

"Of course, my love, we have waited eons for your return." Aadya is doing her best to pull herself together after her outburst. Galen looks at her father who nods affirmatively.

"I will try to start at the beginning. We left in the middle of the night as you know. We were aware of the king's protective envoy almost immediately. And were grateful for them father," she says giving her father an appreciative glance.

"We did our work in the cloak of darkness moving around and keeping our location always secret. We even did our best to keep the envoy in the dark about our movements. Although we were thankful for the provisions whenever we sought them out." Galen stops to take a sip of the tart mullar tea Ali has brought her.

"While we were within a day's journey of Katara our methods worked rather smoothly. It was when we got to the outer reaches of the kingdom, it took us longer to get there and by the time we did, the disease had progressed to the brains of many. They were running amok and terrorizing the healthy people. So, we really had to buckle down and become even more secretive. I was nearly kidnapped twice, and once came close to dying by the sword. One group was extraordinarily paranoid about my abilities and were accusing me of being a whorlwich and talked of my execution."

Galen looks up at Kandar, "My dear sweet husband saved me every time. His courage was beyond heroic, and I realized how important he was to me, and I wanted to make our union blessed by the One True God."

Kandar clears his throat as if to speak. Galen gives him a slight negative nod, and proceeds with her tale. "I expected this was going to be devastating to you mother, but there was method to my madness. We put out the word the healer was with child. This protected me. We did this before it was even true. These ignorants in the outer reaches are led by fear and superstition, but could respect I was pregnant. It made me more human. While they still treat their women like cattle, they are careful not to harm the unborn. And this also put to rest the rumor I was a whorlwich."

Galen sips the tea Ali has brought her and takes a deep breath. "So, I loved this man," she pats Kandar, on the back of the legs. "And we needed to go ahead and make the pregnancy real, so we found a holy man in one of the villages and had him brought to our camp. He performed the ceremony in front of only two people, our closest friends, Jazide and Chesta Wilks. They signed up as brothers, but we later found out Jazide was actually Chesta's wife in disguise.

"Once the word got out I was pregnant, things calmed down a lot."

"But you did this without the sanctity of the Matong." Aadya protested.

"It is odd. I will tell you now," she says meditating on what she shall say.

"There was an exotic bird at our wedding." Aadya lets a smile cross her lips. "This bird appeared early in our journeys. It is a magnificent large red bird with an overarching blue tail. It sings to me with messages from the Matong and has guided us throughout our risky task."

Aadya chuckles remembering the same bird at her wedding. "Galen, we are familiar with the bird." She looks over at Poma as they quietly beam at each other, sharing the memory of the wedding bird from many years ago.

"You are?"

"Yes, but that is another story for another time. Were you able to heal all the people?"

"Most of them. We certainly tried. The ones with brain complications were healed too, although many changed, becoming more docile after their healing.

"Mother, there is still much education needed in the outer reaches. You must continue your push for this."

"I know, but the cataclysm has set us back so."

Galen sighs heavily. "Yes, after many revolutions we have begun to evidence people who we thought were not affected, but actually were. So, I began an initiative to reach more of them with my touch." She takes another sip from the teacup beginning to cool in her hands. "We may have not healed absolutely everyone, but we certainly tried."

"Your journeys are over now. You must take care of yourself and our first grandchild."

"It's a boy," Galen tells her.

"And how do you know?"

"The bird, I told you, shares wisdom in the form of song."

Aadya looks around the room, not wanting to leave but realizing they have detained Galen enough from her rest. "We will let you rest now. We must figure this out, first we must get King Mesa buried. Your abdication must come before the official marriage ceremony. We can have a small wedding ceremony here at Katara for Queen Mesa's sake. We must move swiftly. How far along are you?"

Three moons have passed.

Deep in thought Aadya announces, "We will have to announce your abdication today then. Are you ready for this Ali? Galen's official renunciation will make you Heir Apparent."

"Yes of course," the teenager straightens her posture as if she were already donning royal garments.

For now, Kandar may continue to be your special guard here in your chambers.

"But what about Roark?" Poma asks. "He isn't even here."

"I wish he could have been here for Galen's story."

"He's out hunting," Ali tells them.

Aadya turns to Galen and Kandar. "I can see you two love each other, and while it is a great surprise, I can embrace this union. We will build you a house for your family," she tells Kandar.

"We do not want anything grandiose." Galen tells her.

Aadya frowns. "Of course, you do not. Perhaps you will give me the dignity of living nearby in Compana where I can be near my grandchildren."

Galen smiles faintly, realizing she has won her mother over.

42-Matters of State

"The Great Spirit has been within me since before I left my mother's womb." Galen speaks from a chair which has been anchored to a speaking platform placed at the top of the public stairway on Katara's front entrance. She is still weak from exhaustion, but understands the urgency of the chain of events at hand.

The crowd has been summoned quickly by couriers who run through the streets of Valtar and Compana with brightly colored assembly flags for such occasions. The people have been waiting for news of King Mesa's burial. Instead, they are greeted by a white-haired woman who many do not recognize.

"The prince announced it himself a few minutes ago, before you arrived." One fellow was heard telling another. "See?" he points. "It's Princess Galen, firstborn and great healer. She has returned from her journey to heal everyone in the land."

"I have been very blessed to be bestowed with the gift of healing powers." Galen continues, her voice magnified by the convex metal shield behind her designed to boost her voice. "Today I speak to you to let you know we are back from our journeys. We have traversed the country and sought out all we can to restore the health of those who suffered in the tragic 'Targa' event, almost a complete revolution of Merth now.

"I speak to you today to let you know, although I am the firstborn of the royal family and Heir Apparent to the throne, I am stepping down from such responsibilities to further dedicate my life to healing."

The wind blows against the shiny concave backdrop, creating a brief echoing effect. "My Sister Ali, excuse me, Her Royal Highness, Aella Anemone, will take my place in the Ascension.

"As you know we have lost our great leader, King Larsa, my grandfather. With the many poignant and joyous times, and with my recent return, we wanted you the people to know of my decision. Two days from today we will have a glorious celebration of our king to send him on his journey 'over the bridge.'"

She pauses and swallows some dark red prelita juice, known for its restorative properties, Ali has brought her in a cup. "My dear people, I want you to know in addition to my abdication, I am to marry my trusted friend Kandar Zola, and we intend to begin our own family as soon as possible!" She raises her fist into the air and the crowd cheers as if she has just announced a kingdom-wide holiday. Kandar joins her on the podium and allows the crowd to see him, then steps down.

"Father, you must take over now," she looks to her left where Poma is standing.

He nods and takes Aadya's hand. Galen is lifted off the podium in her chair and the two of them step up.

The crowd continues to roar until Poma raises his fist into the air signaling for quiet.

"My loyal subjects I address you today to announce we will bury my dear father, your leader in two days.

Couriers will let the people know of the particular details. The following day will be the coronation for myself and Aadya as my queen. We look forward to beginning our lives as your leaders. My mother Queen Mesa is grieving over the loss of her lifelong partner. She has asked me to tell you she will no longer serve in a leadership role but is looking forward to spending more time with her grandchildren and soon-to-be-great grandchildren. And to serve the people in less demanding ways

"We as a family, are blessed to serve you with our powers as they are connected to the wonderous Matong in all its majesty.

"I would like you to now hear from my beloved wife, princess, soon to be Queen Aadya."

The crowd, knowing it is Aadya who has looked after them in ways no one on the Planet Merth has ever done, grows more raucous as people whistle, stomp, and throw things in the air.

MY PRINCE YOU ARE SO FINE STANDING THERE, SOON TO BE THE LEADER OF ALL. I HAVE BEEN BLESSED TO BE YOUR WIFE AND CONFI-DANT.

I LOVE YOU MY DEAR AADYA!

43- We Bury the King

"He was always kind to me and indulged my every whim."

On any other day, Poma might have disagreed with Aadya. "He was a great man, but sometimes an exacting father. I always felt much pressure from him to excel."

They sit together in the king's bedroom where Larsa's body, fully dressed now waits for burial. There is a knock at the door as it pushes open slightly, "May we come in father? It is Roark and Ali."

Poma looks up from his daydreaming. "Of course. Please…"

"Are you okay?" Roark asks his father.

"Yes, of course, we were sitting here in peace before the uproar begins" Roark goes over to the side of the bed and stares at his grandfather's face now lifeless and slightly blue. He notices the absence of the heavy monarch's ring on his right hand, always present when he was alive.

"Where is the ring?" Asks Roark innocently.

Buried in his own thoughts, Poma answers distractedly. "What? I'm sorry what did you say son?"

"The ring? The big gold Dalia stone set in plunger's gold the color of the setting star. Where is it?"

"Oh, the king's ring. It will be part of the coronation process. It will be placed on my finger tomorrow and I will not take it off until my death."

Roark studies his grandfather's body more closely, both arms have been pulled straight over the covers and are now stiff, but this is how his body should be properly displayed for the people.

Roark looks to his father sitting nearby in a chair and touches his sleeve slightly. "I would be inconsolable, if I were burying you."

Poma looks up at his son and gives him the most appreciative look he can muster.

"He did not prepare me enough," Poma says absently to the air.

"Do you remember the time Grandfather took us hunting and he shot a pogon bird by mistake?" Roark asks and looks to Ali who has knelt down on the floor beside her father's chair.

Ali laughs, "Oh my, the nasty thing put out such a stink! We were all poisoned with its scent for days."

Poma laughs. "Yes, but King Larsa was a great hunter. I am sure he did it on purpose to teach you children a lesson.

"And there was the time he accidentally drove off the embankment and got the wagon stuck in the stream."

Poma grimaces. "Yes, well kings are not supposed to drive wagons. Let us not dwell on his bad moments."

Roark flashes a compassionate look toward his father. "He led soldiers into battle against the Omis."

Poma stands and stares at his father's body. "When I was a child, I still remember when he came home from the war, he had changed. We all noticed it."

There was another gentle knock on the door. This time it is Prince Parsa, Poma's youngest brother. "I thought you might be in here. How is everyone doing?" he asks as he turns to look around at all the family present.

"Do you know where Bonder is?" Poma asks his brother.

"He is working on the speech he is to give."

"Thank the One True God he is. With my coronation tomorrow, I couldn't be the main speaker today." Poma's words catch in his throat and everyone in the room looks away except for Roark, who has never seen his father this decimated.

Aadya goes to the door and whispers to the guards outside. "This is a good time for the family to gather, please tell Galen, and bring Mother Mesa." Aadya rarely refers to her mother-in-law as 'mother' but at the moment it feels appropriate. "Oh, and please ask Bonder to join us for a minute. You could have someone bring some refreshments too. I do not think the prince ate breakfast." As she says this, she realizes tomorrow he will be king. The fact she would be queen does not really register. *I will be the same person, but Poma, he will change.*

When Queen Mesa arrives, she brings Hoya to lead the family in prayer. When all are gathered, they join hands and Hoya speaks to the One True God with a little extra drama thrown in for good measure. For some this is comforting, for others like Bonder, it is annoying, and he thinks his mother weak for listening to all this mumbo-bumbo through the years.

Later Aadya slips out to visit the Matong and finds Poma already there. She has never seen her husband this broken, this lost. He looks at her trying to mask his sadness and finally speaks.

"Tomorrow I must become king." In his eyes pool tears of regret. "I am not ready. I depend on you for your guidance." Aadya puts her hand on his cheek and kisses him lightly searching for the appropriate words to say. "You will do fine, my king. You will do just fine."

44-The King's Revelations

"Did you feel nothing?"

Aadya looks at Poma curiously. "No? Was I supposed to?"

"Oh, my Aadya! It was the greatest blast of sensations I have ever experienced at once. When the Imperial Cadash anointed me with oil, and placed the crown on my head, I thought I might explode, I was so bombarded with information," he tells her, once they are alone in their chambers. "But it is the ring mostly where the stream of information is coming from because I do not wear the crown now. The ring sends a tiny vibration laden with information. Our whole history as a people is in the ring."

"What are you talking about?"

"It is as if the entire memory of our family history is accessed through the ring. While I wore the crown, I saw generations living and dying before my very eyes. I saw wars and drought and any kind of disaster you can imagine including what happened to us recently. I saw women and men coupling as one, I saw people dying and giving birth. It was amazing. My father did not prepare me for this.

"Aadya," he grasps her hand with intensity, "I saw your father in battle, he was laying on the ground with people fighting directly over his body, then later I saw him get up and leave."

Poma's revelation feels as if someone is choking her. "What are you talking about? My father has not returned home from battle."

"I know, it is what makes this vision extraordinary."

The emotions of being left out worsen with Poma's descriptions of his visions. "I do not understand why all this was not conveyed to me when I was crowned."

"The only thing I can think of is you are not of the direct bloodline as I am. And you do not wear the ring."

Aadya has a sudden urge to jump on her horse and run her as fast as she will go, a favorite activity that always brings her release. "I'm…I have had a long day as I am sure you have. I am emotionally drained," she tells him.

"Yes, if only we could get away from all of this. We should go to the hunting lodge and hide out for a few days."

"Sounds delightful! Let us tell no one."

"We can't. We will let Roark know, he will guard our secret unless we are needed. Of course, we will have to have a small guard detail with us."

"Yes, of course, of course we do." *Now especially, our privacy is sacrificed.*

"But what about the celebrations?"

"We can make a brief appearance then sneak off in the darkness of night," he tells her grasping her around the waist. "It is not unheard of for a newly crowned king to retreat for a few days. And now I understand why."

Aadya grins, "I love it. It is a perfect plan."

Before they enter the great hall of Katara for the inaugural celebrations, the freshly crowned king and queen are ushered into the tiny Matong chamber. A coronation is the only time when the great doors are allowed to be open and those lucky and high-ranking enough will be allowed to peer into the Matong chamber from the hallway.

Perhaps I will have a similar revelation as Poma when I bond with the Matong. But Aadya's hopes go unanswered. Their children, as is the custom, are ushered in, and all partake in the bonding. But all Aadya gets out of the bonding is the simple message BE PREPARED. "I couldn't get a more generic message," she tells Poma later when they are riding their horses through the woods toward the hunting lodge, where once they honeymooned.

He turns his head to her and gives her a compassionate look, while all the time secretly remaining puzzled and overwhelmed by all the information still being cataloged into his brain.

The gentle rocking of being back in the saddle is like music to Aadya who is more than ready for a respite. *I knew he would be transformed, but why am I not?* She urges Bruta on with a gentle nudge and the two of them gallop off into the night, tree limbs whipping at their faces.

45-This Place

"I have always loved this place," Poma says enthusiastically, with the energy of a younger man.

Aadya dips her hand into the still lake and looks at her image in the water as Poma settles back into the bottom of the sturdy oar boat and looks up at the sky. The water is colder than she expected it to be. Her own reflection too is disappointing to her. She pulls a loose strand of her hair tucking it behind her ear, deciding she is looking older than she would like. *I shall be a grandmother soon.*

"This is a little piece of paradise," she says to Poma abandoning her own troubles.

"I'm not supposed to ever take off the ring, but I wish I could take a break from it, it keeps my brain buzzing with information."

"I wouldn't mind wearing it for a little while."

"Oh no, you do not really," he tells her. "I presume the furor will die down after a while but for now my mind is utterly overstimulated. I can't believe father did not prepare me for this."

"Maybe he wasn't supposed to, maybe you are actually wearing all the information you need."

"At least I am finally able to sleep a little."

"Those first nights were stressful."

"I do not know how Ali is going to handle this…maybe we should figure out a way to make Roark the next monarch."

"Do not ever say that ever again! I will hurt you if you do."

Poma sits up and studies her, deciding to hold his tongue and change the subject.

"My advisers are telling me the people are growing afraid because of the 'Targa' event. They are worried it will happen again."

"Does the ring tell you why it happened?"

"No, it provides more of a history of our people. I have not come across anything similar." He swallows. "We may never know."

A soft breeze shimmers along the surface of the water giving Aadya a slight chill. She shields her eyes against the glare and looks across to where a guard awaits with their horses at the little pier where they got into the boat. Bruta is eating the tall grass and stamping her foot. This sight gives Aadya great pleasure.

"We need to go back tomorrow."

"What's the rush?"

"I can't hide any longer."

Aadya bows her head looking at the bottom of the boat, but not meeting his eyes. "We can return whenever we want."

Poma makes a sarcastic noise with his lips which sounds like a wild doma spitting.

"Probably not, but we can try to come more often. Roark and Ali are almost grown."

Poma reaches for his wife and pleads with his eyes for her to join him in the bottom of the boat. She lays down with him despite the discomfort of the hard wooden hull, and lets him touch her intimately. She drinks in his breath. They do not fully undress but continue to chuttle each other until it becomes obvious they would rather complete what they have started in the comfort of their bed.

Aadya sits up and pulls her tunic back on.

DO NOT COVER THEM UP THEY ARE EX-TRAORDINARY.

A smile spills from her lips. "Silly prince, get up." She pulls at him. "I mean silly king."

Poma frowns. "I'm afraid kings are not allowed to be silly."

"You may be king now, but you will always be my prince." The comment meant to reassure him, does. *I can see it in his face.*

Aadya pulls at one oar and pushes it toward him. "Now take us home please."

He stands to button his breeches and sits down to pull the oars. "Okay, but we are not leaving our bedroom until you cannot walk, and I cannot stand."

Aadya gives him a look of disapproval, but it is clear he will have his way.

46-Kandar and Galen

Galen wakes to the sound of the river rushing down the gorge. Unlike other women's pregnancies, Galen and her child communicate with unspoken gestures and songs, visualizing in each other's minds their thoughts and desires.

Galen and Kandar have been camping on their land, in a spacious cloth tent, nearby to where they are building a house. The land was gifted to them by her father, King Poma, for her service to the community as a healer. And while Kandar insists on building the house himself, each day a group of ten or more men show up to help him. People also bring food, clothing, furniture, and anything they might also possibly need. At night friends gather around an open firepit to tell stories, play music, and sing. Ali and Roark are often among the crowd.

Because she is late to rising this daybreak, Kandar comes to the tent to check on her. "I bring you these fruits and cheeses some of the women dropped off earlier. Are you feeling okay my love?"

"Mmm, yes, just a little slow this morning. The baby danced in my belly all night long," she says patting her ballooning girth.

"I guess I didn't notice, I slept soundly."

Galen smiles at him knowingly. "You always do."

"Did mother come by yet?" She says, folding her silky white hair to one side of her face.

"No, I haven't seen her."

"She has some sort of project she wants to talk about with me. She was kind of mysterious." Galen's deep lilac-colored eyes never cease to startle Kandar who is completely devoted to his wife 'the healer,' even if her status keeps her busy with others and robs her of time with him.

"The men say it is only a short time now before our house is completed."

"I do not need to rush, I love the sound of the water here," she says pulling the sleek sheets up around her as she rises. "The baby does too."

Kandar finds it odd when Galen speaks of the baby as if she knows what the little creature is thinking.

"We will have the water sound at our house too, and the baby needs a roof over his head." He reminds her with somewhat of a patronizing tone.

"Have some of these gripples, they are lusciously sweet and ripe." Galen pulls off some of the deep red orbs from their stems and hands them to Kandar by grabbing his calloused hand and dropping them into his cupped palm.

"Mmm, you are right." He says tasting the fruit.

"Aah, I grow heavy with the burden of this child," she leans on a chair back to steady herself. "Perhaps you could ask someone to prepare my bath."

"Of course, there are three servant girls outside the tent waiting to help you."

"I know, if I weren't pregnant, I would relieve them of their duties, but it is really helpful to have them here. It was the only way I could get the 'women' to agree to let us do this." By 'women' she means, her mother, her Grandmother Mesa and Ali. "They are smothering and protective to a fault."

"They do not understand. You lived for nearly an entire revolution in encampments while healing the people after 'Targa.'"

Kandar kisses his wife on the forehead and inhales the captivating scent of her. The time is growing closer when their lives will change, or so he is told. He cannot quite accept the fact, yet he will be a father. Fathers are supposed to be wise and teach their children. What did he know he could bestow upon a grandson of the king?

47-Seeking Guidance

"Oh, there you are. I was wondering when you would show up. Perfect timing to brush my hair."

Galen has gotten out of the heavy metal bathtub brought in for her, and is in the process of dressing when Aadya arrives.

Aadya comes near her to place a hand on her swollen belly. "Is he moving around this morning? Oops, yes, he is. Perfect timing." Aadya giggles, "I can actually see your belly roiling."

Galen takes Aadya's hand and moves it to a more advantageous place lower on her abdomen. "So much energy, he will keep you busy once he arrives!"

"I know," Galen smiles contentedly rubbing her bulging middle. Inside her womb the baby sings to her of love and family. Galen reaches down to guide her pregnant body into her chair before the mirror, a luxury which is exceptionally out of place in the humble tent abode. Aadya standing above and behind her with a brush made from animal fibers and wood begins the familiar activity.

"What is on your mind?" Galen asks.

"As you know your father is inundated with responsibilities now. It is like I have to arrange time to be alone with him, except when he comes to bed and then he falls instantly asleep." She holds a clump of Galen's white hair and pulls the brush through it. "I have no one to hear me out although he gives me full rein. I need the wisdom of another on occasion. Ali is still too young, to guide me, besides, she needs to start shadowing him these days to familiarize herself with the duties of leadership."

Galen sashays her hand in the air, "So, tell me."

"Someone has brought me a painting, an extraordinary painting."

"And?"

"You know Petra Kilver?"

"Yes, we get some of our best herbs from her." Aadya nods affirmatively.

"Okay, do you trust her?"

"I have no reason not to."

"She is the one who has brought me the painting, and says it was created by an Omi woman."

"No way the Omis are letting their women paint!"

"I know." Aadya looks into her daughter's eyes through the reflection of the mirror.

"But she says it is the truth, and I want to believe her"

"You must tread very carefully with the Omis involved. Our truce with them is quite fragile."

"But you went there on your healing mission, did you not?"

"Yes, and it was the most dangerous place of all. You absolutely must consult father on this."

"I was thinking about issuing the woman artist an invitation, through Petra, to come here."

"Sure, it would be your safest bet, but you still have to consult Father. If anything were to happen to her while being here, it might start another war."

Aadya grabs a persistent snarl close to Galen's head and gently picks at it with the comb she has traded for the brush so as not to hurt Galen.

"I had not considered this. I thought if it was her own desire to visit Katara, I would give her an audience."

"You might choose this path, but I still think you must consider a diplomatic envoy to escort her. And what about the Omis even allowing a woman to paint? They might kill her themselves if they learn of her talents." Feeling weighted down by her child, Galen shifts her balance from one side of the chair to the other.

"I must find out more about this by consulting with Petra. I'll make a formal appointment with her and your father, so he can hear first-hand from this Omi woman."

"There you are. A better way to handle it."

Aadya sets the comb down. Reaches down to kiss her daughter hastily on the cheek and rushes out the tent door where Bruta has been idly grazing.

48-Secrets

"If the artist were a man, I would see nothing of it, but…" King Poma turns on his heels and locks eyes with Petra. Tell me again how you acquired this painting?"

Petra Kilver was known for her resourcefulness, she was the one who had encouraged trade with the Omis, even before King Larsa had died. Her cousin was actually married to an Omi and lived in Omi territory. She was not afraid to travel there occasionally and when she did, she had brought back bitterbalm, one of the most powerful herbs of all. At first her trading had been quiet, personal, and small scale, but when Garth Olfen, a high-ranking Omi had suggested to her there might be sweeter deals were she to bring greater quantities of her toku leaves, which were much more potent than what the Omis were used to, she had gained an inroad to larger trade deals.

"I do not think it is any secret I have been trading with the Omis. Your daughter's healers are the beneficiary of my bitterbalm trade, a much coveted herbal remedy."

"Have you registered your activities with our officials?"

Petra glances down at her bejeweled sandals pondering whether she should lie to the king or be straightforward. If it were someone of lesser power she would not hesitate to deceive, but fearing the wrath of the king, lying is something else altogether.

"Not yet, I didn't know it was required."

"How much trade are you actively involved in?

"I go there occasionally with two wagons," she says stretching the truth to suit her needs. With the open door from the Omis and her own people begging for the bitterbalm, her trips had become more frequent.

"I need to consult with Quigley, and it wouldn't hurt to have a few other advisers. "Get Bonder and Parsa and Quigley in here," Poma nods to the aide standing by the door. "And fetch Kandar if you can." As his son-in-law and a soldier, Kandar was being included in more of the king's consultations.

"We need to make sure trade strengthens our bonds between other regions,"

"The Omis have been the most resistant to progress for women," Aadya chimes in.

As the room fills up with more advisers, Poma looks to Quigley, the Minister of Trade, to take the lead.

"We need to devise a thoughtful plan, tying the benefits of trade to our progressive roles for women," the king tells Quigley. King Poma no longer needs Aadya's enthusiasm for what used to be such a radical idea, because he has witnessed first-hand the direct benefits of the many roles women play in their thriving society.

Quigley nods in agreement. "We need accurate accountings of what trade is going in and what is going out."

Petra squirms inwardly hoping the toku leaves will not become an issue, abuse of the leaf was getting more recognition, especially with Queen Aadya's brother Jubal's history. But outwardly she appeared as cold as stone on a winter's day. There might be more regulations, but she would get around them if needed.

"Sir, what about the artist? May I ask her to come visit me? Just an innocent invitation?" Poma turns to Petra considering her request.

"There are many Omis visiting our region now," she adds.

"I suppose it would be acceptable. But she is not to bring any of her work. She can paint for us once she is here. But under no conditions do we want to contribute to her misfortune, or ours, if she were to be discovered doing activities not yet allowed for women by the Omis."

Petra lets her lungs slowly fill with air. She has her own reasons for bringing the woman, she has fallen madly in love with, to Valtar.

49-More Secrets

Alatoi sneers when Petra shows up at her doorstep and tells her she has permission to carry her to Katara for a short visit. "Where will I stay? At Katara?"

"No, of course not. Do not be stupid. You will stay with me, but you will have an audience with the king and queen." Petra secretly wishes Alatoi was more considerate and loving, but once they had been together to fulfill their lusts, Alatoi has claimed the upper hand. Despite this, Petra is hoping, by making this invitation known to Alatoi at the last minute, she will not turn her down.

"Now go get your things. I have to meet my supplier."

It takes Alatoi a surprisingly short amount of time to return to the wagon with a duffle. "You tell me they are allowing women to wear pants at Valtar?"

"Yes, it's true, our queen wears them regularly."

Alatoi throws her heavy bag up onto the cart with ease. This is one of the things which attracts Petra to Alatoi, she has great physical strength like a man, but the body and insight of a woman, making her an ideal lover.

"Are they going to allow me to paint?"

"Possibly, this is the tricky part," Petra shrinks at what she must say as she slaps the reins across the rump of her carriage horse, causing a cloud of musky dust to rise.

"For your protection, and mine, you must be very discreet when it comes to your talents." Petra turns to look her in the eyes. "All of them."

Alatoi smirks at her lover. "I told you, you do not own me. I like being with men as much as women."

Sulking, Petra does not turn again to face her.

"You have bewitched me," she says under her breath.

"What did you say?'

"Nothing, but you need to be careful. Our king is not going to do anything to start a war again with the Omis."

"Let us have a pull on the pipe," Alatoi says, reaching for the long-stemmed smoking pod hanging from Petra's mouth.

"It's frowned upon in Valtar. I told you," Petra says giving her lover a dirty look. But she hands it over anyway.

In her distraction, Petra lets the cart hit a deep pothole and they both lurch causing Alatoi to nearly drop the pipe. "Watch where you are going fool!"

Petra gives Alatoi a sullen look. "You distract me with your wicked ways."

"Really? Well take a look at these." Alatoi pulls her leather vest apart and flashes her bouncing breasts at Petra. Giggling at the reaction she receives, she folds her clothing back in place.

"Maybe we can have a threesome with the king."

"Hush! You will get us thrown into prison with talk like that. The king is not a lecher. He is totally devoted to his wife, he is pure of heart, and leads our kingdom righteously!"

Filled with mirth for the first time since boarding the cart with Petra, Alatoi takes a long drag on the pipe she keeps lit with a small torch box and stem she has brought along for such a purpose.

"Yes, yes, I have the proper paperwork," Petra waves it at the waiting magistrate. "I have had to license my trade as you have, but at least now I can make my trips more frequently, although I shall not be returning for several days this time." The magistrate nods allowing his eyes to wander between the two women, one dressed in bright colors and fanciful shoes with glass beads, the other woman with straight black hair hanging down to her chest, dressed in a provocative vest and simple calfskin skirt. He is somewhat puzzled by the bare arms of the woman in the vest as he does not see this fashion much outside of the toku leaves dens. But he does not question Petra, as her trade is too valuable to him.

"We will arrive before nightfall," Petra hesitates, not sure how to handle Alatoi during this visit. She looks at her and her heart flutters like a bird caught in her chest. "I have decided to pay you while you are my guest at Valtar."

"Oh?" Alatoi puffs on the pipe enjoying the ease and comfort it is exhausting into her brain.

"But you must obey me completely. I am risking a great deal to bring you to our land."

"The money will be yours to do with as you please. But in return you must do everything I say."

A wicked smile creeps across Alatoi's lips. "Every-thing?"

"Yes, everything."

50-An Encounter with a Stranger

The two women journey down the badly rutted road mostly in silence. Petra is quickly coming to the realization Alatoi will just bait her if they stay in conversation long and is beginning to doubt her own judgment about having Alatoi in her home. It is when they draw near to Katara, they see a man napping on the side of the road, using his hood as shelter from the daylight and nearly invisible nestled into the tall grass.

"Stop!" Alatoi commands.

"The vagabond is of no concern to us."

"I recognize him from home," Alatoi says jumping down from the slowly moving cart.

Alatoi squints her eyes to get a better look at the man in the grass curled up like a sleeping dog. "I used to drink with him at the Bondall Tavern," she tells Petra. He has a strange story. I slept with him once, and he had an unusual approach using a long whip to both beat me and tie me up with. It was quite erotic."

Petra recoils from Alatoi's salacious comments.

"Do not tell me of your exploits. Now get back in the wagon!" she says finally slowing the cart to a standstill.

Alatoi turns and sneers at her benefactor. "He looks compromised. Surely, we must help him. Perhaps he is injured."

"Alatoi!" Petra screams between clenched teeth. You said you would do anything I ask."

Alatoi expresses an angry gush of air and begins to sulk, reluctantly getting back into the wagon beside Petra. As they drive off the huddled traveler stirs on the ground, but they do not stop.

"You did what?" Aadya asks her servant incredulously.

"But your highness, he was quite persistent. He said he has information of your father's whereabouts. I thought someone should question him. So, I had one of the king's guards look into it and they locked him up. He has asked to speak with you directly."

"But why would they lock him up?"

"They are concerned for your safety; they say he traveled from Omiland."

This is very curious. My father has been gone for many years. Why would someone come from Omi with word of him? I will ask Poma tonight, when I see him, how to proceed.

But Aadya is fast asleep by the time Poma comes to bed. And it is well into the next day before she sees him again. She is training horses with the groomsman when he shows up to join her.

HELLO MY LOVE. She lets her thoughts into his head. He smiles affectionately at her. I AM SORRY FOR THE LATE NIGHT. WE HAD A COUNCIL MEETING.

THERE WAS MUCH TO DISCUSS WITH TRADE OPENING UP TO THE OMIS.

She hands the lead to the trainer and slips her arm into Poma's. "Have they told you about the stranger?"

Poma gives her a perplexed look. "What do you speak of?"

"Our guards have detained a stranger who says he has information about my father. They say he has journeyed here from Omiland. There's probably nothing to it, father has been gone for too many years."

Poma turns to face her. "We do need to be cautious about this, but we could have someone interrogate him."

"They say he wants an audience with me. I need to know what this is about. You know I have not seen or heard from my father since I was a child."

"This is very curious." Seeing this is important to her, he tells her he will join her.

"Thank you, Poma. It should not take long to figure out what this is about."

51-News from the Grave

It takes another few days for Poma's schedule to become open enough for the interview with the stranger, but finally the traveler is brought to them. I CANNOT BELIEVE THEY WERE WORRIED ABOUT THIS OLD MAN Aadya transmits her thoughts to Poma who nods his head.

AGREED

"Please be seated." she tells the foreigner, who bows and sits in the chair provided.

"What is it you have to tell us?" The man shuffles uncomfortably in his seat finally looking up and meeting her eyes. His voice is soft and gravelly. "I believe you are the daughter of Zolan Wannatu. Is this true?"

Aadya cocks her head to hear him better. "Did you say Zolan Wannatu? How did you come to know this? He has been dead for many years."

"No, your highness he died only recently."

Aadya involuntarily gasps. Realizing, finally, she will not have the chance see her father ever again.

"How do you know this, he died in battle years ago."

"No, he was wounded, captured, and imprisoned. I shared a cell with him for many years, but even so, it was a long time ago. He saved my life in prison, and I owe him fealty, so I became his eyes and ears on the outside, once I was released."

Aadya has many questions, but she does not want to lead the stranger into make anything up, so she listens carefully, hoping his words will reveal only truth.

"There were rumors they were going to release him, but what I heard is there was a newly installed captain at the prison who hated Zolan because he had killed his father in battle."

Aadya's pain leaks from her eyes and trembling lips. The stranger pauses. "I didn't come here to upset you your highness. Your father asked me to find you."

She sucks in her breath and does her best to compose herself. "I understand," she says bowing her head slightly. Poma looks over to her. ARE YOU ALL RIGHT?

YES, WE MUST GET HIS STORY.

"I traveled to your village, and they told me you were now queen of the land. This knowledge frightened me a little. My instincts were sound. I have even been held captive for my good deed."

"Please tell me more about my father."

"He was a good man. We lived together in 10 x10 space for probably six years. I was finally released and went back to my family."

"What was your crime?" Poma intercedes.

PLEASE LET HIM TELL HIS STORY ABOUT FA-THER!

"I lost my position at the Triponia Vinyard and I was caught stealing."

HE IS LYING. I CAN SENSE IT.

YES, POMA YOU ARE CORRECT.

"I do not believe you. Why do you lie to us?"

The stranger bows his head then looks up. "I'm not a virtuous man, sir." He casts his eyes toward Queen Aadya. "But your father was. He was a leader of men. And he deserved a much better life than he had. He asked me to deliver this ring to you." The stranger slips off a cast vadal ring with a modest blue stone from his burly little finger and hands it to her. It drops into the palm of her hand, and she gasps clutching her heart with the other hand.

THIS WAS HIS! I REMEMBER THE RING.

"So, when did he die?"

"Like I said, with the recently relaxed trade agreements, they talked about letting him return to his homeland, but this particular captain caught wind of who he was, and he was found beaten to death several rotations ago. I kept the promise I made to him on my last visit; if anything were to happen to him, I would travel to your village, seek you out, and give you the ring."

He stopped and fished into his pocket. "There was something else, he must have had a premonition he was not going to get out alive. He gave me this note to give to you. I had to sneak it out, I was afraid I might be closely searched, and I was. I slipped it into the lining of my boot, and no one discovered it."

Aadya takes the small, stained piece of cloth and examines it. In script, which could have only been written in blood, are these few short words.

Aadya, if there is any chance you or your mother, are still alive, please know I love you. I had hoped to return one day. You have the warrior spirit of the Lynton wolf. It is you who I pass on my privilege to sit on the

council with this ring. Use this note to rightfully claim your position. And be the leader I know you are.

Aadya's breath comes in short hiccups now. It is as if her rib cage is being squeezed in a large vise.

"So, he never knew I had become queen?"

"I guess not. Word of King Mesa's passing is known, but we do not keep up much with what is happening over here. I guess he had no idea." The stranger says. "We didn't get a lot of news we could trust in prison."

IF ONLY WE HAD DEVELOPED OUR RELATIONS SOONER WITH THE OMIS HE MIGHT HAVE LIVED. I MIGHT HAVE SEEN HIM AGAIN.

THIS IS NOT YOUR FAULT AADYA. YOU HAD NO REASON TO KNOW, Poma gives her a sympathetic look.

"Thank you for your service." Aadya quips as she struggles to process this devastating revelation.

"We are happy to reward you for your information. I will have one of my staff find you accommodations for a couple of days allowing you to stay in the area," King Poma says, "in case we need to contact you. Be assured we will make up for our indiscretions of having you imprisoned."

The traveler grimly answers. "I have no reason to rush back to Omiland, but I will not be held hostage again."

"Of course not," Aadya reassures him looking into his pale eyes, the color of dirty dishwater. "I do not believe you told us your name."

"Cronar, Cronar Devlin."

"Then it is settled," the king signals an attendant to escort him out, as Aadya sinks back into her chair with a vacant look on her face.

52-A Shocking Revelation

Try as she might, Aadya cannot recall her father's face. She remembers the wheat-colored hair which fell to his shoulders. It was soft and silky when he took her into his strong arms and hugged her as a child. She remembers the touch of his scratchy beard, and the clear blue sparkle of his eyes. But the sound of his voice is gone, His smile... *Did he even smile much?*

I should remember. We spent much time together in the woods hunting. "Aadya you have a gift as a huntress. Your prey does not stand a chance," he would tell her.

Zolan Wannatu, impressed with his daughter's skills, started training her to wield a sword, much to the chagrin of her brother, Jubal, who took every opportunity to use his burly size to intimidate her when no one was looking.

My father should have been focusing on training my brother, but Jubal was overlooked. I do not know why. I can't say Jubal was much like us at all. But why did he not bestow the rights of the heir to council to Jubal instead of me? He could not have known of Jubal's addiction to the toku leaves.

"Are you okay?" Poma asks Aadya. He has not left her side since their interview with the traveler from Omi.

"Oh, my goodness you are still here? I thought you were off to attend another counsel. I was thinking about my father. I think I will visit the Matong and see if some of my memories might be restored." She looks at Poma with a quizzical expression "I want to remember him, but I do not even know what I want to remember. It is sad."

"I understand," he nods with a certain regret in his voice. "Memories of my father are more and more at a distance, and he has not been buried long." Aadya reaches out to touch Poma on the sleeve, but he does not linger long. Bonder has appeared in the doorway and is motioning for his brother to come along with him. "They've been waiting on you." Bonder says, trying to mask the irritation in his voice.

Aadya receives only one small glimpse of her father in her Matong vision but the message to send for her Uncle Tabiathin is loud and clear. "Good afternoon," her uncle hugs her. "To what do I owe this pleasant surprise?"

"Forgive me uncle, we do not see enough of each other. I hope you are in good health."

"As good as can be expected for an old man like myself."

"Please sit down, I have some sad news to share with you."

Her uncle's bushy eyebrows arch into the suggestion of curiosity as he sits in an armchair near her.

"Word has it my father recently died in a prison in Omiland."

"I'm sorry to hear this my queen."

"There is no need for such a formality. I am your niece."

"Yes, Your Majesty. Er, I mean Aadya."

"We have recently received this news from a traveler who came here from Omi to tell me and bring me this message." Pulling out the note she received earlier, Aadya shows it to her mother's brother.

"Yes, I believe this is authentic. That looks like your father's handwriting."

"So, tell me what you know about Jubal," she asks.

"Ah, I'm not sure what you are referring to."

"There is something missing in my memories. I do not understand my relationship with my father completely and why he was partial to me and not Jubal."

Tabiathan lets his shoulders slump as if resigning himself to some unwanted fate. "I promised your mother I would never tell you."

"Tell me what?" Aadya lets out a gasp of frustration. "What? Uncle you must tell me."

"It is the shame of the family. But your father and mother loved each other"

"AND?" Aadya motions with her hands in a circular gesture as if to physically rout the truth from her uncle's mouth.

He looks around to make sure no one else is in the room. "Do we have complete privacy?'

"Yes, of course."

"Mayalina" he pauses as if to recapture his breath. "Your mother, was kidnapped and raped shortly before they were to be married."

"No!" Aadya covers her mouth in an effort to smother her shock.

"Yes, it is true," he swallows. "Your father somehow found her and killed at least three men who were holding her captive." Tabiathan lowers his face to avoid eye contact with her. Anger, like lightning bolts, is running through her body. "But it took him nearly a week to track them down, and by then they all had their way with her."

"This is horrifying!"

"No, one in our village ever faulted your father, and there certainly was no trial."

As her emotions rise, it is as if a swarm of honton bees have landed on her, weighing her down with the warmth of their energy. *This explains so much!*

"I guess this has much to do with how you were raised."

"Of course, it does. My father must have secretly hated Jubal knowing he was the spawn of my mother's aggressors."

Tabiathan nods silently in agreement.

"Now I understand. This is why he raised me to be a warrior. It was so I could protect myself."

"He made the noble choice and raised the boy, although no one would have blamed him if he did the unthinkable."

A million memories flood into Aadya's consciousness, and suddenly she can now visualize both her mother and father laughing together, singing songs, and snuggling with her. Her mother's cold indifference to her brother was justified, and unexpectedly she experiences compassion for the foul visage of her brother Jubal. "Where is Jubal these days?"

"He hangs around with those who lurk in shadows. Fortunately, he is inebriated most of the time and does not cause much trouble. I imagine he specializes in running errands for the least desirables of our village." Bitter emotions slither inside of Aadya, as she tries to quell them by distracting herself with thoughts of justice and acceptance.

"Thank you for telling me. I know it was difficult for you, but I'm glad you did." She takes his hands in hers and kisses him goodbye lightly on the cheek.

53-In Memory

"I've gathered you three here for lunch today to let you know of my heartbreaking news," Aadya tells her children as they feast on an elaborate picnic served for them on a huge stone slab table nearby to a thunderous waterfall.

"I love this spot!" Ali says as she picks a bright blue junal berry from her plate and pops it into her mouth. "I haven't been out here in many moons. I do not know how many times we played toss over there in the clearing." She points toward a sunlit meadow beyond a grove of ceylon trees.

"We all love it here," Galen chimes in.

"Yes, I'm sorry, I have to share with you word of my father, who you have never known. This has come to me via a stranger from Omiland." Aadya sips her tangy qultar juice from an earthen mug and takes a deep breath.

"The man was imprisoned with my father for many years and came to tell me of his death."

"Oh, this is heartbreaking." Ali mutters, "What was he doing in prison? I thought he was a war hero who probably died on the battlefield."

"It's deplorable." Aadya struggles to go on. "Apparently, he was caught and imprisoned for many years. If I had only known, I could have saved him."

"Mother, you didn't know." Galen reassures her and touches her lightly on the arm.

Her daughter's touch is like the cooling tingle of a mintus leaf to Aadya.

"I wish I had known him," Roark tells her. Aadya's thoughts are triggered by Roark's surprising statement. She looks at the handsome young man her son has become and realizes he has breached the threshold of maturity when she was not looking.

"You are lot like him physically. He was about your height, and you have the same color eyes. Your hair is much darker though, more like your father's."

Roark flashes her a smile, and suddenly she sees it, the similarity, she is now seeing the smile her father used to give her, only on her son. "You are very much like him. I didn't realize."

"Oh," Galen groans as the baby kicks her hard against the ribs. "I must get back to a more comfortable chair."

"Here I'll walk you back sister," Ali stands up to assist Galen back to her campsite.

Disappointed the gathering is already breaking up and concerned for her daughter's welfare, Aadya suggests waiting for someone to come get her in a wagon. "When will your house be finished? You must have four walls to raise my grandchild!"

Galen turns around grasping her enormous belly. "I'm fine mother, do not worry. It will be finished soon. The fresh air will be good for the baby, but I need to walk this baby out. By my count I am overdue by several revolutions."

"And I have an engagement with a lovely maiden who adores the ground I walk upon." Roark grins and races to catch up making his exit with theirs. Ali reaches around to link her arm in his and gives him a petulant expression for his vanity.

As her grown children make excuses to get back to their lives, Aadya watches them walk away with their backs turned toward her. *I have been watching them leave me all their lives. Why does it surprise me?*

Aadya whistles to Brita who bolts her head up from grazing and comes to Aadya, nuzzling her velvet nose into Aadya's face. Brita's breath is like a kiss of meadow grass as Aadya inhales. She places her palm on Brita's nose and lets the sadness fill her heart. *If I only had a picture of him!*

54-A Child is Born

It is later in the night, as light from the two moons bathes the hills and valleys of Compana in a blanket of luminescent white, a child is born to Galen and Kandar in the humble tent they still reside in. "Kandar, it is time!" Galen shakes him from a deep sleep. She has been pacing around the tent unable to rest, when her water breaks with a resounding pop in the stillness of the night.

He jumps up like a startled crona pig and blinks. "What do I do? What do you need?"

"Send for the women, we talked about. I need some help please." Galen pulls off her wet garments, smoothes the covers to the bed and lays down after pulling on a new gown. She tries to breathe rhythmically, but something is wrong, it is as if the baby is trying to push out her back. It is extremely painful. When the breathing does not soothe her, she calls on the mystery of the Matong to find her here, and to assure the safety of the baby, but the pain continues to grind and rip at her body. Trying to keep Kandar calm, she is unable to withhold a shriek of panic which escapes from her core, curdling into the air with its vitriol. The sound is otherworldly like an animal being ripped to shreds by a bansha leopard. She faints. And when she awakens the two women and Kandar are kneeled beside the bed talking about her.

"Thank the One True God her eyes are open!" Kandar leans toward her awkwardly.

"The baby, is the baby, okay?" She asks.

"He is." Kandar beams, taking the tiny bundle from the woman holding his son.

"But he does not cry? Why isn't he crying?" She parts the delicate cloth he is wrapped in and peers at the velvety face of her newborn child for the first time.

"He's okay, the women say he is okay. They had to turn him. They had to give you a potion," Kandar stammers. With this information Galen understands her babe's docile condition.

"He will be called Jaru." Kandar looks at her stunned. It has been his impression the Matong would name their baby.

Galen smiles at him with the smile only a mother can produce. "It means kindness in the ancient language. He is to be known as Jaru Osen, Kind One."

"But I thought."

The Matong bird visited me in my dreams and revealed his name."

"Of course. It is as you say."

She holds Jaru and sings to him an old-fashioned hymn Kandar has not heard before.

Symin hoda, Jarsufe tru,
Scharon, dilspot, shaman sma.
Hosper talen, fodder fru,
Jason Jaru Osen.

Then she sings in the language Kandar can understand.

Little one, you are new.

We will protect you; we will love you
All your life, through the best and worst
You are named Jaru Osen.

Kandar sits quietly transfixed by yet another surprise his wife awards him. When he notices her perspiring, he lifts the tent door and lets the breeze blow in, and they quietly revel in the solace of their tiny family member freshly delivered unto the world of Merth.

But the peace is quickly broken as word has been delivered to Compana, and horses are already thundering to their modest domicile.

"Ah my sweet Galen," Aadya rushes to her daughter's side. She touches her cheek and peers into the blanket to view her firstborn grandchild. "Are you feeling okay? What can we do to make you more comfortable?"

"We are fine. The women have done an excellent job assisting with the birth."

Aadya stares deep into her daughter's eyes as if she might possibly convince her to do the right thing. "Darling Galen, I have been concerned about you. We must really get you moved into your house."

Galen reassures her with a gentle smile. "We are close mother. Everything is fine."

55-A Deal Is Struck

On the edge of Valtar, in an impressive house built by trade money, Petra is almost ready to pack up Alatoi and send her back to Omi. Her lecherous comrade has exhausted her both mentally and physically, and has now begun to roam the streets at night, getting slovenly intoxicated on drink and toku, and worst of all does not always return until the morning star is rising in the sky.

"I've had it with you!" Petra screams. You are a worthless leach!" She sucks in a breath and tries to compose herself. "The queen has finally granted us an audience. She wants you to paint portraits of her family. You need to clean yourself up. We are to meet later this day.

Alatoi has finally heard the news she traveled so far to receive. She runs her hands down the front of her bodice and sniffs her underarms realizing perhaps she does need to bathe.

"Finally, this is what I've been waiting for. I need to paint. I need recognition for my talents. And most of all," she runs her hands down the back side of her pants and pulls some straw out of the top of her tall boots. "Most of all I need money so I can move out of this house!"

Her words hit Petra like a cold bucket of water in the chest, even though just moments before, she had been scheming about the very same thing.

"Now wait a minute, you promised!"

A sneer swipes across Alatoi's face as she wipes her upper lip with her sleeve. "And when you make bargains with liars, you are nothing but an old fool!"

Petra places her hands on her hips and begins scheming how she can subvert Alatoi to doing her will.

"I will have you chained and beaten if you do not start acting better. And most importantly I will not take you to see the queen unless you get yourself looking like the gifted artist you are, and not some common slutza!"

Petra's abuse actually begins igniting a spark of passion in Alatoi and soon the two are tearing at each other's clothing. When their passion is quenched, Petra shouts orders to Alatoi. "Now get up and get dressed! And do not make me regret all the kindness I have bestowed upon you."

"Kindness? You are such an annoying Bistoide!" Alatoi barks and then slinks off to bathe in the luxurious marstone tub in Petra's house.

Aadya is finishing the task of delegating teachers for the upcoming educational conferences to be held soon. Her committee meets regularly, and she has scheduled this meeting with the woman artist from Omi with great anticipation. *If she is as talented as I have been led to believe, then maybe we can get her to teach us also.*

There were paintings of all the royals over at Katara, but they were all created by men. Since the death of King Larsa, Katara was still the royal residence for Queen Mother Mesa, but Aadya and Poma have remained living at Compana. It would be nice to have paintings hanging on their walls, not just portraits, and if they were painted by a woman artist, *even better.*

When Petra and Alatoi are brought in, they bow with respect, but Alatoi makes a sweeping gesture with her peculiarly outrageous hat, and bows deeply, affectedly, as if she were in a contest with Petra to be the most dramatic person in the room. Petra scowls at her and hisses under her breath. Distracted by her own thoughts of her good fortune, Aadya does not notice their dramatic antics.

"Please be seated. Would you like something to drink?"

"Wine." Alatoi answers, before Petra can speak. Petra flashes her another scolding look.

"Juice or water is fine, thank you, Your Majesty."

Petra clears her throat, hoping to bring the attention back to herself. "Your highness, it is my great pleasure to introduce you to Alatoi Tumbrela as per our agreement."

"Yes, of course Petra you will receive a generous bounty for bringing her here."

The queen turns her attention to the painter. "I am pleased to finally meet you. I know you were told not to bring any of your paintings, so I have arranged a studio room for you, and quarters of your own. We desire you to paint for us."

"Actually, I have brought one small sample I hid in the lining of my jacket."

Now Petra is really glowering at her companion, as Alatoi takes off her waistcoat and pulls at a small painting from within a slit in the backside of her dark coat made from the skins of the kosum balt.

"Oh my, this is gorgeous. It brings to mind a place where I first met my husband," Queen Aadya says as she studies the details of the small canvas. "But can you paint portraits?"

"Of course. I look forward to painting all of your family members."

Aadya eyes the curvaceous woman sporting leather breeches as if for the first time seeing her.

"May I ask ma'am, where my quarters and studio will be? I need lots of natural light for my work."

"Yes of course, I have had our local artists confer on this matter. I think you will be pleased."

As they are shown out Aadya can hear Petra and Ala-toi arguing softly as to the details of this new arrangement, and a smile grows on her face. *What a peculiar pair they are.*

56-Aella Anemone

"You shall be first," Aadya tells Ali. "But why me? Shouldn't father be first?"

How should I word my thoughts? "You are the Heir Apparent and you are also at the magical age where you have passed your childhood, and you are on the cusp of adulthood."

Ali gives her mother a peculiar look. "Really you want me to go first?"

"Yes, I want to see what she can do before we bother your father. You know how busy he is." Aadya peers at Ali noticing her beauty and how she will need to be guided into matrimony soon." *I can't imagine how difficult it must have been for King Larsa and Queen Mesa when Poma brought me home!* "I've set up the first appointment for you tomorrow morning when the morning star is almost straight above. The painter's studio is in the small cottage down the way from Barstow's dairy."

"The one Fartell gutted a few years ago?"

"Yes, she requested plenty of natural light and tall ceilings. We tried to make it comfortable for her, but she said she would mostly be there to paint only.

"And what is her name?"

"Alatoi Tumbrela, she's very, ah, unique."

When Ali arrives for her sitting no one is there. So, she sits and waits for a few minutes and just as she is about to leave, a cart pulls up and a disheveled woman rolls out. Aside from her unkemptness, Ali finds the woman to be allusive and magnetic at the same time, if not downright impertinent.

"You are not supposed to keep a princess waiting," Ali's driver tells Alatoi tersely.

"Yes, of course not." Alatoi swings a leather bag over her shoulder and motions for Ali to step in. The room takes up most of the little building. New windows have been fitted in for maximum light.

Ali watches Alatoi as the disheveled artist sets up her easel and pulls herself together. She has never been exposed to someone like this peculiar woman, and is glad her attendant will stay.

"So, tell me a little bit about yourself," Alatoi says pulling herself into a standing position, paints in hand, as if she were being drawn up with a string from the top of her head. Ali notices the woman's demeanor become more polished before her eyes.

Ali is uncomfortable talking about herself. "I love to read and learn."

"Hhmm, what do you read?

"Everything I can get my hands on. Unlike some women, I have been reading since I was a child. My mother, Queen Aadya, has done much to educate the women of our land. Before she came along women were not offered books to read and they used to refer to women as breeders. Can you imagine?"

"Yes, it is the same where I come from, only it hasn't changed." Alatoi peers down her nose at her work. She has tied her sleek black hair behind her head with a leather cord, and her arms are bare when she takes off her jacket. "You are a most beautiful young woman, a looker as some would say."

Ali suffers the embarrassment, of the painter's comment, feeling her cheeks flush.

"Does it disturb you I said that? Alatoi asks.

"I am grateful for my looks," Ali nervously moves her golden curls behind her shoulder.

"Hah, nah! Please do not move. Didn't they tell you would have to be still?"

"Yes, I'm sorry."

"My lady you are a princess you must never apologize for your actions."

The interaction with this harsh woman, makes Ali even more nervous causing her to fidget again.

"Beauty is not important." Ali defends herself. "I am the Heir Apparent. It is more important I have the ability to lead." Ali looks at the painter to see where her challenge lands.

"Yes, you are right. But physical beauty is a gift we nurture much like our given talents."

As Ali mulls these thoughts over, she decides the painter's words need to be weighed carefully.

"What do you say? Are leaders born or do they learn?" The painter asks.

"Both," Ali snaps back.

The painter studies Ali carefully assessing the girl before her. "Painting someone requires you not only see their image, but the character within. I think we have much to teach each other."

Ali considers this statement totally in disagreement, but she does not want to offend the painter. She acquiesces by becoming still and silent.

57-A Conversation for the Future

"Ali, your mother and I both agree it is time to begin to groom you in earnestness for your role as leader to replace me."

"Father, please stop. You are going to live a very long time." She tells him as they ride a simple carriage toward a favorite hunting spot. Their riding horses follow on leads behind the wagon. They bring the wagon in anticipation of all the meat they will bring home.

King Poma decides to change the subject. "You know when I first met you mother, I had her convinced I did not know how to hunt." He shrugs, "Actually I did, but I did not enjoy it. Today I relish in my abilities to provide for my family, rather than let others do all the work, even if I, myself do not eat the meat."

This fact surprises Ali, who has never known her father not to be a good marksman and warrior. "What I'm sharing with you is that I have changed over time. That is what will happen to you." He turns to look straight into her eyes. "None of us are guaranteed a tomorrow. You were young when the Great Targa Storm occurred, but we still do not know what caused it, or if it will repeat itself."

"I know," she says giving him a look half-buried in skepticism.

"I have only been a king a few full revolutions now, aye, I guess it has been longer, but it is time to pass some information on. You need to learn how to manage yourself in meetings with our counselors and get into the heart of all matters. Your protocol teachings are not enough. It will be an exceptional challenge for you as a woman. There has never been a woman ruler on Merth. When I die, your mother will not rule as she is not of the royal blood line, although she certainly is capable."

"Over there is a good place to tie the wagon," Ali points. "We like to walk into the thicket."

King Poma nods. "I know."

"I can't believe we didn't have to bring an entourage," Ali says.

"I wanted this time with you to myself." They climb out of the wagon and pull down satchels filled with provisions and weapons. Father and daughter walk silently through the tall grass. The dried stalks swish against their breeches making the only sound to their trek into the forest.

Ali has bundled her thick golden curls behind her head for maximum peripheral vision. She readies her bow when she hears a rustle in the trees, but it is only a warmoth bird taking flight, and they are no good to eat.

"Tell me about the ring," Ali asks.

"The ring, what do you know about the ring?"

"I've overheard you and mother talking. I'm no fool."

King Poma allows a perplexed smile to shape his lips as he considers his extraordinary daughter, full of surprises. "Maybe it's just me. I had no idea about the ring. My father never once mentioned the power of the ring."

"Maybe it did not speak to him."

His daughter's words surprisingly shatter Poma's presumptions. "I guess I did not consider this. Why would the ring not speak to all kings?"

Ali shrugs. "Listen, do you hear it? It is the call of the golden birds."

Poma cocks his head and hears the gentle warble of a modest flock of bright yellow birds as they rush out of the overhead branches of a wobblysk tree, its solid branches outstretched as if welcoming them to the woods.

"Wow! They are gorgeous. I've never seen so many."

"You didn't answer my question?"

Ali gives him a contemplative stare and shrugs. "I do not know, perhaps it skips a generation."

"I do not believe this could be true. I will have to ask Queen Mesa what she knows of the ring."

"So, are you going to tell me what is special about it?" She glances toward the tantalizing gemstone ensconced in a swirling setting upon his left hand.

"It is passed on from ruler to ruler. No one else is allowed to wear it, and you are never to take it off."

"I can't put it on now for even a second?'

"Absolutely not."

"What if it is too big for me, should I wear it around my neck?"

Poma shakes his head. "No, as a matter of fact, the ring adjusts itself to your finger. When I first put it on, I was afraid it would fall off."

Ali gives him a look of youthful dissent. "Really?"

"Yes." He takes a deep breath. "I'm glad we are having this conversation. I felt ill-prepared taking on the role of leader. I do not want it to happen to you."

Giving him a sideways glance, she says, "you are not going to tell me more, are you?"

"No, I guess not," King Poma glances down at his hands studying them as if for the first time he has noticed they are attached to his body.

"I want you to start attending all meetings. Unless your mother is there you will most likely be the only woman. You need to hear the voices of men as they discuss grave matters and be familiar with their ways. We are sometimes a crude fardel, but I think your presence will get them used to you."

Ali takes a deep breath, sensing her life is changing in ways she cannot even fathom.

58-She is Just a Child

It is at Galen and Kandar's housewarming celebration when Ali first lays eyes on Coda.

"Do you know of him? Ali whispers to Roark casting her eyes toward the handsome fellow, all the young women are crowded around, as he performs card tricks.

"Yes," Roark eyes his sister suspiciously. "Do not even begin to tell me you are interested in that rogue."

"Why what's the matter with him?"

"That scherfel, are you kidding me?"

"He's just being entertaining. What's wrong with that?"

"Oh Ali, we are all doomed if you are going to be our leader, if he is who you think is desirable. You need to become a better judge of character."

Roark's words sting, and Ali mulls over them the rest of the evening as she keeps to herself on the fringes of the gaggle of girls, who gather around and fawn after this Coda Croff fellow. Even as she is oddly entranced by his engaging manner, she is now wary of getting to know him better.

It is when she is about to leave the party, the youthful rake finally finds the time to connect with her.

"Princess Ali, won't you come join us?"

"No, thank you I was about to leave." She is grateful her curly lavskin coat is already in her hands as the engaging knave seems quite persuasive once he has turned his attention to her.

Unbeknownst to Ali, Galen is eyeing her sister's exchange with trepidation from the far side of the room.

"Mother," Galen says the next chance she has to address the queen. "I do not know if I am the one to best speak up, for my own courtship was unconventional, but it is definitely time Ali needs a little guidance about the other sex. Especially if she is to choose a mate suitable as her royal consort."

Aadya sighs heavily letting her hands fall from her waist. "I know! We must do something soon, before she gets her own ideas about how to proceed."

Galen bounces baby Jaru on her lap and gives her mother a chagrined look. "These are tricky matters. Perhaps we should pull Queen Mesa into this matter for her direction."

Aadya nods no. "She is too old and enmeshed in antiquated ways to guide us on this matter. I will consult the Matong, but I sense we need to preselect a group of suitable grooms and let Ali pick her favorite. We cannot let her select her future mate willy villy.

"Oh, this is going to be some challenge!" Aadya shakes her head and looks at her daughter with frenetic resolve. "I suppose your father might want to participate in creating this list. Think about who you might suggest, and we will start gathering suitors to call on her."

But as Aadya presses her palm to the glowing orb later in the morning, she is confused by the message she receives. SEND AELLA ANEMONE TO SEEK THE CUP OF LIGHT AT THE EDGE OF THE RAINBOW BLUFF. SHE MUST MAKE THE JOURNEY ALONE.

"I do not understand," she tells Poma as soon as she can get a moment alone with him. "What is the Cup of Light? I presume the rainbow bluff is where the Sonatong River flows past the rainbow stones." She twists the bracelet on her right hand distractedly feeling the texture of it. "This makes me most uncomfortable. It could be quite a treacherous journey."

Aadya can see this message also troubles Poma because he immediately goes to the Matong for confirmation. Aadya follows him into the hallowed chamber where they both receive the same message.

Resignedly Poma lets his shoulders fall slightly. "I guess we must prepare her for this quest. I will personally see to her training."

Aadya is sick inside. POMA, I DO NOT LIKE THIS AT ALL. IT IS MUCH TOO DANGEROUS.

YOU MUST HAVE COURAGE. THIS IS NOTHING IN COMPARISON TO THE MANY OBSTACLES SHE WILL FACE AS LEADER WHEN I AM GONE.

SHE IS JUST A CHILD

YOU MUST HAVE FAITH!

It is then the Matong pulses with light in a way neither of them has ever witnessed.

WHAT WAS THAT?

Poma takes Aadya's hand and leads her out of the chamber shaken by the Matong's directive.

59-Change of the Guard

When Ali receives her own message from the Matong, she is filled with curiosity and delight. "This means I will soon be wed!" she tells Galen, who cautiously reminds her "not to get the cart before the horse."

"Father says I will have to do more training before I should go on my quest."

"We often gathered a supply of the luminescent water, at the rainbow bluff to share with those affected by the Targa lights, when we were on our journey to heal the sick." Galen tells her younger sister as she rocks her newborn to sleep.

"What entrapments should I be wary of?" Ali asks.

Galen smiles at her sleeping baby as she pulls him down from her shoulder and lays the precious bundle face-up in her lap. Galen places two fingers near her baby who grabs them with eyes closed and clutches tightly.

Galen lifts her lilac-colored eyes to Ali. Galen is enough older than Ali, she can remember holding her little sister in this same way. "There is nothing dangerous I know of about this place. Your challenge will be traveling there alone."

Ali shakes her head, "I know father will have me escorted until I am practically there. My biggest fear is being alone. I have hardly been alone since my birth; we are so heavily guarded.

"I understand your concern. I have always lived with protection. Even when we escaped to heal the people. I always had Kandar by my side."

"It must be a most comforting feeling to have someone you love to care for you."

"Yes," Galen smiles and looks down at her sleeping baby.

With the idea she is to be married once she carries out the Matong's directive, royal heiress Aella Anemone plunges into her training with the kingdom's greatest warrior Fontar Galraith. Fontar has shining eyes, the bright golden color of the bartar flower, giving him an air of genteelness despite the contrast of his rock-hard warrior's body. He is enough visually to make any maiden distracted, but Ali persists day after day as he tutors her in the skills to defend herself. Surprisingly, no one has foreseen she might fall madly in love with the dashing warrior, but before she can stop the tide of irrepressible feelings, Princess Ali becomes captivated. It is as if someone has surprised her by slipping up behind her and throwing a gunny sack over her head.

"We must do something! All she does is talk about Fontar. This is not what was supposed to happen," Aadya presses Poma. She becomes worried enough to arrange a meeting with Fontar.

"I assure you Queen Aadya, Princess Aella is a beautiful woman, but I understand she is meant for another and must go on this dangerous quest to find her future husband. I love her as if she were my sister." As he says this, the words surprise him as he knows it is not true. "My loyalty is to you and King Poma and our land. I would never do anything to harm Princess Ali."

"I'm sorry Fontar, we are going to have to replace you as her instructor." Aadya watches the young warrior's face change as if a torman cloud suddenly crossed the sky. "I am not one to resort to deception, but we must focus her on the work, not the teacher. I am sorry, with someone as naive and impressionable as Princess Ali, we must be careful. This is extremely important.

"I want you to come up with an injury," the queen continues. "We will get someone to take your place. Who would you suggest?"

Fontar searches for an answer, but no one comes to mind as capable as he is for the job. "What about Jesser Waithe?" Aadya asks.

"Mmm, I guess he would be adequate…I want to reassure you, you need not take me off my duties."

It was then Aadya could see in his face the pain this redirection was causing him, and her worst fears were reinforced. *I must keep these two young people apart.* "You haven't been inappropriate with my daughter, have you?"

"Of course not! You insult me." Fontar looks surprisingly wounded by her remark, as if he might choke, and yet he has remorse his answer has been so rude.

"I want you to visit the physician and have him put a splint on your right arm. Tell Ali you fell while riding your horse."

"Your highness, she will not believe that."

"Tell her a serpent bit your horse and he threw you." Fontar looks down at his feet. He has no more to say.

60-Wisdom of His Words

"What is the Cup of Light anyway?" Ali asks her father as they head out for yet another hunting expedition together. Poma wants to make sure she can feed and defend herself should the worst happen.

"I have asked the Matong this many times myself now, and I have yet to understand."

"Me too," Ali says absent-mindedly grasping a hunk of Elita's mane. She was given the magical horse many revolutions ago when her training began, and they have bonded to the point where Ali merely has to think her commands and Elita responds.

"I think the Cup of Light is not an object, but a person, the person I am to marry."

"I have had similar thoughts myself," her father agrees.

"I think the Matong does not give us clear directives, because it wants us to think for ourselves. We receive information, but it is always cryptic."

The gentle rocking of Kilnor's stride beneath him is soothing, and King Poma takes in a certain comfort in her words. He turns to her "You show much wisdom. I have watched as you have matured, and I have great confidence in your abilities, my daughter." His words inspire a light to bloom in her face and she grows bolder.

"So, tell me the truth, why was Fontar replaced?"

King Poma grimaces with fatherly affection. "Let me say I had nothing to do with it if he was."

"I knew it!" A sharp pulse of anger comes upon her, and Ali urges Elita into a brisk canter. The sleek golden horse proudly arches her neck and her silken tail lifts like a flag as she surges off. King Poma spurs Kilnor on to follow closely behind.

"I am ready for my quest," Ali tells her parents on a mild afternoon when tranquil breezes have spoken softly to her of her future.

"Ali, we are not to rush this," Queen Aadya warns, balking at her daughter's proclamation.

King Poma gives his daughter, who has worked diligently at her training, a thoughtful look. He is so proud of her. She has exceeded all his expectations. "She is as strong and fit as you were when I met you," he says to Aadya. Aadya's face wrinkles up into mild disgust. There are no words she can utter which will change the inevitable.

"The three of us need to seek the Matong's direction for the timing," King Poma says, and they all walk together to the chamber.

Ali blinks as she comes out of her trance. "I am ready," she says. Poma and Aadya squeeze their daughter tightly knowing they have no choice but to let her go.

On the day of her departure, Ali is quietly escorted to the edge of Compana by her father, as if they were departing for one of their many hunting trips together. She leads a pack mulfang, not too unusual on such outings, and as requested by her mother, she has chosen clothing which will make her blend in. Her path has been mapped out to avoid concentrations of population, and it will take her two days just to arrive at the rainbow bluffs. What happens then, no one knows. The Matong, which has been repeatedly consulted, continues to insist she must make her journey alone.

"This is not right, I know something is going to go wrong," Aadya insists when Poma returns "I shall not rest until she comes home." And true to her promise Aadya goes for four days without sleeping. Her demeanor becomes ragged and bitter with distrust and her family begins to avoid her.

Finally, Galen comes to visit her mother and slips some herbs into her tea to make her sleep.

King Poma himself, worried and mystified his daughter has not yet returned, keeps revisiting the moment in his mind when he had to turn and leave his precious daughter behind. He had been unable to utter any words, but held up one hand and gave her a weak smile.

"What did you expect?" Roark asks him as he wanders listlessly about the castle, not attending to business as usual. It is two days travel there and two days back, And the Matong has sent her on a quest, it could be months before she gets back.

King Poma swirls around as if to attack. "By the One True God we must think positively!"

"Yes, Father, I agree. You must do something about your thinking. Ali is going to be okay. The Matong did not send her off to her death"

"I hope you are correct. She is all alone out there. When Galen was on her healing journey after 'Targa' at least she had Kandar at her side."

"My sisters are strong women who can take care of themselves. You have really got to pull it together, at least for Mother's sake. You have got a kingdom to lead. Uncle Bonder is worried about you."

"Why? What did he say to you?"

Roark shrugs, "Nothing specific, but he's been handling day to day decisions."

"I instructed him to do that!"

"Maybe so, but it is in your best interest to get back to business."

"If only I could go after her."

"If I were in your shoes, you know what you would say to me?"

Poma looks at Roark, his tangled anguish visible in his brow. "No, son, what would I say to you?"

"You would tell me to get busy running the kingdom and trust the wisdom of the Matong as it has always guided us." And then he added something which came to him as he spoke.

"To lose faith is to lose hope."

Poma studies his son and realizes it is time to listen to the wisdom of his words.

"I will do as you suggest." He turns and strides down the hall to see if Aadya has yet risen from her rest.

61-The Trek

Ali's first few nights are spent in relative luxury. While the pack mulfang is strong enough to hold lots of gear, its persistent braying is a constant source of annoyance. The mulfang can travel as swiftly as Elita, but has an unexplainable and annoying habit of stopping abruptly and yanking on the lead, making Ali almost topple off her horse on several occasions. Ali even considers releasing the animal and letting it return home, but then thinks better of it because she would not have the luxurious and warm bedding, tent, and many culinary provisions the pack animal is carrying.

When she arrives at the luminous bluffs on the second day, the sight of the shimmering water and unusually brightly colored monumental stone bluffs gives Ali a sense of awe. Dirty from two days on the road, she decides to bathe in the shimmering waters. Cautiously she looks around and finds an inconspicuous spot in the shade of three massive wallan trees, whose water-loving roots have positioned themselves on the edge of a steep pebble bar. Careful to tie Elita's lead and not trust the horse to think for herself, Ali pulls off her boots and walks into the water fully clothed with a bar of her favorite lavona-scented soap.

As she sinks into the crystal water swirling around her, she pulls off her garments and soaps them up, then holds them in the gentle current to rinse them. She leans back and lets the water soak her head fully. The weight of her long hair is lessened when she bends her knees and lowers her whole body into the stream. Once she is refreshed, Ali tosses her garments up onto the tree roots and grabs the plush blanket, woven from the downy underbelly of the lama dama goat, she had left on the gnarly wallan roots. She swaddles her freshly bathed body in it and hangs her clothes out to dry.

Ali realizes her hair presents a problem. Her long golden tresses tangle easily in the wind making it difficult to manage. Fortunately, she has some leather ties to hold her hair into a single bulky braid. She pulls out some fresh clothing and gets dressed quickly.

It is time to select a tent site and eat some supper. She chooses some ready-made provisions from the kitchen at Compana, including berries encrusted in crushed nuts and sticky jam, soft cheese rolled inside of thinly sliced meats, and tasty marmalade-covered meat, seasoned to perfection. As she snacks on the pebble beach in the fading evening light, she decides the canopy of the three gargantuan trees, with their massive branches reaching broadly across the sky, is a logical place to pitch her tent.

That night while sleeping, Ali awakens to sounds of a hungry three-claw smorth prowling nearby. She grabs her bow and positions to defend herself, her animals, and her gear. In the bright moonlight, it is easy to see the monolithic black animal. Elita rears up and levitates upward out of reach, but the poor mulfang, who she has begun endearingly to call Chap, is compromised. The arrow whistles from her bow and the burly animal drops. The carcass is too heavy to drag away from the campsite, and Ali spends the rest of the night in a restless doze, worrying about other predators who might be attracted to the smell of the smorth's blood.

As the morning star rises, Ali considers the burden of the dead animal. *Such bad luck!* She would now have to dispose of it. Too tough to eat, she could not allow the dead animal to rot there in the middle of her campsite. Taking the coiled rope from the loop on the mulfang's pack, she ties it around the neck of the dead animal and then onto Chap's harness. "You are going to pull this beast toward the water, and we will let him float away." Chap gives her a blank stare and Ali considers how nice it would to be at home doing normal activities, and not here struggling with these two dumb animals, one dead, and the other deaf to the voice of reason.

Chap surprises her though and begins to pull. It becomes quickly evident her plan has a major flaw. There has to be some way to release the corpse before Chap gets into the water. If she is not careful, the smorth's body might act as an anchor taking poor Chap down with him. She needs a plan for releasing the carcass before this happens.

Dragging the dead animal close to the water takes all morning, but finally the hulk, quickly growing rancid, is close enough to the water she can create a skid, from a piece of driftwood, to shove it the rest of the way down the steep bank.

62-Riding Hard

When Fontar Galraith awakens after a restless night of dreams marked by frustrating circumstances and terrifying outcomes, he is glistening with sweat. He rolls over and panic snatches him awake as he remembers a woman from the night before.

She was drunk and disorderly and wore pants, a more common attire for women these days, but still unusual enough for him to take notice. And while she was wickedly attractive, there was something he feared about her. Perhaps it was the way she had grabbed him aggressively pushing her body up against him and pushing her tongue into his mouth. Luckily, he did not take the bait, or the black-haired hussy, with the long silky hair, would be there now beside him.

Now all he can think about is Princess Ali. He has no way to know if she has left on her quest, but it was going to happen sometime soon whether anyone could tell him or not. He pulls on his boots and decides to approach Jesser Waite, the man who had replaced him as her trainer.

Jesser has been sworn to secrecy and at first, he is no help. "Who was it saved your life when your horse fell into that pit of poisonous snakes?" Fontar presses him until he begrudgingly admits the princess had left, escorted by her father, several revolutions ago. "I may not be allowed to escort her, but no one can tell me I can't journey to the rainbow bluffs for myself."

Jesser pretends he cannot hear Fontar speak under his breath. To know of his plan is to invite folly.

Upon leaving the stable where he found Jesser, Fontar jumps on his horse and heads back to his lodging to gather a duffle of gear and clothing. He eats a hastily prepared breakfast of grease-laden sausages and stale biscuits, and tears out toward his destination.

The vision of Princess Ali slashing at him with a heavy sword, as they have practiced many times before, becomes a peculiar fantasy as his passion swells into his heart, and spurs him on toward his purpose. The punishment afforded him for his reckless intervention occasionally crosses his mind. But his irrational desire propels him toward his goal and an unnamed destiny he cannot forgo. He rides hard for a day and straight through the night. His sturdy horse is lathered when he finds the object of his desire.

Ali is still camped along the riverbank in the shadow of the wallan trees. She is lying on the bed of river-washed pebbles fast asleep. But Fontar does not recognize this. He sees her there and is afraid she is dead. He rushes to scoop her body up when she opens her eyes. It is a great surprise she finds herself in his arms.

"Fontar? What are you doing here?"

"I could not keep myself from coming, no matter what the risk."

Ali laughs, "Put me down!" He sets her gently down on her feet and she pulls at her tunic.

"I've found it is easier to sleep during the day. At night there are all kinds of wild animals roaming about looking to ransack my food."

Elita snorts and Fontar's deep brown horse neighs softly as he paws the ground with his over-sized hooves. "Is everything okay? Has your quest been difficult?"

Ali laughs, "I have been living the lavish lifestyle of a princess, only more outside than usual."

"Have you figured it out what it is you are supposed to do?"

She shrugs and lifts her arms. "No, I am supposed to find the Cup of Light and by doing so will find my mate. Thus far, I have seen nothing like that. I even explored a cave up there." She points up toward the many-colored bluff, "but found nothing except some old animal bones and a half-broken clay pot."

Fontar gives her a quizzical look. "That does not sound like what you are looking for. Anyway, I am here now. May I stay for a while and keep you company?"

After the many days she has been alone, Ali finds his offer irresistible, even though she's not sure it is allowed." Fontar appears to read her thoughts.

"I did not escort you here. I just happened upon you. Better me than someone else."

Ali drops her head in thought. "I have not been worried about the wild animals, but…"

"But what?"

"I sure wouldn't want to have to kill a man, if you know, someone should accost me."

Fontar bristles at the thought. "This is ridiculous, you shouldn't be out here unprotected. You are heir to the throne after all."

"My family does what the Matong decrees."

Fontar kicks his boot at the pebbles on the ground. "I cannot understand this folly."

"Look, you are here now, let us cook some dinner. I have some small game hanging, ready to cook, and I gathered some mussels this morning. They are over there in the river in a bag tied to the roots of the tree. They sent me with enough food for an entire army."

"Sounds good to me," Fontar says rubbing his hands together. He has eaten nothing but morsels of nuts and biscuit crumbles from his coat pockets for the last two revolutions and the invitation is welcome. He had not entirely been sure how his appearance might be received.

63-The Cup of Light

As the fire pops and crackles in the open hearth, Ali built from stones as heavy as she could lift and carry, the two lounge on a cozy woolen blanket and let their food digest.

"Cooking over an open fire always makes everything taste better," Ali says offering Fontar some crystalline sugar-covered Fanti flowers packed safely in a box. "They are divine," she says. But Fontar is not familiar with such delicacies and holds his hand up in protest. "I have eaten far too much, thank you," His emotions percolate within his chest uneasily as he recognizes he is sitting with the woman who holds his heart.

"You are quiet," she says.

"Yes, I do not know whether I should stay or go."

"It is nearly dark you can't go now."

He looks up at her. The setting star is casting a mystical array of colors across the sky as it lowers, and the two moons are rising on the other horizon. He is completely mesmerized by Ali who has been transformed in this natural setting with her hair bound and her clothes rumpled and slightly dirty. Even so, she is completely unapproachable.

She stands up and dusts off her leggings reflexively. "I'm going to make some tea." As she lowers the kettle onto the spit, they had cooked most of the meal on, she picks up the broken clay bowl she had found up in the cave, to hand to Fontar.

He takes it from her and clutches it in both hands when something very strange happens in the dwindling light. Fontar's face is lit up with light emanating from the modest crucible.

Ali drops the kettle in her surprise and Fontar is transfixed on the fiery flow of light. Neither can speak. It is as if they have been caught in a spider's sticky web. The campfire sputters as the tea kettle spills, almost extinguishing it. Ali places her palms together and bows her head. She understands she is in the midst of a Matong manifestation. Once the power leaves her, she recovers the tea kettle and places it back onto the spit. "My sister Galen speaks of these moments when the Matong is present outside of its globe," she whispers.

Frozen in his tracks Fontar asks her. "Must I keep holding it?"

"Close your eyes and enjoy the warmth of the message."

"I do not believe what it says!" Fontar says setting the cup down softly.

"What did it tell you?"

"It said I have been chosen to be your protector. This will be my job to my final days."

Ali giggles, allowing her glee to pulsate through her body. She wants to say something wise and comforting, but all she can do is lean over toward Fontar and let her lips reach for his. They both perceive a pulsating buzz as their lips touch and then they break away.

"I will sleep outside your tent tonight and begin my duties as your protector," he smiles as widely as a child discovering a toy.

"But I'm not even tired, I napped most of the day," she says playfully.

Knowing how utterly exhausted he is, Fontar begins planning on how he might actually stay awake to protect her. "Then I will rest here beside you until you retire to your tent." He lays his head down next to her with his arm around her legs as she sips her tea and listens to the sounds of the night— the river churning, the insects buzzing, the occasional call of a neton cat to its mate with its guttural growl and intermittent yipping—and, of course, Fontar's snoring.

64-Duty Above All Else

The light of the morning star is shaded by the huge wallan trees above, and yet Ali is awake by first light. She tiptoes over Fontar's body, which is crossways across the tent entrance, and begins to restart the fire and boil water for tea.

"Good morning," he says sheepishly as he awakens and realizes he has not maintained his objective to stay awake all night.

"Good morning," Ali says cheerfully. "Can you hand me the bag of tea over there?" She points to the wooden table she has fashioned out of driftwood. Fontar looks at the table confused by which bag she might mean and opts for the smallest one he sees. "No, the other one."

Utterly dazed by the events of last night and waking to the presence of Ali, Fontar continues to wonder what was a dream and what is reality.

"Er, I will be back shortly." He takes off for the cover of the woods to find a tree and when he returns, Ali is stripping off the skin of a small woosan she felled with her bow and is pulling out other dried provisions.

"Hungry?" she asks.

"Yes."

She looks at him warily. "Did you sleep well?"

"My intention was to not sleep at all, but the hard ride and heavy meal did me in I guess." He looks up at her self-consciously. "It seems I have already let you down."

Ali lets out a hearty laugh and shakes her head. "And here I thought all along I was doing fine on my own quest," she says, turning the meat on the spit, and allowing the tongues of flame to merely kiss it. The dripping fat occasionally produces a hissing noise.

"Seriously, that wasn't merely a dream last night. We must talk," she says. "But first let us eat something." Having Fontar's company is uplifting, but underlying this pleasant surprise is knowing she will come to know this man, who throws her off balance with his edgy smile, kind heart, and luscious physique, as her husband.

"We never even kissed until last night," she tells him as she spoons the last bit of citrus sauce over their fire-roasted meat. His grin is telling, unrestrained, as if he would allow himself to boast in her presence, which he does. "And what a kiss it was!"

Ali, not entirely ignorant of the effect she has on young men, feels vulnerable down to her marrow. "This might be the most difficult thing I've ever had to do. But I must resist you until we are wed.

"But I get ahead of myself," she says throwing her long braid over her other shoulder. "You haven't actually proposed."

Fontar immediately sets down the plate of food, she has just handed him, and kneels before her on both knees. "Ali, my one true love. Will you give your heart to me and do me the honor of becoming my wife? I promise to always protect you with every fiber of my being."

Ali reaches for his outstretched hand when an enormous red bird swoops down so close they experience the brush of wind caused by its flaying wings. Startled, they both grab for each other blindly while tracking the bird with their eyes. It lands on a branch above them, and Ali lands in Fontar's strong grasp as he shields her from the bird's claws and pulls her into his arms. Ali's surprise goes from fear to joy as she realizes the beautiful bird is the Matong manifested.

With both arms wrapped around her, Fontar holds her tight as she melts into his embrace. "Fear not Fontar. It is the Matong here to bless us." It is then they kiss deeply, passionately, and if it were not for their sworn duties, they would have become one.

Fontar stands and lifts her to her feet. Ali is barely able to speak, but she musters the staff of leadership now buried deeply into her heart. She will not ever succumb to her own personal interests before her duty to her people.

Awkwardly they pick up their plates and begin to eat. "I'm not sure the quest is over," she starts. "But personally, I sense it is." The enormous bird overhead begins to sing a mesmerizing lyric, hypnotizing them both.

"I will do as you say, should you desire to return home today." Fontar finally says without looking at her, hoping with his very soul, he will never be separated from this woman who holds his heart in her hands.

Ali hears the bird's mystical song and instantly knows she has found the cup of life. It is her whole life ahead that is the prophecy. Fontar is the beginning to the vast adventure which stretches before her like a ribbon with many twists and turns.

65-How Will I Fit In?

The two of them take their time packing up the campsite, but decide to stay one more day for an early start the following morning. They leave the tent up for shelter and gather most everything together, leaving a few provisions out for preparation of dinner and some cold provisions for breakfast in the morning.

"I will cook for you tonight," Fontar offers.

"Okay, but shall we hunt more meat now while it is still light?" She asks thinking they might fare better by doing something to keep them busy and away from temptation.

"That is probably a good idea," Fontar agrees, but they do not ever get around to hiking into the woods to find more game. Instead, they swim in the effervescent aqua waters of the river, lounge in the sun, and swap stories about their childhoods.

Fontar shares how he grew up in a family filled with laughter and games with two older brothers who were "always teasing me and roughing me up. Although I know they loved me."

"As you might suspect, I've been groomed from early childhood to become the reigning heir of the throne," she tells him. "As soon as Galen officially abdicated, my childhood was over, and my training began."

She looks at him suddenly. "How much older are you?"

"Than you?"

"Yes."

"I will be twenty-eight revolutions during the next cycle of the moons."

"Really?" She tosses some sun-bleached pebbles at him in an awkward attempt at frivolity.

"You mean I am marrying an old man?"

His expression sours as he does not know how to answer, realizing how much his bride-to-be intimidates him. This is confusing to Fontar, who has never been afraid of anything before. Even as a child he was fearless and sought the life of a warrior at an early age.

"I am teasing you. I will be twenty-two revolutions after the Feast of Fellows."

Fontar lays in the warm daylight on his back in the softness of the beach sand and looks up at the sky. He loves everything about Ali. Her voice, her beautiful body, her golden curls, her eyes—especially her eyes which sparkle with generosity.

"How will I fit in?" he asks.

"What do you mean?"

"You know what I mean." He sits up and looks into her eyes. "You will be queen and leader of the land. I will be your husband. Will there be purpose in my life? Or will I sit on the sidelines, watching the children?"

Ali chokes back laughter and considers his words.

"Oh, I should think you will lead a very full life, because of your position. While I will have the final say on all decisions, you will be my partner. You will share your viewpoint and knowledge with me and guide me. Like my mother guides my father." As the words leave her mouth, she regrets the part about her mother guiding her father thinking he might be offended.

"And as my spouse, you will be privileged to know the Matong." Her voice grows more serious. "That, in and of itself, is reason enough to marry me. To know the Matong is to exist in an entirely unique and special way. You will have Kinetic Sight and we will be able to communicate without speaking."

Fontar cannot even begin to imagine exactly what she is talking about. It is the first time the topic of the Matong has been broached with him. All he wants is to have Ali as his wife, and the sooner the better.

They fall asleep after a light, but tasty dinner, under the night sky as the wind gently rustles the many leaves above them. Fontar wakes up and pulls their blanket up around them after adding more wood to the fire. He intends to keep it burning all night to keep wild animals at bay. He nestles his face near to Ali's and listens to her breath and wonders if he should awaken her and get her into the tent, but the night is mild, and he does not want to disturb her.

66-Heading Home

"We could stay here a few more days." Ali offers even as she and Fontar begin to load up Chap and the other two horses with bundles.

Fontar grins. "Believe me it has occurred to me, but I know your family awaits your safe return. Besides the sooner we return, the sooner we can marry."

"This is true," she says cinching up Elita's saddle girth with a hefty pull.

"What if they do not accept me as your mate?" Fontar blurts out the one troubling thought, which has haunted him ever since he held the glowing cup.

"Oh, they will, if it is the will of the Matong. Besides, we are taking the crucible with us to prove you are my rightful groom."

"Where is it?"

"Over there," Ali points to a pile of clothing she has clumped together but not yet packed.

Fontar searches the heap but does not find it. A bit panicked, he feels his chest constrict.

"I do not see it."

"Yes, it is in there, I am sure of it." Ali drops Elita's reins and comes over to show him, but she does not uncover it either. She kneels to get a better look and continues to rummage through the clothing. "Oh, now I remember, I put it in the tent yesterday to safeguard it."

"But we've already folded the tent and packed it." Fontar is now becoming more and more ill at ease.

"Maybe it is over there by the kitchen table." Ali points and Fontar scrambles to the table, where he finds it.

"How did we overlook it?" he says picking it up, but the broken chalice does not light up like it did the evening before last. A sinking sensation overtakes him, and he almost drops it.

"It did not light up like the night before!"

"Relax Fontar, it was dark then and the light faint. It will light up when we return for all to see." Even as she says this, doubt fills her mind and makes her voice unsteady.

"We saw it." She touches his hand reassuringly. Maybe we are the only ones who need to see."

Typically fearless, Fontar abruptly allows doubt to flood him like puddles of cold rainwater in an unexpected downpour. The only antidote to his desolation is to pull Ali close and kiss her.

They both experience, a slight tingle of energy, not visible, but it plays across their arms and down into their hands. Fontar releases her, fearful he will not be able to stop kissing her.

"We must hurry home now," he tells her.

They pound the turf on their spirited horses toward Compana for several miles until Chap defiantly digs in his hooves, and nearly knocks Fontar down off his sturdy brown warrior horse.

"Ah crynon! You bloody beast. You nearly caused my horse to fall! I should pull on your over-sized ears until you squeal!"

Ali turns around and laughs, her jovial mood is contagious and Fontar begins to laugh too.

"I have half a mind to turn him loose and let him fend for himself."

"Don't you dare, we need our gear tonight to make camp."

Fontar sucks in a breath and listens to the voice of reason. "You are right of course."

"I'll show you where I camped on my way out here," she tells him. "If I can find it, it was off the trail a little on the edge of the woods." She turns around to him placing her hand on Elita's round butt as Elita continues walking forward. "There is no rush we still have plenty of light before the setting star lays down for the night."

Fontar notices the way Ali talks to him. She is confident and reassuring. And yet he knows his presence is also what builds her courage. The physical draw of her is like a gravitational pull he does not have the strength to resist.

67-Sharing the Good News

When Galen first sees Ali ride up escorted by Fontar with Chap in tow, she is both surprised and distracted. The baby is crying despite her attempts to walk and bounce at the same time, while several men are asking her where she would like furniture placed. The house is receiving the finishing touches by craftsmen who have turned the mundane lines of construction into an artistic display, of sculptural shapes and silhouettes, mirroring the images of nature. The filigreed wood is masterfully cut into shapes of trees and birds. Where normally walls would stand are sculptural works more art than structural support. Even Ali, who is bursting to tell Galen her news, is captivated at how beautiful and unique the house is.

"You've returned! Did everything go okay?" Ali dismounts and consciously affects a casual manner. She has chosen to approach her sister first with her impending betrothal to Fontar, but she remains unsure in her mind how this announcement will be embraced by the family.

Galen first notices an unseen warmth emanating from her younger sister. She turns her gaze to Fontar, unsure how to react to his presence.

"It was an amazing adventure. I should do it more often." Galen continues to stare at Fontar surprised by her younger sister's words.

"So, what happened?"

When Fontar dismounts he proceeds to Ali's side, mindful she is struggling with how to tell Galen. He takes Ali's hand in his and this ignites Ali's purpose.

"Fontar and I are to wed. He is the Cup of Light."

Surely this is not true Galen wonders. *If Fontar was supposed to be Ali's mate, why had the Matong made it mysterious and difficult? Perhaps the wisdom of the Matong had another purpose in this adventure.*

"Come let us have tea and you can tell me all about it," Galen hands the baby off to one of the maidens who are always in her company and takes Ali's arm pulling her away from Fontar.

"Sister Ali, you look radiant. I am thankful you are home."

Galen can see Ali is trembling. "I'm glad too. It is all overwhelming." Ali finally admits to Galen.

Galen takes them to an inner courtyard where flowering bushes and dozens of butterflies flit from one flower to the next. "Please, have a seat Fontar," she motions to the stone wall nearby and places Ali delicately between them.

"I was alone for several days, I took care of myself just fine, though it was very lonely," Ali admits, "then Fontar showed up. I had found a broken chalice in a cave when I first arrived and when he held it, it lit up."

"What were you doing there?" Galen turns her gaze toward Fontar who is trying not to let doubt overtake him.

He does not speak at first knowing this question will be asked of him many times before he will be allowed to take Ali as his wife.

"I had a compelling urge to find her. It is really unexplainable."

Galen takes in a breath wondering if this is truly what the Matong has in mind for Ali.

"It would be best if you went to the Matong to verify this."

Ali looks up at her sister and casts aside the little sister persona she has carried with her these many years.

"By your abdication, I am to become ruler." She says to Galen as if to convince herself.

"I am confident of the events which took place. Fontar is to be my husband." Ali stands up and presses her hand toward Fontar who takes it and understands implicitly all is as planned.

"We must go find my parents and tell them the good news."

68-An Urgency Unleashed

As the young couple rides toward home to tell the king and queen, they glide in the safety of their unspoken questions. Until Finally Ali speaks softly, "Fontar are you willing to tell me anything I ask?"

He looks over to her as their horses slowly walk in unison toward what feels like a looming storm. A smile, sincere and kind, gently builds across Fontar's face. "Of course, Ali."

"Will you always try to be truthful with me, even if it seems awkward, or you want to protect me from harm?"

"Of course, we must trust each other."

She tugs at Elita's straw-colored mane, searching for the words. "This partnership of ours, will it be awkward for you?"

Fontar sucks in a full breath and lets it flow out noisily. "Truthfully, I am sure there will be times when I will become frustrated, or angry, or feel boxed in, but if you are to be mine. Then what should I care?"

His words are like seductive vapors filling her lungs. Ali sinks into her saddle and Elita pricks up her ears. Ali smiles suppressing her own giggle and looks into his eyes. "We will be fine."

Word of their arrival spreads across Compana like a wind-whipped brushfire. By the time they reach the threshold of her parent's home, both Poma and Aadya are gathered together to greet them.

"What is this about Fontar?" King Poma squares his shoulders in a defensive manner as he sees the two of them approach. Queen Aadya looks a bit pinched as if she has been holding her breath for too long. Ali grins at them confidently, suppressing any misgivings she might still cling to.

"Fontar saved me."

Fontar gives her a confused look questioning her words.

"From boredom." Ali laughs even as she regrets her frivolity, but unable to pull her words back as they have left her lips, and now she sees her mother is visibly agitated.

"Can we sit? Fontar and I have been on horseback since first light."

They gather in a private parlor near the front entrance. Aadya motions for refreshments to be brought. "I know this might not be what you expected," Ali says, "but Fontar is my Cup of Light." She looks over at him, beside her on a plush settee made for two, and takes his hand.

Aadya folds and unfolds her legs and Poma shifts uncomfortably in his seat. "So, what is your story?" he asks eyeing the two of them.

Ali slips the broken crucible out of her satchel and hands it to Fontar before he can think. He fumbles to grasp it, but as he does it glows with a soft luminescence, even in the small room where open window shades allow the space to be drenched in light.

The fact it glows fills Fontar with immense relief, as he halfway believes it is all a big mistake.

"I see," Poma says leaning over toward Fontar and delicately takes the crucible from his grasp. When he does the light quickly fades, and Poma thrusts it back into Fontar's hands where it begins to glow again. The powerful affirmation makes a believer of King Poma.

As Fontar and Ali recount their story, which will become legendary in the many years to come with embellishments and twists not yet foreseen, the family listens intently. The queen is slow to accept the man she worked to protect from her daughter, and now he will be the father of her grandchildren.

Aadya looks at Poma and places her thoughts into his head. THIS IS CERTAINLY NOT WHAT I EXPECTED. Poma lets a subtle smile cross his face and turns to her.

NO, MY LOVE THIS IS ALMOST TOO GOOD TO BE TRUE. HE IS EXACTLY WHO I WOULD HAVE PICKED FOR HER IF IT HAD BEEN UP TO ME. BUT THE MATONG HAS CHOSEN AND THEY OBVIOUSLY ARE PLEASED WITH EACH OTHER. IT REMINDS ME OF OUR YOUTH.

Aadya blushes remembering her early days with Poma and the passion they shared. Poma clears his throat. "Of course, we must visit the Matong and have all this confirmed," he says apologetically to Fontar. "On your wedding day you will bond with the Matong and become part of our family."

Fontar bows, perching on one knee with the deepest respect to his king. And Ali, lightheaded, sets out for the Matong chamber with eagerness to begin the process of preparing for their wedding with the urgency of a caged kiter bird ready to join with its mate.

69-A Hefty Ransom

It is with extreme surprise and horror Cronar Devlin hears an arrow whip angrily past his right ear. Shocked by the assault, his recently eaten muldar stew comes back up into his throat as he ducks and pivots wildly to spot his aggressor.

"What the falk?" he screams when a racing horseman swoops up behind him, comes to a screeching halt then plunges down to his side, grabbing his arm roughly and yanking him up, only to plunge a fist into his face. The attack is made all the more devastating by the articulated metal glove his attacker wears.

Cronar struggles to open his eyes as blood, warm and fluid, surprises him by trickling down his cheek. Since his interview with the queen about her father, he has been awaiting contact, but never expected Larson Quell to jump him like this.

"Just what the falk do you think you are doing?" he punches wildly back at his attacker who still has the element of surprise on his side.

"You could have killed me!"

Pulling off a helmet typically used in battle, Quell laughs. "You stupid bugger, you were supposed to have found me at the toku den five days ago."

"Wha? No, I was told you would find me."

"And so, I have done."

Brushing off his pants at the knees where his body hit the dirt road, Cronar is still boiling with rage from being attacked.

"Well? Did she buy our story?"

"Hook, line, and sinker. We are positioned for a fine reward. Are the plans still the same as before?"

"Yes, you are to get an audience with the queen. Tell her you have been contacted by a group of kidnappers who indeed have her father to deliver in exchange for the ransom of twenty-two Qualtars. We are still counting on her to be so grateful he is not really dead; she won't hesitate to pay."

Cronar is now dusting off his sleeves. "It is an ingenious ploy. We will all be rich."

Quell remounts his fiery tempered horse and talks down to Cronar. "Do not disobey me again. Follow orders and be prompt. We will meet at the toku den tomorrow, one hour before closing."

"But it may take some time to get an audience with her."

"No, you must not delay. Start by telling her gatekeepers her father is alive; barely, but still alive."

Cronar continues to brush himself nervously as if he might rid himself of the taint of shame for trusting such ruthless men as Larson Quell and his cohorts.

The queen, immensely relieved to discover her father is not dead, is so appreciative of Cronar's message she rewards him with 1,000 kilters before he leaves the castle.

He tells her he does not know when or where, but the exchange will be very soon.

"I can't say I trust these men," he tells her. They approached me when they overheard me telling a comrade the sad news about your father, then all of sudden I learn he is not dead. I thought it was a ruse until they covered my head with a grain sack and took me to see him. I was shocked by his condition.

"They wouldn't tell me why they were holding him, but anyone who demands a price for his return is crooked, and what a price!" He nearly moans in his delivery. "Twenty-Two Qualtars is an enormous sum."

King Poma could not agree more but knows immediately Aadya will be willing to pay any sum for the release of her father.

"We must gather our advisers and plan his safe return. Raising that kind of money will be a monumental task in and of itself."

Aadya abhors the guilt of paying such a generous sum for the return of one man, when the same money could educate, feed, and clothe a hundred citizens of Merth for many years.

I AM SELFISH ALLOCATING THAT KIND OF MONEY FOR MY OWN PERSONAL GAIN.

Poma takes his wife into his arms and hugs her tightly without projecting his thoughts to her, he is thinking there is another answer.

70-A Meeting of Minds

The group gathered includes Galen and Kandar, the king's brothers Bonder and Parsa, Ali and Fontar, and of course the king and queen themselves, as well as Roark. "This is highly private, no one is to know about this except for the soldiers we will enlist once we have a plan," Poma tells them.

"If we can turn the tables and somehow get these thugs to reveal the hiding place of Zolan, we can rescue him, and forget about paying a ransom to some very evil men."

"I agree," Fontar steps forward. "That much money in the hands of evil doers, Omis especially, we could possibly be financing our own misfortune. We must avoid paying a ransom at all costs. We have trained soldiers to handle this. And I believe we can do it with little bloodshed."

Poma looks at his newly designated son-in-law with fresh eyes. As a much-decorated soldier, Fontar is displaying leadership qualities he had not recognized before.

"I believe Fontar is right," Roark adds. "This could be a deeper plot than the ransom. The Omis have been our biggest challenge in recent years, perhaps they are planning to overthrow your rule."

Kandar and the others nod affirmatively.

Ali listens to each and every one as they make their thoughts known, and while there is agreement, no one is focusing on how all this can be accomplished. "I have an idea," she says. As all eyes turn to her, she speaks.

"While I'm not sure we can trust her complicitly, we might be able to motivate the artist Alatoi to become a spy for us. She is after all an Omi, and she has a dark heart."

"Go on," her father encourages her, impressed his daughter is engaged with solving this intrigue rather than focusing on her elaborate wedding, which is to take place before the completion of the moon cycle.

"I happen to know she is a creature of the night, she roams the streets and gets in bar fights, and I'm pretty sure she does not spend a night alone unless she chooses to."

"And you know this how?" her father glares at her.

A smile springs to Ali's face. "I recently posed for my portrait. I spent hours upon hours with her. She is very entertaining."

"I had no idea," Aadya gives her daughter an alarmed look.

"It is true, I know you see her as a talented artist, but I think she can be motivated to help us in finding my grandfather."

Poma and Aadya's eyes meet in agreement. "Send for her at once." The king says.

It is decided Fontar, Ali, the king, and Kandar will meet with Alatoi to discuss the strategy and what part each player will have in the scheme. When Alatoi arrives escorted by two armed guards she gives Ali a puzzled look.

"What is all this about Princess Ali?"

"Please have a seat. We have a…special request for you, and it requires the utmost trust between ourselves and you."

Alatoi grins and utters a stifled, guttural laugh. Looking around the room at the venerable personalities involved she assesses each one by looking them square in the eyes as if to draw out their secrets. But none of the players are seduced by this inscrutable temptress.

"You will not betray us," the king speaks. "If you do, you can expect to have your entrails eaten by our pet lepotons. They always have a hefty appetite," he says with an uncharacteristic malevolent tone.

Facing him undaunted yet respectful to the full degree she is capable, Alatoi bows to him deeply and affectedly, but it is not discernible what degree her respect is, only that she knows how to physically lower herself in servitude posture.

"I should say my king, it would be very unwise, and how should I be rewarded should I participate in this intrigue?" She asks with one eyebrow arched in skepticism.

"Very handsomely." King Poma announces, his authoritative tone leaves no doubt in anyone's mind, he will honor his word. But Alatoi persists with specifics.

"I'm certain your word is good, my lord, but I need details."

"A thousand Krontars"

All are astonished, but even Alatoi gulps at his words. "That is very generous indeed, Your Majesty." She again bows in servitude. This time with a little more sincerity.

"Ali and I are now going to depart, for our security and yours. We are not to know of the details. You will meet with Fontar and Kandar here and determine the best course of action."

71-A Lead

Alatoi twists around to see the two men approaching through the crowd. She lowers her eyes and pulls up the hood of her robe. She is anxious to tell them about her discovery, but does not like the meeting place, too many eyes and ears.

"Why did you pick the market to meet? We have no privacy."

"It is in everyone's best interest to meet openly." Kandar says.

Alatoi rolls her eyes. "I disagree. You two innocents have obviously never done anything like this. Meet me at my studio later when the evening star is still high in the sky. I have news." Neither men are comfortable with her controlling their meeting, and they both hesitate without a response. She shrugs her shoulders and throws up her hands twisting on one boot heel as she does. "Dah! I will paint your portrait while we meet. It is perfect. Do not be such pistoids!"

When they come together with her later, she tells them how she found a woman beaten and raped in the alley near the Whistler's Tongue Inn the night before.

"Bow to the honor of the One True God. I hope you helped her!" Kandar roars.

"Of course, I did. That is how I got my information. She told me she had been smoking toku leaves, with her friend's lover, when she was taken as a servant by some really nasty men, who made her cook for them and their captive, and of course they had their way with her. Their prisoner was a fragile old man who was kind to her and told her he would pay her if she would help him escape." Alatoi stops talking and finishes some sketching she is doing on her easel as she talks.

"So then?" Fontar raises his eyebrows in anticipation of her words, and Kandar leans toward her as if to make his physical presence even more intimidating.

"Some of the men grew suspicious of her and that is how she landed in the street. They left her for dead."

"Where is she now?"

"I thought about bringing her back here. But you both warned me about keeping my distance, to keep the royal family out of this."

Kandar nods affirmatively. "Yes, you did the right thing. How do we find her then?"

Alatoi flips over her paper with the likeness of the girl in question. "I gave her a coin to find a room for the night, allowing her to stay off the street for a few days."

Fontar snatches the drawing from her and looks at Kandar. "We will find this girl, and she will lead us to the men and their captive."

"But where did she go?"

"I'm not sure but there are not too many options around here. She had no transportation to go over to Valtar. But who knows?"

Kandar scowls. "Why didn't you have her stay at certain lodging to make it easier to find her?"

Alatoi shrugs, "for all I know she took the coin and bought more toku leaves. You know the type? You boys will find her, alive or dead. Besides I am sure they have already moved him again. But, if you will let me finish…I have two names for you, Caulera Somes and Eulal Coper. They are the men who took her as their slave. They have also been known to associate with a Larson Quell."

"I want you to go look for her immediately!" Fontar growls. "We will have these men questioned."

"Ah, you might go easy with this idea if you want this to remain private. You tip off these fellow's associates and they may kill their prisoner, rather than have you find them, and worse the royal family is implicated."

It is obvious in Fontar's glare he does not like Alatoi's directive, but senses she is right.

He ponders what to do looking at Kandar. "We are too close to this; we must get some trusted warriors to carry this out."

Kandar nods yes, thinking of his gifted wife and precious child at home—wanting no harm to come to them.

72-A Warrior Rescued

Kandar and Fontar assign a dozen men to work with Alatoi beginning immediately. When she and her men find Zolan late in the night he is dehydrated and listless, but they are successful, and no ransom is paid.

"You made quick work of this," Fontar tells her when she and the men return with Zolan.

"Yes, but we lost one soldier in the capture, Politar Vicker, I am told is his name. It was a bloody exchange. I am not trained in combat, so I was not of much help. The queen's father, however," her face lights up, "was amazing despite his weakened condition." Fontar looks over at the tall angular man, with a white beard and disheveled ponytail astride a tall black mare, and winces.

"We must get him cleaned up and rested. I will arrange for a meeting with the queen later."

Alatoi gives him a puzzled look. "You need to take him to her right now. Scrum to the presentation."

Fontar realizes she is right and walks over to the man still tall in his saddle despite his recent ordeal. The mare lifts a hoof and stomps, swishing her tail to fend off a pesky flyn.

"Sir, I would like to take you to the queen." A broad smile spreads across Zolan's parched lips.

"Yes," is all he says.

"By the One True God you are safe and alive! Queen Aadya rushes to her father's side wondering if, after all the time has passed, he will still be familiar.

"Aadya, my darling Aadya," he says taking her into his arms and squeezing her tightly.

"Let me look at you," he politely pulls back suddenly realizing he has the repellent stench of captivity hanging on him strong enough to make her choke. "Forgive me, I am filthy."

"After all you've been through? You need not apologize for anything. I am most grateful you have been rescued. What an ordeal for you." Aadya opens her arms to direct him.

"Please go with Larton here. They have prepared a bath for you and some provisions. We will gather and talk later when you have had a chance to rest." Zolan's shoulders drop slightly, and, as he walks out, turns back to her and Poma.

"Thank you, Aadya. And you sir, you must be the king?" Zolan turns his head down to honor the presence of the king with as much physical energy as he can gather.

"We will have plenty of time to get to know each other," Poma also gestures with his arm, "Please take your time and collect yourself."

Once Zolan is escorted out, the heated, but muffled conversation Fontar and Alatoi are having in the corner of the room becomes more apparent.

"No, now is not the time," Fontar tells her, but Alatoi does not back down.

"Queen Aadya,"Alatoi dips slightly to be recognized. "May I say something?"

"Of course, I want to thank you for saving my father."

Having the queen's attention, Alatoi balks. "We lost a man, I'm sorry to say."

"Fontar has told me. I'm sure all fought valiantly, and my father has been returned to me unscathed."

A willful smile creeps into Alatoi's expression. "Your father is quite the fighter."

"Is that what you intended to tell me?"

"No, Your Majesty, I wanted to tell you how everyone praises your work to create a better world by educating all, but…"

The room suddenly becomes noisy as Ali and Galen join the gathering. "Did we miss him?"

"He has gone to get refreshed. But yes, we have him back. You will now get to meet your other grandfather!" Aadya tells them cheerfully.

"I'm sorry Alatoi can we save this conversation for another time? There is much rejoicing to do. We will keep our promise and pay you handsomely for your endeavors."

"Yes, Your Majesty," Alatoi backs away toward the door realizing Fontar had been right. Now was not the time.

73-Effle, Fonin Plont!

"Please father, won't you tell us your stories?" Aadya has been waiting all afternoon to speak with Zolan, but he had laid down after his bath and slept the afternoon away. After her first encounter with him earlier that morning, she is surprised by his physical energy when he joins the family for dinner, and the way he makes a fuss over Jaru, taking him out of the arms of Galen and carrying him as he greets the rest of the family.

"My dear daughter, I have been through much, but tonight I want to reacquaint myself with you and your beautiful family." A shadow crosses his freshly shaven face, transformed from his afternoon of rest, and then he succumbs to a hearty grin. "They are my beautiful family now."

"Yes, of course I didn't mean to pressure you. We are immensely pleased to have you home. It truly is a miracle."

Zolan turns around looking to assess the massive family dining hall, with its lofty ceilings, and hand-hewn beams, the roaring fireplace as tall as a man, and the trays brimming with food of all kinds, being brought out by smiling staff. Jaru begins to wriggle with impatience, and his mother comes to pull him out of Zolan's arms.

Ali approaches him with Fontar in tow, and the old man beams. "You must be Ali. The staff, who helped me, were all abuzz about the upcoming wedding." Ali turns to introduce Fontar when Roark steps up to the conversation and hands his grandfather a large stein.

"They tell me this is your preferred ale." Zolan thanks his grandson with lifted eyebrows and a nod.

"You mention something in passing and the staff learns to read your thoughts. Thank you, son," he says not quite sure who he is talking to yet.

"Grandfather this is my betrothed," Ali gets the conversation back on track as she pulls gently on Fontar's arm. He turns to greet Zolan with an awkward and humble smile.

"Yes, well, fine looking pair, the two of you. I'm looking forward to the festivities."

Aadya returns to the group, her luminescent pale green gown reflects light with a shimmering effect, giving her an extraordinary radiance. The simple golden crown she wears is an impulsive action as she has broken her own rule not to wear a crown except for official business. "Father please may we be seated. They are bringing out the food and we do not want to let it get cold."

"I am in a daze; this is like a miracle to be surrounded by family at last." Zolan grins and sips on his heavy stein while allowing her to show the way to his place at the huge round table recently sculpted by Galen's craftsmen with massive, gnarly tree roots for legs.

Aadya looks around the table listening to the growing chatter, and is elated by having her entire family there together. *I am greatly blessed!*

Roark stands and offers a toast. "Please join me in the traditional welcome toast, of the old ones, to our Grandfather Zolan who has been returned to us."

He raises his stein into the air and all join in as the sound echoes throughout the grand hall. The reverberations make it sound like there are hundreds assembled not just the immediate Karda family.

"Samna, dar, oten par, plebus, nonar, fote,
Venan, teffle, flargen, pont,
Effle, fonin plont!"

"If only I could keep this moment captured in my mind forever," Aadya leans over and tells Poma who responds with a warm-hearted expression of love and squeezes her hand.

"Mother, you could you know," Ali who is sitting beside her, says impulsively joining the conversation. "You could send for Alatoi and have her sketch us. That is how she starts with a sketch and then she paints from it."

"That is a marvelous idea! Let us see if we can reach her at this hour." Aadya nods to a nearby staff member and requests someone to find Alatoi and summon her at once with her sketching materials.

74-A Sense of Urgency

As the night's festivities ripen with conversation, wine, and stories, fabulous food, and stringed instruments softly filling the air with a serenade to the family's happiness, Alatoi appears uncharacteristically slipping in unnoticed. Laying her cape down on the floor she takes to sketching the family gathering.

She is there long enough to make several detailed sketches before anyone notices her in the shadows of the dining hall. Ali, lost in conversation with Fontar and Galen, had meant to keep a look out, and when she finally sees her, quietly goes over to peek at her work.

What she sees is beyond her expectations. Alatoi has been able to capture the kinetic energy of all her family members. "You are amazing!" She touches Alatoi slightly on the sleeve to make eye contact, because the artist is engrossed in her work of capturing spontaneous gestures.

Alatoi, sitting on the floor, looks up and beams. "Yes. Thank you, it is hard to portray everyone honestly, but by being discreet, I have captured them in casual poses, making the images more authentic. Ali continues to examine the quick sketch of the group and the detailed portraits. "It's difficult to get the expressions of the ones who have their back to me, but as they turn to talk, I am able to add more detail."

"I see that, very clever."

Ali slides back in her seat unnoticed as the servers begin to bring out tall, plate-sized cakes sculpted personally for each member of the family in their own likeness.

"Oh, how delightful!" Aadya exclaims. "Tell Carlin to please come out and speak to us, He has outdone himself."

As the group begins to disperse, Ali holds tightly to Fontar's arm. Pressing into him, she gives him a disparaging look. "Only three more revolutions and we will be together." She whispers into his ear, close enough she can feel the velvety texture of his ear lobe on her lips.

"Yes, my sweet Ali, I cannot believe it, and I cannot wait."

Aadya, who spotted Alatoi hard at work, even before Ali spoke to her, has been watching expectantly as the artist tears sheet after sheet of sketch paper, and lays her work down gently on the floor beside her. Aadya drops her napkin on the table and urges Poma to follow her to where Alatoi is working.

"Let us have a look," Aadya says to her.

"Your majesties," Alatoi stands to bow and then begins to hand them her sketches.

"These are wonderful," Poma, who as he has gotten older and become statelier in his role as king, has become a man of fewer words. This in large part because as king, his words carry such weight, it is less complicated to parse them out sparingly.

"You must make an extravagantly large painting of this. We will hang it here in the dining hall. You have done a wonderful job, Alatoi." Aadya tells her, feeding the artist's swollen sense of self-importance.

There is no subtlety to Alatoi's reaction as her pride simmers like a boiling pot with a lid. "I plan to paint it on the wall there."

Aadya turns to look behind her. "Aye. That would be spectacular."

"Ah, your majesties, may I have a word. I need to request something of you."

"Yes, of course is it what you wanted to speak of this morning when you rode in with my father?"

"Er, yes. There is an urgency of sorts."

"Go on," Poma nods.

"You may not realize the undercurrent of evil on the streets. As you know I come from Omi, where crime is much worse of course, but..."

Poma grows tired of her doubtful hesitancy. "What is your request?"

"I am fearful for my life; I have placed myself in danger to deliver Zolan from some very evil men."

"We have imprisoned them."

"Yes, but there will be more to replace them." She looks directly into Poma's eyes and then to Aadya for the answer she wants. "I need to be trained to defend myself."

Poma continues to deliver his focused attention on her. "You want more than training. You could have asked Fontar or Roark for that. Why do you approach us with this request?"

"I believe once I am trained in the martial ways of warriors, I could be of great service to your kingdom. I will be much more valuable to you as a covert scout. You need me."

She turns to Aadya. "Everyone knows you both have worked to create a steadfast society fair to all, but until you recognize there are tensions and flows of evil among us, on the streets where your children walk, then you are setting yourself up for reprisal. This is especially so since we thwarted the forces of evil who captured your father, and who would have ransomed him handsomely without our intervention."

Poma tilts his head slightly, surprised one so talented at creating vivid images with paint and canvas would be interested in pursuing this path of a warrior.

"We will consider your request." Poma tells her then leads Aadya off to retire for the night.

75-What Could Have Been

Ali, who, now that the process has begun, cares nothing about the details of the wedding, goes riding with Fontar every afternoon rather than get stuck in endless meetings about the wedding rituals. Fortunately, there are plenty of royal staff to take charge of the details. Not even Aadya seems to have her heart in it as it means spending most of her time at Katara where the wedding will take place. The event promises to be every bit as spectacular as the last royal wedding between Aadya and Poma over thirty-five revolutions ago. Queen Mother Mesa, now slowed by age, consults the Matong frequently for guidance and often it is her vision which is the deciding factor in the choices made.

"We must not let any detail escape us," Queen Mother Mesa is frequently known to say as she pads around Katara in her fleece-lined slippers, which have become her favorite footwear in her advancing years.

The wedding dress, like Aadya's, will be pressed against the Matong before Ali makes the transformational walk down the aisle. There will be many other infusions of the Matong's power in the preparations and final ceremony.

As Ali and Fontar thunder across the plain on their horses, with the light of the afternoon star bouncing off the tall wheat-colored field, they both enjoy the freedom despite four warrior horsemen who now ride at a distance from them. It is a precautionary measure Fontar has requested, despite its intrusion into their privacy, but with the heightened dangers from the recovery of Zolan he knows it is necessary.

"Any of the royal family are targets," Alatoi has warned. "We need to maximize our protection of each and every one of you."

When they slow to a walk to head up the wooded path, toward a lookout point the are both fond of, Ali pulls her horse Elita, up to his side and whispers to him. "Only two more nights I sleep alone." Fontar turns toward her, his delight stretches across his muscular face. The horses gently collide as the two riders allow them to come close side by side.

"Yes, my love soon, very soon." He reaches down and clutches her knee, and they both experience a jolt of passion pass through them.

It is just before they reach the winding path, approaching the stone outcropping, where they are stunned by shouts and curses as four men leap from the tree branches above them. Ali is knocked off Elita who rears and stomps her front hooves into the face of Ali's assailant leaving a bloody imprint. Elita blocks Ali's vision of Fontar, but she hears him draw his sword as she jumps up to calculate what her next actions should be. Ali can hear the shouts of their escort riders as they race toward them.

Fontar is in full attack mode, and she wants to assist him, but all she has with her is a hunting blade, which she pulls out, and braces herself for plunging it into the heart of the next man to approach her. Her assailant comes from behind and knocks the knife out of her hand. "Ali, are you all right?" Fontar cries out, not able to see her, as he engages in sword fight with a bearded aggressor.

At this point, Ali has been taken in an arm lock from behind. Their guards have arrived on the scene, and Ali gasps as she sees one of them struck down. The clashing of swords gets louder as the mortal exchange grows. Her assailant tries to haul her off, but she punches him hard with her one free elbow, and somehow twists loose kicking him sharply in the groin with her knee. "Sossa, faw!" she hears him curse. She searches the ground for her blade and sees it just out of reach. Fontar is now engaged in sword fight with two of the marauders. She picks up the knife, but as she does someone kicks her from behind so hard, she lands forward on her head. The sound her skull makes hitting the ground is like a ripe melon splitting open on a flat rock. She is temporarily dazed. Fighting for her life she grabs the knife, now beneath some of the warriors engaged in a sword battle. The knife is seen by Fontar who kicks it her way. She picks it up and charges at the man behind her who is now brandishing a knife of his own. She makes quick work of him using her skills to throw him off balance with her leg, and then using the full force of her body to plunge the knife, through his thick leather tunic, all the way into his heart.

Meanwhile, one of the guard detail has downed another assailant, and has joined Fontar in his sword battle. The noise of swords slashing metal on metal becomes deafening as the men, sometimes grunting, try to slam their swords hard enough to break the grip of their opponent, and gain the advantage to pierce their sword into the chest of their rival.

Ali situates herself behind Fontar's opponent and stabs him savagely in the back. She is unable to pull the knife back out of him and now remains weaponless. The pain only exacerbates the raider's fury, and he does not turn to stave her off, but lurches at Fontar wildly and successfully slashes his neck close enough to his critical artery. Blood begins to pump grotesquely out of his neck as Fontar thrusts back at the wounded man.

Ali watches the blood pumping from Fontar's neck like a primed well pump, one, two, three surreal slurps as he staggers, determined to keep standing.

She is immobilized for the briefest moment and sees the other guard has successfully cornered his opponent against a tree. She turns looking for a sword to snatch up and help Fontar, the blood now flooding down his neck and soaking his leather garment.

"AAH!" she hears a groan coming from the cornered man and sees the guard has completed his task. She picks up a sword on the ground, it is heavy and crude; and using her training swings at Fontar's attacker with all her might. It knocks him off balance and he crashes to the ground. Fontar rushes up and plunges his sword into the chest of his attacker now twice wounded, then Fontar stumbles and falls.

"Fontar!" Ali screams rushing to his side. "Fontar!" She presses her hand to his neck to compress his wound laying his head on her bent knees, but she knows in her heart he is mortally wounded.

"Your highness," the guard rushes toward them. "Are you all right?"

"By the One True God, Fontar," she shrieks. His forehead is clammy and his lips cold as she bends over to help him.

He opens his eyes for the briefest of moments and all life passes from him.

76-Lost

Ali, immobilized by grief, sobs over Fontar's body while being aware, in her peripheral vision, the last surviving royal guard is going around to each body and plunging his sword into the chest of the enemy. There will be no doubt anyone will walk away from this tragic and bloody battle.

"Why?" she shrieks with her chin raised to the sky. "Why have you done this? You made me go on a quest, you gave me the man of my dreams. Then you cut him down like a he was nothing more than a wormoccle. What is wrong with you?" She curses the One True God.

Quintoff, her only escort now, gathers up the horses, and straps the bodies down to them hurriedly. His skin crawls with the impending danger of another attack, and he gently touches Ali on the shoulder, even though this is not protocol, to convey the urgency of departure. "Your Majesty we should go in case there are others who will come."

As if in a dream, Ali tells him to put Fontar on her horse. "He will ride with me."

With each stride Elita takes, Ali hopes for Fontar to lift his head and let his lungs fill, but he does not. The two riders make an informal death procession as they wend their way back to Katara where they are received by astonished villagers.

"I want to take him to the Matong," she tells her mother who has gotten word of the tragedy and has met her at the gates of Katara.

"My darling Ali, you must accept this, we have sent for Galen, but not even she can bring the dead back."

"Maybe he's not dead." Ali wipes the warm, liquid drooling from her nose with the back of her sleeve as her tears, like salty acid, etch her cheeks."

"I came as soon as I heard!" Galen comes running up.

"Oh my God please save him!"

Galen immediately touches Fontar's body still draped over the withers of Elita, but all she senses is the stone-cold answer of death. He has bled out and his heart has stopped. Turning to her sister, she grabs Ali by the shoulders and forces her to lift her head and look her in the eyes.

"Listen to me Ali, he is truly gone. It was his time."

"NOOO!" She lets go a blood curdling scream. "What about the Matong? The Matong set all this up how could he die? Let us take his body to the Matong and see if he can be revived?"

"Listen to me," Galen shakes Ali gently. "One thing I have learned as a healer, not all people, not all situations even, can be healed."

"I'm going to try anyway."

"Ali, listen to me, you are making this worse for yourself. He has no life left in his body. He is truly gone."

Ali looks at her sister, her face grossly contorted and splotched with red patches. "The Matong is capable of miracles. I have to try."

Galen slumps as Ali pulls away and leads Elita to the ramp to take Fontar's body to the divine chamber of the Matong. By now the crowd has grown and Quintoff is being greeted by other guards who are helping him to remove the horses laden with bodies from the scene.

Galen reluctantly follows Ali and her horse to the Matong, and as she expected there is no reprieve from death for Fontar. She places her hand in unison with Ali to hear the heartbreaking message. FONTAR IS TO BE NO MORE. PATIENCE BELOVED ONE. The tall chamber door opens softly and one by one, as they are made aware, of the tragedy, Ali's family gathers around her. Her body shudders uncontrollably as if there is ice in her veins.

It is Roark who takes the reins away from Ali to lead Elita outside and make arrangements to have all four of the mortally wounded men's bodies prepared for a hero's burial.

77-A New Start

Aside from the burial ceremony for Fontar, it is many revolutions before Ali will leave her quarters despite the best efforts of her family to ease her grief. One day when he can stand it no longer, King Poma comes to her chamber and pounds on the heavy door until it looks like he might vibrate the massive metal hinges loose. "Aella Anemone, you come out right now or I shall break the door down!"

She comes and opens the doors in silken lounging robes she has not changed for days. "Has the Matong given any indication of why it struck Fontar down?"

King Poma looks nervously at her. "Not yet, your mother consults every day."

She looks at her father with scorn. "Then I'm not coming out." She drops her arms to her sides and gives him a sidelong glance as she walks away from him. "You are not behaving in a royal manner by hammering on my door."

King Poma's anger leaks out of every pore. "And you are not acting like a daughter of mine! Royal heir to the crown my foot!"

When she hears his harsh words, she begins to cry, falling into his arms. "Why did the Matong do this? It is grotesquely cruel!"

King Poma hugs his daughter and holds her in his arms for as long as she will allow. "My wonderous daughter, the Matong is not our wish grantor. We do not always know the wisdom behind the Matong's actions, but we are the noble Karda family, and we must have faith to guide our people and lead them to their destiny."

Ali pushes away from her father's grasp. "I am lost, I cannot lead anyone anywhere."

"You will find your way. But right now, you need to bathe, get dressed, and join your mother and I for a meal. You must put one foot forward and then another."

Ali looks around the devastation of her bedchambers and a spark of energy ignites in her dulled brain. She turns back to her father and gives him a slight nod making his face brighten.

"Do not even think of suggesting a replacement for Fontar," Ali says as she sits down with her parents for the first real meal she has had in days. Poma and Aadya look quizzically at each other, for neither of them would have even thought of such a thing considering how broken their daughter is. Their own hearts still hold a void as Fontar had been beloved by them both. "I will pull myself together and lead this land." She says heavy with remorse. "Roark is probably already rejoicing thinking he will be the next king."

The two of them decide to ignore her unexpected diatribe. "Let us only focus on today, this meal, Ali." Poma says to her softly. Aadya looks at him sideways and gives him a nod. YOU HAVE ALWAYS BEEN ABLE TO

REACH HER BETTER THAN I CAN. Poma gives his wife a compassionate smile and begins to eat.

"Oh, I almost forgot!" Aadya says unexpectedly like she has just told herself a private joke.

Ali, whose eyes normally are the color of the pale green silica flower are still dulled by grief, looks at her mother like she has lost all sensibility.

Aadya wipes her mouth with her napkin and beckons to a nearby server. Whispering in his ear, she returns to the conversation smiling.

"We wanted to wait until you might appreciate your gift."

"What gift?"

"You'll see," Aadya tells her daughter.

They continue to eat their midday meal with sluggish stabs at conversation until a man approaches them holding a furry white pup in his arms. Ali is intrigued as the puppy is brought to her and placed in her lap. The bright blue eyes and tiny pink tongue gleam with innocence while the sweet, pure puppy smell engulfs Ali. "He is so beautiful!" Her eyes light up with the first spark of life her parents have seen in her in weeks.

"We didn't' know about him at first." Aadya explains. "The breeder came to us after the tragedy." She hesitates hoping not to set her daughter off with uncontrollable grief again. "He is your wedding gift from Fontar."

Emotions swim up and down Ali's spine, like a water snake in a storm, as she cuddles with the soft little furball who, will grow into her most steadfast protector. "He is of the Mortar breed," her father tells her. He has not been named yet. It was Fontar's desire you should name him."

As Ali presses the soft puppy to her breast and squeezes, she feels the pup's life source beckoning her to respond. Hot tears burn her cheeks as she both sobs and laughs into his fur.

Robick, as Ali names her dog after the legendary folk hero, who leads all stranded warriors home, never leaves her side. She decides to name him this after a conversation with her Grandfather Zolan as he recounted his travails and decades-long journey home. "It took you nearly a lifetime, but Robick did eventually lead you home."

"Yes, and look at me now, I am merely a relic of the man I once was."

Ali had hugged him, noticing he still carried himself proudly. Even though it was a complete fantasy, she wished in the most secret part of her soul Fontar, too, might someday be led back home.

78-The Work Begins

One morning as she makes her way to the great hall to join Roark and her mother for breakfast, Ali, and Robick, carried in her arms, come across a crew who are putting up scaffolding. "What's going on?" she asks Aadya when she gets to the table where the family is gathered.

Aadya beams, "Alatoi is about to begin the mural of our family at the celebration dinner of Zolan's return." A spark of energy jolts Ali as if someone literally tapped her on the shoulder when she remembers, what must be ages ago, but in actuality was recent, how they had gathered to celebrate the return of her Grandfather Zolan. The energy source is her remembrance of Fontar by her side as they giggled, and held hands, and blew kisses to each other. Ali sucks in her breath and holds it as she realizes Alatoi has images of her beloved.

But Alatoi has not shown up. "What's wrong with you?" Roark asks Ali as she nervously looks about the room.

"Oh, nothing, leave me alone!" She snaps. Aadya and Roark both give her a sidelong glance and then look at each other with perplexed expressions.

"Your father says you are resuming your duties at council and have plans to return to your horseback rides together," Aadya intercedes.

"Yes, we are riding this afternoon, as a matter of fact." She turns away before she finishes her sentence when she hears Alatoi's demanding voice.

"You men weren't supposed to get the scaffolding out until all were done with breakfast."

One man bows his head slightly having learned it is best to treat the venerable artist with deference.

"But Queen Aadya said she does not mind; she is looking forward to seeing the painting completed."

"Oh," Alatoi spots the queen and her family. Going over to them she apologizes for the commotion. "I requested these, clowns, er, I requested they not disturb you." An incredulous smile crosses Roark's face, Alatoi always amuses him.

"It's quite all right. We will be watching this project unfold for many moons to come, I'm sure."

"Alatoi," Ali breaks in "have you brought your sketches with you?"

"Of course, Your Majesty."

"May I see them?" Alatoi points to the empty space on the far end of the dining table and goes to lay down her leather portfolio."

"Have you any of us, Fontar and I together?"

"Yes, I'm sure I have several of the two of you."

"Oh Scwarta!" Ali feels her chest release. Robick, still in her arms, squirms to be put down so he can search for food scraps beneath the table.

As Alatoi pulls out the many sketches she made of the gathering, Ali is overcome by a surging joy. There on the table she sees the expressive face of Fontar, his slightly dimpled chin, his round eyes filled with promise and love. *What a gentle soul he was.*

Aadya comes over and rests her hand on Ali's shoulder, still grasping the soft napkin most recently in her lap. The two women meet each other's gaze and smile. OH, MOTHER I AM LOST WITHOUT HIM, BUT HERE ARE THESE BEAUTIFUL IMAGES.

Aadya is immensely grateful this is happening for her daughter and is once again reaffirmed in the goodness of life, but before she can respond, she feels Robick tugging at her pants leg and looks down to see the naughty puppy chewing on her leather legging.

"Aach! Off with you!" Aadya shoos him.

Ali picks him up and then pauses, THANK YOU MOTHER FOR THIS GIFT. I SHALL BE ABLE TO RE-MEMBER HIM WITH THESE PICTURES!

Alatoi, who is not privy to the private thoughts of the two women, begins to fidget as she is eager to begin her mural, a project greater than any she has ever attempted before.

79-Metal Magic

"So, let me understand this. You are telling us, after this lengthy investigation of the Great Targa Storm, you have determined there are metals, not native to Merth, which fell through the 'Great Immense'?" One of the four experts nods affirmatively to Prince Parsa who has posed the question.

"We have taken our time, and pored over the evidence countless times, your highness," says one of the investigators, an apprentice in charge of collecting the items.

"And how do you know these all came from the Immense?"

"Our findings are documented by first-hand sightings," says Faynyl, the one woman on the team. "We even have the shard which wounded Queen Aadya."

"You have been very thorough then. I was hoping to avoid seeing the sickening death projectile again." King Poma strokes his chin and looks toward Aadya.

THIS IS ALARMING!

I KNOW STAY CALM.

The presentation of the investigative committee has gone on for some time, and everyone in the council meeting looks mentally drained.

"Then what do you suggest we do about this?" Roark pipes up.

"We would like more funds to study these metals," Jars Oldam, the senior investigator tells them. "As we have stated, these metals have properties unlike anything here on Merth."

"Roark, you seem to have interest in this mystery. I want to appoint you to the team allowing you to report back to us frequently," his father tells him. "You will meet with our committee members and keep us updated. And we need more exploration of what these materials are capable of.

"Now I think everyone will be most excited to call this session of the council meeting closed. Excellent work team."

As everyone files out, Poma nods to Roark, "I think you should take some of these metals and bond. The Matong might provide some insight."

"Sure, that is a great idea."

"And, son, everyone in the room can see how you looked at Faynyl."

Roark grins, "was I that obvious?"

Poma gives him an annoyed, dispassionate look. "Keep it straightforward my man and focus on the task." He says as he gingerly places a strong hold on Roark's shoulder.

"Kysal, wait up," Roark hails the team member he has known from childhood. "Let me get with you about the tests you are performing on the materials. I want to check it all out."

"Stand back!" Kysal tells Roark. "We have found when we strike this metal, it gives off sparks." As he slams the hammer down, flashes of bright light fly everywhere, and even though he was warned, Roark is surprised by the intensity as he has never seen anything like it.

"By the One True God! That is amazing." He jumps backward to avoid getting sprayed with the high intensity flashes. "Ouch it kind of stings when it hits you."

"Yes, we have to be very careful," Kysal tells him.

"Is it hot to the touch?'

"No, that is what is remarkable. The more you strike this metal, the colder it gets."

"I need to take it to the Matong and see if I can get any information about what this is."

"Sure, is this piece too large?"

Roark eyes the thin metal sheet. "I think it will work." He takes the metal piece from his friend and turns it over in his hands. "Amazing how cold it is, unbelievable really."

"I wish I could go with you into the Matong chamber," Kysal says hoping by some remote chance Roark would acquiesce. Kysal's curiosity of the omniscient orb is piqued by his scientific training. Roark gives him a stern look. "Absolutely not, it would be your death and mine!"

"Be careful. No telling what might happen." Roark shrugs, he has not had an unpleasant experience with the Matong yet.

80-The Study of All Things

With nothing particular to do, Roark takes the metal to the Matong straight away.

When he enters the chamber, the hypnotic globe immediately begins to hum and glow. Because of this unusual reception by the orb, Roark suddenly has a flash of doubt, and he sets the metal down on the floor and touches his hand to the globe, now pulsing with light.

YOU HAVE QUESTIONS ABOUT THE METAL DROPPED DOWN THROUGH THE IMMENSE. YOU WERE RIGHT NOT TO TOUCH IT WHILE BONDING. THIS METAL IS BEYOND YOUR PEOPLE'S COMPREHENSION. THERE ARE USES FOR IT TO BE DISCOVERED.

As soon as Roark is released from the Matong's hold, a curiosity strong and unavoidable, pops into his mind. He places his hand back on the orb and asks, "What is the Immense?"

YOUR QUESTION WILL NOT BE ANSWERED AT THIS TIME, YOUR PEOPLE MUST EVOLVE MORE BEFORE YOU WILL BE ABLE TO UNDERSTAND. EACH STEP TAKEN IS BASED ON THE ONE BEFORE. YOU CANNOT LEAP TOO FAR FORWARD OR YOU WILL FALL. THE ANSWERS LIE WITH THE ONE TRUE LEADER, AELLA ANEMONE.

Roark looks around, the Matong is typically not this revealing, and yet he is disappointed by the information he has been given. *Perhaps this is a chance to get the orb to open up about some other questions like why Fontar was killed after he became the chosen one for Ali. I'm rather sure Ali has probably asked the Matong this question every day since Fontar's death, but it's worth a shot.*

THIS IS NOT YOUR QUESTION TO ASK.

The Matong roars inside his head. He shakes off the vociferous proclamation, picks up the metal, and leaves feeling useless as he has not received the information he had hoped for.

"Nothing," he tells Kysal later when they meet. The Matong won't explain the Immense either." Roark's royal training has not included scientific exploration, although he had studied several courses in class which alluded to such matters. Kysal on the other hand, has devoted his education to scientific theory, a quickly developing area of education on Merth.

"We really know little about these things. The folktales…"

"I know what the folktale says, "A warrior threw the Matong at Merth and it caused the sky to rip. We call it the 'Immense' because we do not know what else to call it," Roark all but growls at his friend.

Kysal nods in agreement. "I have studied all things about our natural environment. I can tell you about the cycles of life, I can name all the species which walk and swim upon Merth, I know all creatures which fly or flutter, the plants that feed us and our animals, but we know nothing of the sky. We have no way of going there to try and find out the mysteries of the heavens. Much of our planet remains unknown to us." Kysal says folding his thin hands into his chest.

"We must do something about that." Roark muses, looking at his impassioned friend. It is then the seed is planted in his soul, a purpose, and direction he has not been drawn to before.

As the two men walk together, Roark asks Kysal. "How do I educate myself in this line of work, this science you call it?"

Kysal pauses, startled to hear his cavalier prince friend show interest in such scholastic pursuits. "You should come with me to where the sacred books are stored. We are adding to the knowledge of them nearly daily. If it weren't for your mother, only royals would have access to them, and I would venture to say, you've never spent much time in the vault."

Roark laughs and pats his friend on the shoulder. "Ah Kysal, you know me too well."

As Roark spends more time in the sacred book vault, searching for answers about the properties of the now sacrosanct metals collected from the Targa Storm, he becomes obsessed with seeking answers. After each day of study, he bonds with the Matong for further knowledge. Roark's educational journey makes him more sensitive to the nuances of the ecosystem enveloping Merth. He is beginning to see a course of action to discovering answers to so many of the mysteries of that plague his people. But of course, running into Faynyl frequently offers its own set of rewards. Aside from his mother and sisters, Roark has not known a woman so educated and clever.

Book III

Jaxyl

Moon Date - Clovis 212

"I wish your father could have seen your coronation, and know you were finally installed as his rightful heir."

"I wish he could have gotten to know Jaxyl." Ali peers down into her baby's tiny face, ogling her with the adoring fascination only a parent can have, as she leans over her day cradle. She looks up at her mother who has aged gracefully, but noticeably since her father's demise. Gratitude surges through her like she has just eaten a clutch of crystalline flowers. Their sweet, concentrated flavor always gives her an energy burst. To have survived these past few revolutions—and now to have this astonishing baby, and a husband who she loves and who loves her passionately—is truly remarkable.

She picks up Jaxyl who is beginning to stir. "We've been through much these past few star revolutions, haven't we?"

"I'll say." Aadya's voice cracks, and in a moment of weakness she lets out her regret with a small shudder. "I miss him."

"I know manona," Ali uses the familiar grandmother sobriquet as she stands to hug her mother tightly with, the now fully awake, baby squeezed between the two of them.

81-The Border Wars

Moon Date - Clovis 212

When the first night raids began, people were startled by the noise and bright lights, and many thought the Targa Storms had regenerated. The sieges on the villages surrounding Compana, and Valtar lasted for nearly an entire cycle of the moons, until enough soldiers were engaged to push the marauders back. It seemed like everything was going to be okay until the Omis united with an outlier group known as the Fythls. The Fythls were barbaric and known to cut their captives up into pieces and feed them to their drazons, a species they kept locked in cages to enhance their ferocity, allowing them out only at night to patrol the perimeter of their battle encampments.

The war forces the Karda family to put all societal advancements aside, as they rise to the obstacles of warfare not encountered, in such massive proportions, in any prior historic era.

Zolan, Queen Aadya's aging father, who could have easily sat by the fireside without judgment, was one of the first to fall in battle. His actions inspired many others to enlist in the pursuit of securing their homeland from the ravages of the marauders.

Roark, with his idea to make shields and swords out of some of the seemingly magical metals of the Targa Storm, brought to the bloody battles innovation, and thus an edge, sparking success on many fronts. They found, with the ample supplies of the metals harvested for study, there were some metals best suited as swords, which homed in on the enemy leaving the warrior only having to hang on, and the sword itself would engage terminal blows. Another metal, while lightweight, was particularly suitable for shields as it was impervious to blows. Still another metal, because of its reflective properties, was assembled for mirrors to blind the enemy, even in the weakest of light. A fourth material was ideal for its elasticity and could be sewn into protective clothing, which looked and felt like a supple, copper-colored leather. While it took some time to fabricate these weapons, as each day passed, more of King Poma's warriors were suited out with these remarkable materials. This gave them the advantage to push the frontlines back to the borders of the Karda reign.

Prince Roark and Princess Ali, along with their father, and his brothers fought purposefully with their warriors. While Kandar was assigned to protect his wife Galen, the healer. Only Addya and Faynyl stayed at home, to care for the growing brood of grandchildren. At the time of the beginning of the Border Wars, Aadya and Poma had three grandchildren, Jaru, Olza, and Borzok. Jaru was Galen and Kandar's firstborn, followed by their daughter Olza, and Borzok was recently born to Roark and Faynyl.

For a brief time while the weapons were being constructed from the omnifarious Targa metals, Roark was able to remain in Compana overseeing their production and could thus stay at home for the time being. But once all the materials were made into weapons, he was compelled to ride with the other brave souls, seeking to rid the kingdom of the savages who had invaded them.

82-Roark's Departure

Faynyl's pale yellow eyes flood with tears and, then like a cup tipping over, cascade down her soft cheeks. "By the One True God, our baby is barely four moon cycles. Can't you stall a little longer?"

Roark kisses her softly on the forehead and wipes at her tears with his thumb. "My darling, I have stretched this out as long as I can. I leave with the last delivery in the morning. My time here with you and the baby has been a gift, but my reprieve has run out. They need me, besides our family is greatly protected. My father lets none of us join him at the fore front of the battle zone, where he and his brothers are an inspiration to the fighting men. They are constantly flanked by a score of special warriors who shield them. I am to stay behind the scenes with Ali. We are only involved with the strategists not in the fighting. It is a smart plan, no one is trying to be a hero. We are systematically rolling these monsters back beyond our borders. We are actually expanding the Karda domain."

"That sounds aggressive."

"No, no my love, it is all for the best. These people will eventually receive the benefits of our society."

Faynyl laughs nervously as she cries. "You make it sound so, I do not know, like this war is something honorable."

Roark adjusts his posture becoming taller. "No, war is never a proper solution, but we must not let these monsters overtake us either. Remember how frightened we were when they first began their attacks? By the One True God it seemed as if they were going to beat the gates down here at Compana."

Faynyl shudders, she had given birth only three revolutions before the attacks started. She was barely out of her birth bed with complications, which might have ended Borzok's life before it began, if Galen had not been there by her side.

"Okay, but you are allowed time to return home periodically," she turns to him and looks him directly in his eyes. "You need to take your leave periodically and check on us." She frowns at him with the intensity of a new mother, "I mean it!"

Her stern reproach sets Roark to reflecting on how Faynyl has changed since becoming pregnant, once fiercely independent, *she now worries more and depends less on her education for assessing outcomes. Curious.*

"My love will you please help me pack? I do not want to forget anything important."

"Yes," she tells him, "Your son is crying, we have spoken too loudly. You should pick him up and hold him, it may be your last chance."

"You are being way too dramatic," he scolds her but does as she says, thinking the same thing she has dared to utter out loud.

"Hush little baby don't you cry," Roark purrs into his ear as he bounces the baby, but before long he realizes Borzok wants only what his mother can supply."

"Here he needs you." He holds the baby out at arm's length.

The knock on the door comes before daylight and Roark is not eager to answer it, but as the morning ride toward the battle grounds progresses, he finds his heart turning toward his duties and less toward his family he has left behind. He brings with him over 300 protection suits, 120 swords, 175 shields, and thirty light-reflecting panels. Recognizing his contribution toward the safety of his men with these innovative weapons, he is less disappointed he and the other scientists have not been able to answer the questions of how they arrived on Merth, and why the 'Immense' exists.

83-Roark Arrives to Camp

When Roark arrives at headquarters, he is surprised to find out Ali is not there, but has joined the king's squad. "Do not worry Prince Roark they are heavily guarded and well-armed with your weapons, and they all ride Matong horses. She wanted some first-hand knowledge of the battlefront," the freshly decorated warrior tells him. Roark hands the reins of his horse to him and strides briskly over to the healing tent, hoping to find his sister Galen. She is there but too busy to stop what she is doing. There is a lengthy line of injured warriors waiting on her to have their wounds healed. Roark watches her as she sits in a chair and has each of them sit across from her. She takes their hand in hers, smiles, at each one straight into their eyes, and whispers a quiet absolution. Some of the injured stand up ready to go back to battle immediately, and others rest in a nearby tent where fresh air is allowed to flow freely, and they are fed a hot meal. Those who do not make it back alive are taken to wagons to be removed and buried.

"Why has Ali been allowed to join the fighting?" he asks his sister crossly.

Galen looks at Roark, and flashes him a scornful look. "I'm not happy about it, but you can't hold the woman back. She is just like our mother."

Roark shuffles his feet uneasily, "I'm starving can I get a meal in there?" He points to the resting tent.

"Sure, it's the best meal out here," she says without looking up from her patient.

As Roark sweeps open the tent, the aromas of freshly prepared food reach him. He looks around. Alatoi is over in a corner chatting animatedly with a warrior. He goes to fill his plate at the serving table and sits nearby, giving her a nod when they make eye contact.

"Oh, please join me Prince Roark, Shoten is about to leave and head for the front." Roark picks up his plate and sets it down across from her as her acquaintance stands to leave. Alatoi gives the departing warrior a loaded wink, and Roark is again reminded, of what a lascivious nature Alatoi has. A snide remark is on the tip of his tongue, but he holds it.

"So, here you are. Your weapons and shields have revolutionized our fighting. It looks as if we will all be able to go home soon."

"Wouldn't it be nice," he says between swallowing large mouthfuls of spicy burgon and pletos.

"So, how is fatherhood? I'm sure you are not pleased to be joining us."

He looks up from his food and says dutifully, "It is my obligation to be here fighting beside my family." His tone yields no regret.

Alatoi peers deeply into his eyes making him uncomfortable. "And why are you not out on the battlefield?" he asks her. "Didn't we give you the honor of becoming a trained warrior?"

"That you did," she says sipping on her hot cider. "But the uppers say I am more important as a spy. I have crossed the enemy lines many times now and have taken up with one of their high-ranking Chosars."

"That sounds like very dangerous work." He says cutting his tender meat and pushing another flavorful morsel into his mouth.

"I am suited to the role," she gives him a demure smile and takes another sip.

Roark swipes some dark gaifar bread through the syrupy sauce on his plate and fills his mouth again. Wiping his lips with his napkin he stands. "If you'll excuse me, I really need to report to my regents."

"You must be eager, you made quick work of your meal, a luxury in these surroundings."

With his hunger satiated Roark is ready to jump on his horse and join the fighting, but it is not to be. "I'm sorry sir, with Princess Ali at the front, you are the next in line as heir. We have been given strict orders for you to remain here, until she gets back, which will probably be before dark."

"Sharza!" He slaps his gloves on the table. *Once again, my sister usurps me.* He wrestles with his anger as he stares at the messenger, the aide to one of their highest-ranking officers. He looks away disgustedly and locks onto a scene outside the headquarters tent. It is a man he has never seen before, talking to Alatoi.

"Where is Master Tzunard?" he demands of the Aide.

"I'll go get him," the young man says apologetically.

Roark looks toward Alatoi's direction again, the two appear to be arguing now. Suddenly Alatoi slaps her arm up in a derogatory gesture and stalks off. *She is so insolent!* He thinks as another smile breaks across his face.

84-Desperate to Find Her

The night air is brittle as Roark waits impatiently for Ali, but when she does not return, and her horse Elita does, search parties are sent to find her body. "She was right there with us one minute, the next she was gone" the senior officer in her detachment tells them, shame bleeding through his words. "We were on the edge of a gradual versant. I do not know how she could have disappeared like that."

King Poma and the rest of the Karda royalty have been brought back to the central quadrant to assess the situation. They listen grimly to the accounts of all four warriors who were there to personally protect her. "She was fine, carrying one of the Targa swords, all she had to do was hold on. I could see her shield resist stroke after stroke."

"One minute she was astride her horse, then suddenly she was gone. I did not see the horse until I returned here."

Another guard explains. "It was as if she was taken by magic. I've not experienced anything like it."

Alatoi, sitting on the far side of the room, stands and pushes her way toward the center of the conversation. "Did anyone see a flash of light?"

"Just the flash of steel swords in the sunlight." One of the guards offers.

"I might have seen something out of the corner of my eye," another one says.

"Really? Is it possible our own weapons may have been used against us? Could the enemy have captured one of our mirrors and used it to cause a distraction to capture Princess Ali?"

"Do you have knowledge of this?" King Poma demands of her.

"I would like to speak to you sir, and a select few. I may have some insight."

"Clear the tent, Parsa, Bonder, Roark, and you Kefle, please remain. We have things to discuss." Guards, maintain a perimeter around the tent to protect our privacy."

"So, what's going on here?" Roark glares at Alatoi suspiciously.

King Poma holds up his hand. "Let her speak."

"As you know sirs, I have been commissioned to confer with the enemy, and share what I learn with our side." She gives Roark a meaningful look as if to let him know he just arrived and should not be sticking his nose into her affairs; and yet he is a prince, and she knows it is counterproductive to splash vitriol his way especially within certain company as this.

"There has been talk of capturing some of our weapons while in battle, and this is certainly feasible. While I have no confirmation of this, I have met a man doing the same thing I am doing, going back and forth across enemy lines, he disguises himself as a service ward, hauling food, water, and burying trash. He calls himself Yani, but he is much more sophisticated and intelligent than he lets on. I am building a relationship with him, but I do not know I can trust him yet."

"We must find my daughter, the sooner the better. Without her horse she is most certainly in harm's way." King Poma's voice is measured but breaks at the end. "We cannot, absolutely <u>not</u> allow this capture to continue." He looks around at each individual carefully as if gathering information on how he should tell them. "I would lief surrender myself for her return, but I do not believe it is the soundest measure to take for our people. They need a leader."

"No, sir,"

"No, Your Majesty"

"Absolutely not!"

The king holds up his hand for all to quiet. "I want ideas now! How to end this. Do we forfeit land? Do we crush them with force? Do we offer a trade? Our weapons for our daughter? Do they know who she is?"

"We strike now and capture their leader for a trade. We fight all night in the darkness if it will bring back my sister," Roark demands.

The king holds his hand up once more. "Fighting at night is not practical with their use of caged drazons. We would certainly suffer gruesome casualties.

"Who is willing to be a messenger and tell them we want to negotiate?"

"Sir," please let me do my job, I think I can bring about a successful return if you will let me," Alatoi says. Her voice is the most conciliatory anyone has ever heard her speak.

"Alatoi, I'm not sure how you can help at this point. If she falls into the wrong hands, she may already be dead, or worse."

"I know Your Majesty, but I doubt it. They will certainly know she is someone special. She was not wearing the royal seal on her clothing, and thank the One True God, they did not capture her horse, but I know she always wears a locket with the royal seal on it. If she is captured, she can use this to identify herself if needed, or keep it concealed should it be detrimental."

"I cannot sit here and wait for ransom. We must do something now!"

"Then send me to make inquiries."

The king takes his sword and stabs the ground forcefully with it, which causes it to sing with reverberation and sway back and forth as if to mock him.

"I will give you three men to take with you in your stealth. I give you only until the evening star sets, then we raid those somas sonts with all ferocity tonight. Shawt to the drazons."

"Respectfully sir, I am better off alone. You send me with others, and I will be discovered for who I really am. Send me with a sturdy horse and a mulfang with bags of grain on it where I can conceal weapons instead. If I find Princess Ali, I will send the animal back to you. If there is a red scarf tied to his mane, you will know I have found her, if there is a green scarf, you must start a raid immediately."

"That is not much time," Roark's voice comes out with a quiet whistle.

"It's all you've got Alatoi. Need I remind you of the importance of your mission?" The king grabs at his sword, pulls it from the ground and swings it toward the sky.

85-You Lie!

It is not until Alatoi is almost to the enemy's encampment, when she notices she is being followed. With the time constraint, she has been riding hard forcing the mulfang to keep up, which is not in its nature. Occasionally the animal plants its feet stubbornly, sending Alatoi into a rage of cursing. Finally, she stops and gets a stick to beat it with. When she looks behind her, she sees Ali's Matong horse, Elita, racing after her, sometimes springing into the air to pass over obstructive bushes or fallen trees.

Shawxa! That is all I need right now. There is no time to stop and argue with that horse. It seems to have a mind of its own.

With the stick in her hand, the mulfang is more compliant and she draws further away from the loose horse arriving at the enemy camp without her unofficial escort. Alatoi lets her Omi persona wash over her becoming the person she needs to be.

Rather than look for Yani, she decides to start with Omlhen Dargle the officer she has become intimate with. He is busy in the command tent discussing something, she can tell by his distinctive voice, which sounds more like a dog's bark than human. She walks past the tent slowly, shielded between her horse and the mulfang, but there is no talk of capturing a valuable female warrior.

She turns and begins to look around for Yani. She most often finds him near the dining hall tent, but today she has no time to waste, and he is not there. Curiously Alatoi hears a muffled whinny and sees the magical horse again stomping its foot impatiently on the edge of some nearby trees. Alatoi mounts her horse and slowly walks over toward, Elita, whose coat is gleaming in the bright afternoon light. The horse turns and walks off, goes a few paces, and then turns to look back to see if Alatoi is following her.

Alatoi looks around suspiciously, but no one seems to notice her. Following Elita for some way beyond the encampment, she becomes optimistic the horse knows what it is doing. She understands vaguely the horse is special, but does not know the full extent of what it means to be a Matong horse. Her only knowledge of the Matong is what she has been told. If she did manage to get past the heavily guarded doors of the Matong chamber, it would mean immediate death to anyone who was not a member of the Karda family.

On a lead behind her, the mulfang appears to be co-operating because of the slow pace and the stick in her hand. Alatoi certainly does not want to attract attention. She is almost out of sight of the camp when a rider races up to her.

"What are you doing?" Yani grins and hails her.

"Where have you been? I have been looking for you. I have an urgent need."

"Yes, what is it?"

Alatoi studies Yani, her blood suddenly runs cold, and she hesitates to ask him what he knows. *Can I trust him?*

"It must be about the female soldier who has your people turned upside-down."

"What do you know?"

Yani shrugs, "I was hoping you were going to tell me what you know. I just came from there and your head-quarters is buzzing with speculation."

Yani's version seems unlikely as such great care had been taken to keep Ali's disappearance confidential only to the leaders.

"I do not know what you are talking about," Alatoi lies. "Surely, if this were true, I would know about it. The Karda troops do contain some women, they are enormously proud of their inclusive policies, but I have heard nothing of this nature. They do not treat their female warriors with special favors. I think you may have been misled."

"I know this capture to be true. I have seen her"

"You lie!" Alatoi hisses.

"No, it's true I've seen her."

"Then prove it and take me to her."

Yani gives her a crushing smile which lights a spark of lust, but he does not yield his secret.

"I must go, I do not have time to deal with you now." She kicks her horse and tugs at the mulfong. She takes off parallel to where she last sighted the golden horse, not wanting to give her position away.

"Where are you going?" Yani calls. She thrusts her arm at him in a derogatory gesture and trots off in the opposite direction she had seen the horse go. After a while when Yani has traveled out of sight toward the enemy's encampment, Alatoi turns to try and catch up with Elita. As she rides hurriedly through the woods, she does not see the horse, but hears it whinny occasionally. It is like playing the childhood game of hot and cold.

When she finally comes upon a tiny cottage in a clearing, the Matong horse has led her to, Alatoi is disappointed to see Yani's horse.

86-Surprise Attack

Alatoi's instinct propels her toward the house. Princess Ali is surely in there, but there is no way of knowing without investigating for herself. There is no time to waste given King Poma's declaration, or she could stay there on the edge of the trees until nightfall, or perhaps Yani would leave. Alatoi starts to pull weapons out of the bags of grain and is tempted to tie the red scarf onto the mane of the mulfang. But then she realizes it would be better to send her own horse who would run fast and hard back to camp, whereas the mulfang, as obstinate as it was, might take its bloody time. It seems like a fair risk to take considering there are now two more horses potentially available.

Alatoi arms herself with one of the mirror shields to blind her opponent, but first she needs to look into the window and see if her instincts have guided her correctly. A twinge of doubt trickles down her spine as she takes the red scarf out and ties it onto the mane of her horse, not the mulfang. Creeping slowly toward the cottage without any nearby trees Alatoi hopes she is not detected. Despite the reflective properties of her enchanted shield Yani spots her as if he has been waiting for her.

"I wondered how long it would take you to get here." Yani opens the door and shouts as she approaches. "Come join the party, your friend and I are about to have tea and tolta."

Alatoi is now faced with how to walk up the steps of the front door and not be disarmed, or worse, by Ali's captor.

Yani holds his hands up in a peaceful gesture. "It's all right you can come in. I won't hurt you."

"Let me see the girl. Is she unharmed?"

"I knew she was valuable the minute I laid eyes on her." The intensity of his voice betrays his delight. "And no, I won't bring her out here, you have to come in."

Alatoi braces herself mentally for what her next move should be. "Wait, in my haste I forgot to tie my horse." She backs up slowly to the edge of the woods watching Yani carefully until she is within reach of her horse. Hopefully, she is shielded by enough trees he will not see what she does next. Giving her horse a healthy whack on the hind-quarters she sends him off.

"Aw Shawxa!" Alatoi shrieks.

"What happened?" Yani asks as she again approaches with a slight limp. "The cursed animal stepped on my foot, pulled loose, and took off."

Yani laughs at her casually as if their relationship is based on friendship not deception. "You really must come join us."

"You first," Alatoi points her sword at him and covers her heart with the shiny shield.

"Ah, you brought me another magic shield. That is how I captured this lass to begin with."

Alatoi does not take the bait, but concentrates on the small knife in her grasp behind the shield she carries and, how she is going to get it to Princess Ali when she enters the room.

To her great relief Ali appears unscathed. She is standing against the wall with her hands tied behind her back.

Alatoi nods to Ali and uses her sword tip to push back at Yani. "Untie her," she growls, but Yani only laughs.

"I think not."

"So, what is your plan? Why have you captured this woman?"

"And why have you come to her rescue? Is she someone special to you? Omlhen Dargle brags about your willingness to allow another woman into his bed with you."

"I do not even know her." Alatoi snarls. "I followed you here to see what you were up to. I could smell your mischief." Alatoi still stands stiffly close to the door not quite sure what her strategy should be. "I thought we agreed we are both profiting from this war, and we give tit for tat."

"Yes, but that was before I landed this big prize." Yani looks over at Ali, who has lowered her eyes to the floor so as to give off a defeated demeanor. "I think I will sell her to my King Brechnole. He must see first-hand how the Karda's regard their women with such disrespect by allowing them to participate in combat."

Alatoi holds back all the fiery words she wants to shout at this idiot, and instead spits at his feet. She immediately regrets it. The anger in his face gives her the sense he is going to lurch at her, but her sword still points his direction.

"You barchlar! Put down your sword or I will slash this woman's face."

"What a fool you would be to diminish her ransom." While keeping her sword raised and ready, Alatoi walks closer to Ali and pushes her chin up with the edge of her shield in a desultory manner. She spins around and as she does pushes the knife into the back of her trousers hoping Ali will be able to reach it with her bound hands. It is a risky move, the knife could drop to the floor, or perhaps Ali will not be able to reach it. At the same time, she dips her shield slightly in order to flash a blinding light into Yani's light-sensitive orange eyes. As she does so, Alatoi steps in closer to Ali, who is able to reach the knife.

"Hey, go easy with the shield, would you?"

"What is my share in this treasure?"

"It depends, you need to tell me her value, and then perhaps I will share her ransom with you."

Alatoi gives him a scornful look. "I need more assurance than your word."

Suddenly there is a huge commotion at the door and Ali's Matong steed, Elita, comes charging into the room snorting and whinnying as if she has wings. She knocks Yani over, and he grabs at Alatoi's ankle. Alatoi stomps on his wrist with her other boot, but then loses her balance, and falls to the floor. She keeps a firm grip on the sword and slashes toward him.

"Stop! Do not kill him," Ali shouts. "We need to question him."

It takes all of Alatoi's strength to keep the momentum of the miraculous sword, with its mysterious powers, from striking. Ali cuts through the sisal rope and rushes to assist Alatoi, but first slams her fist into Yani's face bloodying his nose. Elita is prancing wildly and taking up much of the space in the tiny room, as she snorts and kicks at Yani knocking him over again.

Ali holds her hand up to signal Elita to back off, helping the wounded Yani into a chair where they bind him with the same rope, he used on her.

87-The Point of Diminishing Returns

"We have no time to waste," Alatoi says generically to Ali. "There is a deadline for my return." She wants to divulge as little to Ali in front of Yani as possible, giving Ali a single finger in front of her closed lips, out of Yani's vision, to signal the necessity for discretion. They manage to force him to climb on the mulfang, where they tie him securely. If he slides out of the saddle on purpose, he is still attached to the saddle and his brains will be pummeled as they charge along the tundra, back to camp and out of enemy territory. Elita bears the two women, and nudges the mulfang with her muzzle, occasionally nipping at his hindquarters. There is a lot of whinnying as if Elita is cussing the obstinate animal, but the mulfang responds and breaks into a choppy gallop.

Yani's head hangs low as he bounces along, as if he has been swung like a doll by his hair and his neck has come unscrewed. By the time they arrive at Karda territory, a charge is already being assembled. Once they are spotted, Ali's royal guard swoops up beside and escorts them into the encampment. Yani is taken as a prisoner and the wheezing mulfang is allowed to drink his fill of water.

"I think this was random luck," Alatoi underscores the word luck with demonstrative hand motions. "If you allow Princess Ali back in the field, I will personally thrust this knife through my own heart!" King Poma looks at Alatoi trying to hide his amusement and nods slightly.

"Short of imprisonment I will not comply!" Ali strikes her words sharply across the tent. If they had been in the great hall at Compana, her words would have echoed across the expanse like the reverberations of a hammered gong.

"Ali," the king speaks softly but firmly to her. "You are not acting like a leader. You must think of your people first and your own *sava* last." Ali scowls, allowing her shoulders to drop, and decides to listen and not speak.

King Poma addresses all the high-ranking leaders assembled by meeting their eyes around the room as he speaks. "It is clear we have come to a point of diminishing returns. I reluctantly withdraw from battle and request you heroes finish the job we have begun. We shall depart at once."

"But I have just arrived," Roark says lacking a certain gusto in his proclamation.

"You have a newborn at home. You will see combat another day." Poma commands.

The walls around Ali seem to compress in on her; she has been restless and irritable since returning home. Memories of Fontar wash over her like scorched bath water, which turns the flesh rosy from too much heat. These painful memories rush in on her when she least expects them. Not even Robick's playful antics can seduce her into happiness.

To calm herself she goes for a ride on Elita at break-neck speed, but Fontar is not there, and the loneliness produces a sour taste in her mouth, which seeps up from the back of her throat. Instead of returning home, she guides Elita to Katara and like a magnet, is pulled to the Matong chamber. Ali throws herself on the floor and weeps. The stone floor is cold and damp, but it is soothing to her feverish body. She lays face down until her tears pool on the floor making her face puffy and soggy, then she pushes herself up to the orb's pulsing light.

Without touching it, she takes in the radiance of the Matong's power. Its power surges around her, and she hears the message it has to deliver.

MAKE KATARA YOUR HOME WITHOUT DE-LAY.

She looks up at what she now believes is a specious power and shouts "Why? Why did you let Fontar die?" It is the same question she has uttered a quantum number of times only to be rebuffed with silence.

YOUR JOURNEY IS LONG BUT YOU WILL PRE-VAIL. DO NOT DOUBT ME. The voice thunders in her head like a menacing pain pulsing inside her skull.

"Princess Ali are you okay?" A muffled voice comes through the heavy door. The security guards have strict orders not to open the door, under any circumstances, no matter what they hear inside.

Ali stands and tugs at her tunic, wiping her tears on her cheeks using the back of her hand and some of her sleeve she pulls down to sop up the unwanted signs of grief.

88-On the Move

Katara? Why must I move to Katara? Before leaving for her quarters at Compana, Ali seeks out her grandmother, Queen Mesa. She finds her sitting in an enormous cushy chair upholstered in a variety of lush and color-coordinated velvet prints. She has her three little white dogs, Mooshu, Motsie, and Poluun assembled in her lap. Queen Mesa is brushing them and cooing love words. Their eyes gleam with appreciation and unconditional love. The unexpected intimacy of the moment brings a smile of distraction to Ali's self-righteous state. She knocks lightly on the open door.

"Hi, can I come in?" She sits down across from her grandmother in a equally luxurious chair and allows the familiar surroundings to comfort her.

"What is that busy mind of yours telling you now?" Queen Mother Mesa asks Ali, sitting across from her, the same granddaughter who once crawled across this very floor and pulled herself up on the same chairs, to stand and wobble and stare.

Ali hesitates, but realizing the Matong will give her away to Queen Mesa soon, anyway, goes ahead and shares the Matong's decree. "It looks like I will be joining you here at Katara."

The news spreads across Mesa's face with the subtlety of a cloudless sunrise. She continues to brush her dogs and does not ruin the moment with her own personal delight. "I've been warned," She says coquettishly, toning her joy down to a mere smile.

"Really?"

"This huge place needs more smiling faces. I rattle around here like a lost feather in a whirlwind." She looks up from her grooming to meet Ali's eyes. "But I'm sure my comfort isn't the purpose of the Matong."

Ali sucks in her breath and lets it out with the power of a bellows. "I've become distraught. My faith in the Matong is…should I say waning?"

Queen Mesa looks at her granddaughter and touches her lightly on the arm. "My dear, you've been through a lot. It is only natural considering your circumstances. We all go through this at one time or another."

"You know! You are right." Ali fans her hands in the air. "It's as if I am caught in a never-ending loop of bad chotzwa. I am absolutely furious at the Matong, and have lost confidence in its powers." To give voice to her blasphemous rage gives her physical relief.

Queen Mesa squeezes her granddaughter and commiserates silently. Her own face mirrors Ali's mood.

Finally, she speaks. "The change will reinspire you perhaps. You can have the entire Voldar Wing. We won't even have to see each other if you do not want to."

"Robick will have fun playing with these guys," Ali leans over to pat them, and Mooshu jumps up in her lap, sneaking a quick lick in, giving Ali an uncomfortable smooch with her hot silken tongue.

"It is settled then." Ali stands up and Mooshu jumps down.

The move takes place quickly once Ali tells her mother, the only one disappointed in the exodus. "Galen lived over there before Kandar came along," Ali justifies. She is trying to have compassion, but it is hard to suppress her distaste for her mother's unusual pitch for drama.

"I need my own space, now as I am never to marry, I must pick up the pieces and ready myself for the crown."

Ali's words are like a knife thrusted into Aadya's heart, but she sucks her hurt inside, only emitting a quiet murmur of despair. "Who says you are never to marry?"

89-Diplomacy

Not two revolutions after the royals have returned home from battle, word is received the Omis want to negotiate an end to the fighting. Ali is still unpacking and making her new quarters her own when she receives the information.

Council is called, and while he was only there a brief time, it seems odd without Zolan present. "We shall invite the Omis here to Compana and show them the many advances we have made with our people. We need to organize legally their participation in our government," King Poma begins.

"I suggest we wine them and dine them for a few days," Queen Aadya says. "We have had great success with our hospitality as a negotiating tool."

King Poma frowns, "If it were only that easy, but I am sure you are correct. Treat them like family and let them know the benefits of joining us officially." These tidings bring everyone in the room into a state of mild disgust.

"We must also show them our power," Prince Bonder hammers his fist on the table for emphasis.

"Yes, Your Majesty," Roark does not use the personal expression of Father when in council. "We need to show them our might and power. Our beautiful gardens and intelligent women, will not seduce them." Everyone in the room chuckles at Roark's comment while most agree.

"Let us send word they should expect to stay three days with us at least." Poma's voice is low and even. "It's settled. Form committees for the negotiations and for the celebratory events. They will be mostly housed in Katara with the most gracious of accommodations to comfort them." As soon as the words leave his mouth, Poma is reminded Ali now resides there, and he gives her a questioning look.

She nods to him. "It's fine. We will be heavily guarded, and it will give me a first-hand experience with them."

"You are quite brave for someone who was held hostage by them."

"Fortunately, it was a brief detainment," she says distractedly.

On the day the Omis march into the Katara compound, all the people, with trepidations vibrating through the collective bloodstream of the community like a milchup avoiding a poisonous cavatar, gather to watch a handful of high-ranking Omis parade in on black horses foaming at the mouth, and biting at their bits in defiance as if they have been tethered too long and need to seek vengeance. It is an intimidating display. King Poma, Aadya on his right with Princes Bonder, Parsa, and Ali; Roark and the recently appointed captain of Defense, Chartain Corflu, Fontar's replacement are on his left.

The Omi King Brechnole balances a sneer and a smile on his lips, while his subordinates stay on their angry horses. Brechnole dismounts to greet King Poma who is now walking toward him. It is a historic moment and Alatoi is on a nearby balcony quickly sketching the players. The two leaders eye each other with nothing more than a powerful handshake. Finally, King Poma says, "welcome."

Brechnole nods slightly. And then spits out appropriate words in response. It is an awkward moment, but they both are acutely aware they must exude confidence.

"Allow my grooms to take your horses and stable them. I would have you shown to your rooms so you may refresh."

Brechnole nods no. "We are ready to begin talks." As if he cannot imagine being here one moment more than he must.

"Very well, my guards will take your horses, stable them, and you may join us for peace talks immediately." Poma gestures for Brechnole to join him by his side, and they strike up a simple conversation about the ride in, the weather, and ask about each other's families as they proceed to the great hall where they will begin their peace talks. The others dismount and follow them.

As all the players gather, refreshments come streaming in by the platter full. The Omis hesitate to fill their plates and drink, but they have been riding since before dawn and are hungry. Prince Olafar, Brechnole's son is the first to sit and eat, encouraging his brothers, two of them, and his brothers in war, to be seated and relax.

"We will be better negotiators if we have eaten, than if we are starving mad." He has been known by his family, since childhood, to have a hearty appetite. Roark takes the place beside him and before another Omi can join him on his left, Ali slips in, smiles, and welcomes him.

"Is this part of your strategy to entice me with food then surround me?"

Ali laughs, "Of course not, I am Ali, and this is my brother Roark, we only want to welcome you. Roark can leave if you are uncomfortable." Aghast a woman should be so forward, Olafar looks suspiciously at Ali. Already struck by her beauty, he does not have a smart comeback.

Accustomed to using his charm to seduce any woman he wants; the brawny soldier is caught without a word to say to this puzzling princess. "The food here is very tasty." He manages to mutter.

Sensing his awkwardness, Ali seizes the opportunity to advance her stand for peace. "There are many benefits to our people working together as one."

"Let the man digest his food, Ali."

Roark's familiarity with his sister causes Olafar to become more relaxed. Others are beginning to eat also.

King Poma stands. "Please everyone eat and we will begin our talks, after we have filled our stomachs. Later tonight we have prepared a little entertainment for you. We are hoping to provide you with a respite after our diligent peace negotiations."

As the afternoon proceeds, no one rushes into specifics. Instead, the two groups swap stories and begin to acclimate to each other. Some strike up conversations about how it was many revolutions ago when the Omis and Kardians were not so separate.

90-Dining with the Enemy

Despite her opinion Prince Olafar is a spoiled, pompous ass, and his compatriots bullies, and his father a monster, Ali dresses in a golden lantéé floor-length gown to dazzle. Its fluidity is surreal as it floats around her body, which is typically layered in practical riding wear. She has both her beauty and her brains as weapons, and Omis will be unsuspecting of the latter, especially if she disarms them first with her beauty. There are no Omi women present to balance the severity of their men, further holding the Omis at a disadvantage by the Karda family and their people; a detriment begun on the battlefield.

As the piercing music of the stringed instruments peals through the great hall, Ali drinks from the golden goblet she has been brought and tastes the rich red wine. A chill runs up her spine lodging itself on her upper lip. There is a frosty swirl forming on top of the wine, which wanders like a ground fog. She looks for the server who has brought it to her to ask him what it is, but he is gone into the crowd. She has been seated on the left of her father with Olafar in between them. King Brechnole is on her father's right and on the other side of him is Aadya. Father and son are surrounded by Karda royalty. *There's no escaping us!* She laughs at the joke she has told herself.

Out of respect and necessity, King Poma spends most of the evening engaging King Brechnole in conversation.

This leaves most of the weight of the conversation with Prince Olafar, up to Ali.

"Princess Ali, I understand you participated in the recent fighting. Is it odd for you to be here sitting next to your enemy?" The pressure to be diplomatic boils and simmers as Ali smiles noncommittally stalling for the appropriate words.

"Of course, this is all very strange, but I have to admire your father's courage to submit to peace talks."

"Is it true you were captured by an Omi?"

Doubt now floods Ali with confusing currents. She does not want to talk about the incident. Most of her people do not even know of it, and yet there are murmurs of indiscriminate origins, surfacing around her brief capture. She laughs from a deep and abiding fear of this becoming known, "What an obscure idea. Where did you hear something like that?"

"You hold Yani Yacovickle behind bars."

"Who is Yani Yacovickle?" She stares straight into his shining eyes which are the turquoise color of the luminous Sonatong River.

Her steady gaze disarms him slightly and he loses his train of thought.

"Oh he's, a somewhat of a scoundrel we keep around for unsavory tasks."

She struggles not to let her voice betray her bitterness. "I do not know the nature of his imprisonment, but perhaps he was detained for his participation in one of your unsavory tasks."

Olafar laughs and turns in his chair to meet her gaze more directly. "I salute you Princess Ali, future queen of all of Merth." He says raising his goblet to her. His tone wanders between respect, conciliatory remorse, and vengeance. Ali's skin crawls with trepidation, and they continue to spar convivially through dinner until the plates are cleared and speeches are made.

King Poma stands to greet the Omis with a toast. "I welcome all of you attending and thank you for your bravery in doing so." He pauses, looking down at the table before him. "We begin these peace talks in the morning, not to take over your lands and your people, but to enfold them into our society of prosperity—with all credit going to my dear wife, Queen Aadya," he turns to acknowledge her. "We have been on a most needed cultural journey to include our women into the realm of decisions and discussion. At this time, peace is our telic, but our society has much to offer."

King Brechnole peers up at King Poma as his counterpart speaks, his posture is stiff and unforgiving, but he stands to address the gathering as he is invited to.

"We are the mighty Omi, we have always been on the fringes of Merth, but today we join together with those who, in the not-so-distant past, have been our allies. Though we tried and failed to conquer, we will embrace the advantages of our distant kin, taking what we see fit, while maintaining our own cultural character." His small band of selected leaders whistle and stomp, making as much noise as possible.

"Aye, we are the powerful Omi," one warrior stands and urges his companions to rise and make noise in a display of raucous bravado.

King Poma quickly stands to reinforce his authority. "Now we have feasted, please join us in a celebration of joy, music, and dance."

"This may be too much of the king to ask the women of Katara, but perhaps you will join me in starting the festivities?" Ali asks of Olafar.

The prince smiles at her and apologizes, "I'm not much up on the dancing steps of your people."

"Do not worry, dance leaders will take us out onto the floor and all we have to do is follow their lead, and others will join us. It will show the others we are cooperating in all things." Ali nods at the dance escorts who come and get them to begin the dancing.

91-The Art of the Dance

"You are not such a bad dancer after all," Ali teases the prince who, when the dance routine collects the participants up into couples again, tries to provide engaging conversation remaining confident with his way with the ladies, but it is all she can do not to grimace at his attempts to be congenial. *Clearly, he only relates to women as breeders and not as equals.*

The peace accord starts out with a bad turn the very next morning when King Brechnole lashes out at King Poma. "You offer us nothing we do not already have."

"What is it you would most like to achieve in these talks?" Poma asks.

"We won't relinquish our rights to self-govern. We are not going to become a puppet of your reign."

King Poma eyes his opponent and thinks of what Aadya has planted in his brain. *The idea to relate to one another on a more safe and social experience.* "King Brechnole, may I suggest we take a break from these talks, just you and I and a small group of our elite advisers, and let the bulton counters work out the details? I am sure they can come up with a satisfactory peace accord palatable to all."

King Brechnole grimaces, but thinking of how much more enjoyable it would be to hunt than sit in these uncomfortable chairs, eyes King Poma and grunts. "My ass says it would be a much better idea," and then he lets go a guttural laugh. The stocky king stands at least two hands shorter than Poma, but he has a way of puffing out his chest which makes him appear larger than he is.

It takes them a painfully long time to even select who should go and who should stay, but it boils down to four guards each and no others.

"We want recompense for our dead soldiers," Prince Olafar demands as he slams his fist on the massive table.

"You want us to pay you because you attacked our people? I think not." Roark struggles to keep his voice to a reasonable level as he rises from his chair instinctively.

Prince Olafar's shoulders buckle up, his expression oozing with resentment. Prince Bonder intercedes. "May I make a suggestion here? As a territory of our kingdom, you will be levied taxes, at reasonable amounts, and in return you will receive services and goods, such as improved roads, water accessible to all, and education for all at no expense. You are new to our ways, let us show you the ledgers which will reveal how much you will benefit from your alliance with us. I have asked our royal artist to help us draw up the way this works. If we could adjourn for a brief interval, serve you food, and provide some inspiring entertainment perhaps."

Even if all concessions were made in the Omi's favor it would never be enough, Olafar admits to himself. "You people keep stalling and feeding us, can't we get on with it?"

As he makes his tactless statement, he realizes the depth of their losses on the battlefield and acknowledges to himself their resources have been severely depleted. People are going hungry back home. This occurred during the disastrous, historic Olfang dynasty uprising. History would repeat itself.

While they enjoy a recess, Olafar and his crew are entertained with singing and dancing by the Merry Martas troupe. Alatoi slips in and out with the needed documents, careful not to draw attention to herself. She has not discussed with anyone her fears about being discovered as an Omi woman, a person of no significance in her own land, but here in Katara, a most important and useful asset.

When the negotiators reassemble later in the afternoon, Prince Olafar has his finance minister ready to pore over the financials submitted by the Karda family. Also, present for the first time is Prince Olafar's youngest brother, somewhat of an enigma. When he enters the room Ali feels herself being pulled toward him as if by a strong magnetic pulse, and she has the strange sensation he can read her thoughts. Prince Tildyn's nearly white hair is unusual for someone his age. Cropped short, it stands straight up on the top of his head in what looks like wind-blown tufts. A curious style for sure, but on him it is awkwardly engaging. His pale blue garments, stand out against the muddy brown of the Omi soldiers

leather armor, reinforced with metal bandalos for protection.

Even Prince Tildyn's accent is slightly off from the
other Omis, especially his brothers, who speak a wran-
gled patois of their language with spare words thrown in,
perhaps from the ancient languages. When he walks his
movements are fluid, as if he floats, rather than steps, to
make his way across the room. Ali is curious to find out
more about this newly introduced brother.

92-Building Trust

"What a remarkable weapon! The shot came out of nowhere." It is the first positive thing Brechnole has said all day. King Poma has found his sullen company quite tedious, and without anyone save his protection detail; there is little conversation going on despite the purpose of the mission to hunt and bond over putting food on the table. King Poma gazes down at his wrists, where the solid dart has come from. "Oh, these wrist darts are about the only weapon I can outshoot my wife with. She is very skilled at hunting."

King Brechnole's bushy eyebrows go up in an arch. "You mean Queen Aadya is skilled with weaponry?"

"Indeed, she is. She defeats me every time at the bow and arrow and is especially skilled with the crossbow."

Brechnole seems to want to say something but holds back. Then he chuckles and whistles softly. "I guess it could be quite dangerous around your household if you let your women be armed." King Poma lets out a heavy breath as he remounts after picking up the colorful game bird off the ground. "Sir, I do not think you are ready yet to have a detailed conversation with my wife on this topic." He grins as he swings around to mount his horse. "It's best you stick with the weather on that one."

Brechnole frowns. He is completely flummoxed by the situation he finds himself in.

When the hunting party returns to Katara, several bucks weigh down the horses as well as a sizable collection of fowl including poltas, gheehas, and a rare cotel, which King Poma regrets was shot by Brechnole, but they had to praise his kill despite the bird's imperiled status.

Aadya greets them cheerfully. "It certainly looks like a successful hunt; we shall fill the tables tonight with your hard-earned bounty. Poma gives her a look as if he is in dire need of sympathy.

IT IS BEEN A LONG DAY

She gives him a knowing smile and merely bows her head softly to Brechnole. "When shall we get to meet the women of Omi?" she asks

Brechnole thinks about his young bride at home, his third wife to date, and what a dull creature she is, but having been a doldar most her life, she is extremely talented in the bedroom. And for her talents he tolerates her inexperience in matters of state. Having her meet this amazing woman, who practically shimmers when she speaks, he is ashamed to reconcile such a meeting, even in his thoughts.

Brechnole bows his head with respect, and mutters, "In due time, Your Majesty."

"I would like to invite an envoy here of your women. We are eager to share our knowledge and skills with them."

Suddenly this woman of light makes him feel weak. He stammers out, "Soon, very soon."

"Aadya my dear, please allow us to refresh before the night's festivities. I'm sure King Brechnole would like to bathe."

"Actually, if you do not mind, I'd like you and I to go back to the bargaining table and see where we are."

"Of course, let us go."

SHAWZA I AM SO TIRED OF THIS MAN.

Aadya smiles sympathetically at him. YOU MAY NOT REST UNTIL THE PEACE TALKS ARE CONCLUDED. YOU ARE DOING AN EXEMPLARY JOB, DO NOT DISPARE NOW.

"I will see you later then." He lets out a subdued sigh and kisses her on the cheek. The unexpected intimate kiss, in the midst of his critical duties, softens her heart, and her mind drifts to a time when they were younger and how utterly smitten, she had been of him.

93-A Conversation

The Omis linger in the halls of Katara much longer than anyone would have suspected. After the first few awkward days when negotiations created a natural surplus of tension, like static in the air before a storm, they seem to relax and enjoy the diversions their hosts keep offering.

Ali experiences unwanted pressure from King Brechnole and his son Prince Olafar, through veiled remarks, as if there might be some interest in the two of them creating an alliance through marriage, but the harder Olafar presses her, the more she becomes repelled by him. She reassures herself in the knowledge of the Matong, there was still someone for her who would be her "Cup of Light," or she still wishes, even if she is not ready for such a resolution. Despite her hopes, the Matong continues to torture her with silence on the topic.

It is at a chance meeting where Princess Ali literally runs into Prince Tildyn, as she playfully dashes though the hall with Robick, and runs into him as she rounds a corner. Both startled, Ali laughs. "Oh, please forgive me. I did not mean to offend." Prince Tildyn, who has proven to be one of few words, appears awkwardly pleased to have met her in the hall with the opportunity to interact. He reaches his hand out to grasp hers not knowing of the inappropriateness of it. Surprised, she makes a conscious effort not to recoil.

"The fault is mine, I assure you." But the energy she feels at his touching her, the tingling now, climbing up her spine awakens in her something she has not felt since Fontar. It frightens her, *he is an Omi after all.*

"May I take this opportunity to converse with you?"

"Yes, of course."

"Shall we take a walk outside in the beautiful courtyard I awaken to every morning?"

"There is one closer through these doors," she points.

They sit on a wooden bench facing a nearby stream and settle in.

"So, tell me about yourself," she begins.

He lowers his chin a bit. "I am nothing like my brothers, if that is what you are wondering."

Taken aback slightly, she pulls back to meet his gaze. "No, I can readily see for myself you are greatly set apart from them."

"I have a different mother."

"I see."

"It is of no consequence; she was not an Omi. Some say she was from another place altogether. But she is gone now."

"Dead?"

"Yes, although we say she has passed over the bridge."

"We have a similar saying here, but it is more of a compliment. If someone is amazing or does something miraculous, we say they have crossed the bridge—the bridge between the two moons, of course."

"Yes, I know what the bridge is."

"Anyway, it has been suggested some of us remain here at court to build relationships with our, ah, new partners."

"Yes, I have been privy to all the negotiations."

He smiles and again lowers his head, then looks into her eyes directly. "Yes, of course. This is my way of suggesting I might be a member of such a delegation."

Checking herself she is not sure what to say. "I can tell you a number of people who I hope shall not stay."

His gentle smile springs forth as he takes her hand. "Prince Tildyn, it is our custom not to touch the royals. Is it not also your custom?"

He lets go of her hand as gently as if it were made of glass. "Please, I had no intention of impropriety."

"It's a minor infraction, but if you must know, had my personal guards been closer, they might have flashed their swords at you." Ever since her capture, she has been more cautious. She turns to look behind her, wondering where they are. Despite the conflicting directives she has given them recently, to give her space and to tighten perimeters with the Omis housed at Katara, they have done fairly well to keep her safe without smothering her. She looks around and there are two by the doors at a distance. Still, she sits with the enemy in a private conversation but senses no threat. In fact, Prince Tildyn's presence feels weirdly comforting.

94-Building Bridges

Moon Date – Clovis 213

The friendship between Princess Ali and Prince Tildyn becomes a model for what may be possible between the two factions of the Karda and the Omi. It is no surprise when he invites her to visit his homeland for a brief holiday.

"Do you know what a logistics nightmare this will be?" Roark scolds and her father frowns.

"It will be difficult to protect you. You have already been held captive by them before. Have you not forgotten?" Queen Aadya all but shouts.

"It's been more than two revolutions since we have made peace with them. We have all kinds of intermingling of our two states." Ali remarks, though doubt still settles upon her in a heavy wave.

"Let us plan the upcoming holiday festivities to be here as an excuse to invite them back for an extended stay." Aadya looks into her daughter's eyes empathetic to her doubt, now building like slow growing mold within her. "Just because you were invited does not mean you should go. I know you and Prince Tildyn have become close, but really Ali, you have your duties here to consider."

Even as her mother speaks, Ali is comforted by her reasoning, however flimsy.

When Ali declines Tilydyn's invite, she sees for the first time the anger seething beneath his soft facade. "But why would you listen to your family? You have always shown me your independence. Is our relationship all a lie? A false alliance you have created for the 'looks' of it? Are the Omi really supposed to trust you when you are this shallow, so resistant to our culture?"

"Tildyn, please, this is not something to get upset about. I am heir to the throne and as such cannot indulge in every whim I have."

"You left your home to fight us." She looks at his now twisted face and does not see the same person she has come to adore.

"We were defending our home, the lands you would take from us, our people you were killing!" Her voice grows in intensity, as she verbally defends her actions.

"Well," Prince Tildyn smooths his light-gray leggings and tries to compose himself. "I should probably take leave of Katara and return home. I have a life there to resume."

"I thought you found your family distasteful in their hostile ways." Prince Tildyn looks at her and pulls a smile back up on his face. "Forgive me lovely Ali," He takes her hand in his and kisses it. It tickles where his warm lips have touched, and she allows him this indiscretion. "But it is time for me to go."

"As you wish," she answers him softly, not able to completely hide her disappointment.

Later as she watches the two moons of Merth rise, Ali mourns her loss of Tilydn's company, even before he has left. He had been a friend the likes of she had never known before. Now he was leaving in the morning, she wonders if she had been too open with him, too honest with her optimism to share the wonders of her culture. Had she shared too much?

She did go to see him and his escort detail leave. Many Omi people now made Karda their home, and he had a large following of his people who were equally disappointed to see him go. Perhaps emboldened by his presence, they would no longer have a high-ranking Omi to represent their needs, though they all recognized, especially the women, how much better it was to live in Karda underneath the 'flag of truth' as the royal banner had become to be known.

After Tyldn's departure, Ali goes to the Matong to take solace, and upon reaching the door of the hallowed chamber, runs into her sister Galen, the healer.

"Sister, you look disturbed."

Shaking off her remorse, Ali smiles. "No, just said goodbye to Tyldn."

"Oh, I know how fond you were of him."

"He wanted me to visit Omi as his guest, but everyone thought it ill-advised." Galen puts her hand on Ali's arm and pulls her close to hug her. Even this simple gesture is healing to Ali, who knows her sister must be stingy with her hugs as anyone, but her husband and children deplete her abilities for healing with even a slight touch.

"I am going to pray with the Matong and find my way again.

"Then I depart, motherhood calls."

Upon entering the warm chamber Ali has an unusual back and forth conversation with the mighty orb.

YOU HAVE HAD A PERFECT OPPORTUNITY TO KNOW YOUR ENEMY WHOM YOU BEFRIENDED. BE WARNED HE WOULD HAVE ENTERED THIS CHAMBER IF I HAD NOT BLOWN HIM BACK.

Ali was stunned. Tyldn had mentioned he would like to visit the Matong with her once, when she first began to know him, but because she warned him it would be his death he never broached the subject again.

I HAVE GIVEN YOU EVERY OPPORTUNITY TO PREPARE YOURSELF FOR LEADERSHIP, BUT YOU RESIST. SOON YOU WILL HAVE ANOTHER LOSS AND YOU MUST PREPARE FOR THE INEVITABLE.

What a vile messenger of the One True God. Why do we follow?

The pedestal beneath the orb begins to shake and the orb lights up with lightning bolts within. I KNOW ALL YOUR THOUGHTS. PREPARE AND GET READY!

95-The Cup of Light Continues to Elude Her

Moon Date – Clovis 214

For the next revolution, Ali spends her time looking over her shoulder for what might manifest itself as tragedy in her life, based on the Matong's warning, but it never seems to come. Ali is now at the age, if she were a peasant like her mother once was, she would practically be considered too old to marry. *The Cup of Light does not appear as the Matong once promised.*

Led by the king and queen's commitment to build their nation strong, and to lead all into progress, there have been many exchanges of goods and services between the Karda, the Dupes, and the Omis.

"We will be able to access the sky someday like the birds do," Roark was known to say as he pursued scientific theories with his group of rising-star scientists. "Then we will finally be able to search the 'Immense' and have the knowledge of the moons at our disposal."

But no matter how she throws herself into her work, Ali longs for the companionship and the touch of a man. The taboos for her as heir-apparent are too great for her to void, so she stays celibate. She allows herself to flirt, which only leads to frustration for herself and her male friends.

"There must be some way to distract myself from these terrible longings!" she declares to Galen one day. "I have not broken down and allowed myself the pleasures of the flesh, but it's absolutely killing me. What can I do?"

Galen, who has noticed her sister's tendency of late to imbibe in too much drink, has already been giving this some thought. "I will mix some herbs for you to take. Come to my house this afternoon and I will have them ready."

As Ali's horse, Elita, pounds the path in a mad gallop toward Compana and Galen and Kandar's house, Ali relishes the wind in her hair and a wild rush of lascivious thoughts picturing her would be suitors naked or in thrust with her. The power of her horse beneath her mocks her and her unsettling lust until she pulls up with a jerk at the door of her wise and wonderful sister.

"Is there a way to be one with a man without getting with child?" She asks the minute they are alone.

It is hard for Galen not to let a smile rip across her face. "Ali, drink this and drink it now." She hands a golden goblet to her, swollen with the intoxicating aroma of clive and chloe.

"Seriously, am I too innocent?"

"First of all, yes, of course there is a way to be physically intimate with a man without getting pregnant, but it is very tricky and ill-advised as nearly all sexual activity leads to the final act between man and woman.

"Maybe I should abdicate like you did and let Roark become king. He is dying to take on the role."

"No! Do not ever speak of that again. First of all, you are going to be the first Descendant Queen of our people. You are a perfect choice."

Galen searches her soul, remembering how it was for her before Kandar. "I have perhaps, a solution, a temporary one, and I really know I shouldn't propose this. You must promise me you won't fall in love with this man."

"What, what is it? You speak of?"

"I have a patient, a beautiful, and kind man, who was married at one time, but his wife has died, and I know he is sterile. It was the tragedy of their marriage as they both wanted children but were never able to conceive."

"But it could have been her body which was unable to conceive."

"You are correct, but they came to me and asked me to test him, which we can do. And it was he who did not have the seed enough to conceive although he was virile in all other ways."

Ali clutches her hands to her heart in anticipation of what Galen is going to say. "So, would he be willing?"

Galen holds back another deep smile, limiting herself for Ali's sake. "My dear sister, you are beautiful and 'champing at the bit' as the stable boys would say. Drink this now. See how it works for you and we will proceed from there."

The effect is almost instant. Ali sits down in a chair beside Galen and lets out a long breathe from the bottom of her diaphragm. "The physical yearnings are gone, but I still want emotionally to be with a man."

Galen sighs, to look at her sister she can see the turmoil in her heart, her longing to be complete through marriage and to have children. Not everyone had this deep need for connection so fulfilling for herself, but most did. Even her scruffy little brother Roark had found someone willing to put up with him and bear his children.

"I do not like doing this, I know the Matong will send your Cup of Light one of these days, but until then, this may be a way to distract you from the intense disappointment you are living."

She turns and pulls out more herbs and places them into a small drawstring pouch. "I will send Martyl to you tonight, after the castle has settled down. Before he gets there, make some tea from these herbs and drink it. It will allow you to follow your desires without the distraction of love. This liaison can never lead to love. You will one day be united with your Cup of Light and marry. Now go before I change my mind."

On the ride back, Ali finds herself apathetic, she lets Elita pause and eat grass. Something she would normally not allow the disciplined horse to do. She stops at a stream, strips off her clothes, and dives into the icy water hoping it will calm her. Her mind wanders to the time with Fontar on the Sonnatong River at the Rainbow bluffs, and she lets her hands graze across her belly, until she touches herself and allows her mind to let loose her lust. *So much for Galen's potion.* She laughs, dresses, and returns to her castle to dine with her Grandmother Mesa before retiring to her chambers.

96-A Night of Bliss

Having drunk the tea, Ali is surprised at how her heart pounds. *I should be more indifferent like I was this afternoon.* But when Martyl enters her chambers, her mind spins with anticipation.

"Princess Ali, your sister assured me this is what you wanted," he says taking her hand and kissing it.

"Yes, it's strange to say the least, but there are many constraints on me, I cannot continue forever waiting for 'the Cup of Light.'"

"Galen explained. I am honored to be here with you. You are a stunning beauty."

"You are too, by the One True God look at you!" She declares as he pulls his loose linen tunic over his head. He is muscular, but not too broad and big, rather svelte and compact, but also solid. She cannot stop looking at his bare chest.

"Please, let us have wine first." She sits down on the bed and pours a rich pontou wine from a carafe on the bedside table. The heavy crystal stemware twinkles in the dim light. He sits down beside her and touches her hesitantly; softly pulling her long curls gently back behind her shoulder. She shudders. *Do not back out now* she warns herself. Handing her wineglass to him, she sits up, and pulls back the silken brocade cover to reveal midnight blue sheets, also glimmering in the flickering light of several candles. She takes her crystal stemmed glass back from him, and swallows the remaining wine. Setting down her glass, she pulls off her linen lace garment and crawls under the covers. The silken sheets tantalize her bare body, and he slips in beside her after pulling his pants off. There is no hiding his desire for her, and she allows him to entangle himself in her body. They persist for hours with fluid motions, slippery tongues, and deep, penetrating kisses.

When the cold hard light of the morning star slashes oppressively into the room, Ali panics. He is still there with her. She lets her fingers wander across his shoulders and marvels at his muscles as if he is the first man she has ever seen. But there is no attachment, like what she had with Fontar, only curiosity for what else there might be. A deep satisfaction grows inside of her. She will never be the same. *If and when the 'Cup of Light' shows up, he will not be the first, but it is okay. I will be a ruler someday. Why should I be more constrained than a man in my place?*

Ali shakes him. "You must awaken, the castle is beginning to crawl with life. You must not be discovered in my bed." But it is too late, the maids are already preparing her morning bath. "Quick, out on the veranda!" She grabs his clothes and shoves them at him.

When he is gone, she is disappointed she has treated him rudely. *But surely, he understands the ground rules. We will have to talk and be clear the next time I see him. Hopefully tonight.*

"Your father requests you ride with him today. He has had the hounds prepared for a hunt." There is much excitement in the air. Ali is nervous the handmaidens will notice something unusual about her as if they could tell by looking at her, she had spent the night with a man.

She rushes into the bathing tub and Robick bounds in to check on her. She wonders why he did not bark last night at Martyl, but then quickly gets distracted by the soothing sensation of the handmaidens scrubbing her back.

She smiles thinking about Martyl struggling to get off the veranda without being seen. As she remembers the events of the night before she is astonished how quickly he had her into bed. A smile, one not meant for anyone else other than herself, creeps upon her. *It is probably best; I might have backed out had he gone slower.*

97-The Chase

What was meant as a spontaneous event, with only a few chosen family members, grows into a larger crowd of Kardans. It is the fine weather, and the promise of a feast afterward, which draws the neighbors and their kin. King Poma does not mind, it is a great opportunity to be with his people. Queen Aadya already had plans to speak at an educational lecture, but Prince Bonder, Prince Parsa, Prince Roark, and Galen's husband, Kandar are all present. Galen would never kill an animal and was too busy anyway. The family would all gather later for the feast.

"Father looks blissful, does he not? He's truly in his element." Ali mentions to Roark as they make their way to the starting point of the hunt. Her horse side steps with anticipation of the jumps they will make, and the hard ride as they chase after hounds, who are chasing after a diminutive molaton, whose fluffy fur makes up half its size. If the poor animal is caught, he will become the signature dish of their feast. The animal's sumptuous coat will be awarded to the hunter who shoots him; and likely would become a warm muffler, or a collar on a winter coat.

All the flags used to mark and alert hunters locations are brought out for display, and local musicians play a brief cantata before the hunt begins. The sound of the horns will be used to signal the start of the race.

Mingling among the crowd is Alatoi with her sketch book to document the games, she watches children playing, and tries to capture their motions as they run and chase. Even the street vendors have appeared, hawking their items to the growing crowd.

"We have the advantage, those of us who ride Matong horses," Roark tells Faynyl as she lifts Borzok up to him to ride around with his dad for a minute. "But that is okay, it was supposed to be a small family hunt."

Ali stares at Borzok and is strangely engaged with his childish movements while Roark playfully rides him around in a tight circle. It is as if she is seeing a child for the first time. Her mind wanders to the activities of last night and she wonders if she will ever be a mother. Her sessions with the Matong have not revealed her future and it pains her to imagine a life without a mate. Roark hands Borzok down to his mother, and she and Roark make their way to the starting line.

When the horns begin to start heralding the beginning of the race, Elita's prancing becomes more pronounced, her hooves barely touching the ground. A murmur grows among the crowd as the molaton, with an identifying red ribbon collar, is ceremoniously released. The music plays to the action with the delay of the hounds being loosed, and eventually the hunters and their horses are allowed to take off in pursuit.

With the wind now in her face and the rhythm of the pounding horse's hooves beneath her, Ali readily admits it is not the ridiculous pursuit of the animal, but the magnificence of the chase which draws them all out on a fine day like this.

"Wheee," she whistles under her breath as Elita takes the first hurdle. The beauty of the horses, with their tails raised high, manes flowing in the rush of air, and as hooves pound the fertile earth, ripping at the soft green grass while hurling it in clods behind them, is totally seductive. It is a sensation of freedom, like no other as they take hurdle after hurdle. The dogs baying, the flag bearers with their colorful flags, and her father the king, leading the pack on his magnificent black stallion, Brodynhelm, is like a streaming banner in her mind.

As they thunder toward the finish, still miles away, Elita's ears prick up followed almost instantly by a sickening squealing. Numerous riders turn their horses and Ali jerks Elita to a sudden stop. Something has happened up ahead.

98-How Can This Be?

"Father, Father!" She hears herself screaming. She is not aware of how she even came to be at his side. Brodynhelm is on the ground thrashing, his heavy fetlocked hooves precariously close to King Poma's body, as the horse struggles to get his footing in the sand. Several men are working to calm the majestic steed, but the horse is more heartbroken than hurt, and he will not stop panicking and whinnying as if he were being beaten with a stout pole. Ali looks in horror at a sharp branch protruding through her father's chest. His lifeblood pulses in spurts around it, and his eyes are open, but no sign of life escapes his pale gray eyes. The scene is too similar to her loss of Fontar, and Ali cannot contain her grief. Her screams heighten Brodynhelm's panic, and her logical side tells her she needs to remain calm, or the inconsolable horse's hooves will strike her father, further decimating his body. She chokes her agony down with the maximum control she can muster and puts herself in harm's way to reach for the reins of Brodynhelm. As she begins to talk the horse down, stroking his muzzle as if she were talking to Robick, she gets the the Matong-blessed horse calm enough to make a lunge for harder ground. Pulling himself upright Brodynhelm shakes so hard his saddle stirrups flap, but when he sees his master laying there, his body pierced by the deadly limb, the horse stomps the ground and lets out high-pitched screams as he tosses and arches his neck obsessively, pulling angrily against the control of the reins.

Ali hands the reins back to one of the riders standing nearby and drops to the ground again to be near her father. By this time other family members have gathered, and as she hears someone shout to summon Galen, she knows in her heart, Galen will not be able to save him. Then a silent scream runs like ice through her veins echoing the horse's terror, she realizes it is up to her now to lead the kingdom, something she is not ready for, but something she was born to. How many times had her father encouraged her, she would be ready, this enormous responsibility would be hers some day and she must prepare.

It is like everyone is sleepwalking as they tend to the matters of picking up the pieces of this fateful accident. Known for his skills as an expert horseman, warrior, marksman, and a great and caring leader. The people are in disbelief this has happened to their king.

The joyous crowd of the morning has turned to a sluggish sea of muddied souls as people speak in hushed tones, if at all. Like aimless creatures the people now limp through the actions needed to be taken to clean up this disastrous turn of events. Brodynhelm is the only one who can be helped. Galen lays on her hands and he has been calmed from destroying himself by charging at trees, and bucking and kicking aimlessly, but he would never be the same; nor would Aadya, who does not utter a word for a full rotation of the moons.

Ali resists advisers who insist the coronation must be huge and public, but in the end, she acquiesces, knowing they are right. Without Aadya to help her, Ali depends heavily on her father's brothers, Parsa and Bonder, who are remarkably loyal to her. "I should think they would be eager to steal the throne from me," she tells Galen one afternoon shortly before she is to be crowned.

"They are honest men who honor their brother's decree."

Ali spins on her heels. "I need mother's help. I need her strength!"

Galen casts her eyes down to the freshly swept stone floor and touches her sister's arm gently. "There is no time to waste. We do not know how long she will be in this cave of sorrow."

"Can't you heal her? Bring her around? It is heartbreaking to see her this way, her and that sorrowful horse who won't stop trying to pound his way out of his stall."

"I know, I told the grooms to let him loose and let him run his anger off, but they are afraid Brodynhelm is so distraught, he might run off a cliff or something."

99-Grieving

"**O**kay big boy, you and I are going to take a ride." Ali tells Brodynhelm as she strokes his glistening black coat. She has had to saddle and bridle him herself as the horse will not let anyone else touch him. For her, the stallion is maintaining an edgy peace as he vibrates with energy and nervous prancing. Still, she moves slowly and determinedly, hoping this contact with her father's horse, using the very saddle he rode into his death, she might gain some peace before tomorrow when she would be crowned queen of all of Merth.

The groomsmen feel they are not serving her well and watch her guardedly as she mounts and walks off on the possessed horse. Ali is as surprised as anyone to see Brodynhelm is cooperating.

They walk for a long while before Ali asks the horse to canter, which he does gratefully, ready to release his jittery grief. For whole moments, Ali forgets her troubles as she enjoys the rhythm of the horse's powerful gait. With the wind pushing its way into each breath she takes, and the afternoon starlight beaming softly down to light the way, she is as connected to her father as if he were there riding with her. For the first time since his death, she does not see the horrid image of him impaled by a *flowkin tree branch!*

They ride on the edge of bountiful fields and down several dirt roads until she stops in a secluded spot where she might rest and meditate, knowing her entourage guarding her, will keep their distance, but not let her out of their sight. When she sees a bed of feathery grass protected from the wind by a small escarpment, she dismounts and lies down feeling sleepy for the first time in many days. Laying her head on a soft growth of moss she allows her thoughts to loosen and as she relaxes, falls asleep. Brodynhelm, feasting on the soft grass, moves closer, his velvety horse lips searching for the most tender blades of grass in frenetic munching. When he draws close enough, he gently nuzzles her and whickers softly.

Half conscious, Ali inhales the warmth of Brodynhelm's grassy breath and feels his soft muzzle against her cheek. Then the sound of her father's voice comes to her projected into her mind.

YOU SHALL DO FINE MY DAUGHTER. DO NOT FEAR. YOU WILL BE A GREAT LEADER AND YOU SOON SHALL HAVE SOMEONE TO SHARE YOUR LIFE WITH. BE READY TO BEHOLD THE CUP OF LIGHT.

Ali jumps up, not sure of what she has just perceived inside her own head. Her sudden movement startles Brodynhelm, and his head snaps up jingling the beautifully ornamented bridle he wears. There has been no word from the Matong concerning her finding the Cup of Light, the Matong's promise to her for a mate, but this surprising message, delivered prophetically in her dreams, fills her with a sliver of promise. The losses in her life mount, first Fontar, now her father, *when does it end?*

Ali looks to the sky and observes the afternoon star is close to setting. The hues of violet, magenta, and oranges stretch across the sky. She knows if she does not return soon, people will worry. She whistles to her guard captain to let him know they can join her in riding back to the stable.

"I appreciate your respect for my privacy on this particular day before my coronation," she tells Wylnym.

"Of course, my queen."

"But you can't call me queen until tomorrow," she scolds while still flashing him a warm smile.

"Just practicing," he says.

100-The Prophecy

Ali concedes to make a brief appearance at dinner, despite her family's grief they must show support and strength to the kingdom. Their combined sorrow, at the sudden death of the king, feels like an oppressive dampness which hangs in the air before a storm. Ali always knew her crowning would be at her father's death, but this is not what she expected. She assumed he would live many more years as a vibrant king and leader. Queen Aadya is the only family member absent at the great hall, but she has sent word, she will be present tomorrow at the ceremony.

Katara is filled with guests from the far reaches of the kingdom including the Dupes and Omis and even the small tribe of Wokutons, from the swampy regions, are represented. It is awkward for Ali to greet Prince Tyldn. At first, he is friendly, but when she does not ask him to sit beside her at the head table, he has a hard time disguising his bitterness.

Ali is able to give the required welcome speech but tells her guests she will address all Merthians tomorrow after she is crowned. The food on her plate is like an obstacle she must hurdle, but she is unable to do more than push her delicious meal around the ornate silver plate. Finally, she sees her opportunity to excuse herself, she can either walk past Prince Tildyn, or leave the other way, which seems cowardly.

"Forgive me prince, we have much catching up to do." She touches him gently on the shoulder. Perhaps you can come back and visit later, after the coronation. I must leave now for my Asencia." He manages a feeble smile which clearly does not match his mood.

Ali's Asencia maids follow close behind and there is no way he can detain her. Ali's head throbs and she is anxious for her prayer vigil to begin, hoping she will receive the guidance she desperately desires. The ring! She remembers the ring she will be blessed to wear tomorrow. *Father would never tell me everything about it. Perhaps I shall find the answers in the revelations of the ring.*

The prayers go on for most of the night in the chapel near the Matong. When Ali hears a ringing in her ears like a distant whistle; it is a call by the Matong. Without saying a word to her prayer group, she gets up and goes into the Matong chamber. For the first time she has ever experienced, the Matong does not speak, but hums comfortingly to her as she embraces it with her palms. Not wanting to let go until she has received guidance she is discharged from her grasp with a slight push. Startled she tries to touch it again, but this time she receives a minor tingling shock. She is tired and leaves discouraged, hoping to catch a short nap before being awakened for the preparations of the ceremony. The Ascenia maidens follow her silently and take her to her bed. She sits limply as if in a trance as they dress her in a silken sheath and lay her down into the lush bed dressed in pearly linens and piled deep with billowy pillows.

In her dreams the Cup of Light comes to her, she cannot see his face, but he hands her a small bundle. It is a baby. *It is a baby? But why does this man hand me a baby?* Many other incidences occur in her dreams during the night, but upon waking the only vision she remembers is of the baby she held in her arms. It is a little girl, and she will be loved by all Merthians.

###

Books by this Author

Beyond: A Tale of Discovery on the Other Side of Life

Imagine a world where ghosts can be seen (but not heard) on computer screens via artificial intelligence and the collaboration of 'seeing' dogs. Follow the story of Laura Haskell, a fantasy writer, and her beautiful white German Shepherd, Cloud.

Laura is a successful author who needs to get sober. She lives in a haunted hotel in San Francisco with Cloud, who can see the ghosts. When Sean Wilson appears in her life, everything changes.

Ghosts have puzzled the living for as long as humans have walked the earth. Beyond takes the reader on a journey which reconciles the questions of their plausibility. Sean and his crew revolutionize how ghostly apparitions are perceived through the use of Artificial Intelligence. This leads to discovering who Laura's mysterious grandfather was and sparks an unlikely romance between Laura and Sean, but will they stay together?

As Laura sobers up her life changes for the better. She finishes the book she has been struggling with, captures Sean's heart, and has a faceoff with an Etheric Revenant. Once the family ghosts have been identified, the ratings for Sean's reality ghost show skyrocket and Cloud becomes famous, creating a new set of challenges.

Readers are in for a rollercoaster ride as they suspend their belief and get to know Cloud and his unique perspective as well as the ghost of Laura's eccentric grandmother who once was a celebrated Madam, serving the elite gentlemen of San Francisco. If you are one who enjoys a fast paced, exhilarating read with mind-expanding ideas presented in a skillfully written and entertaining fashion, then this book is for you.

If you enjoyed the *Two Moons of Merth*, please write a review at https://www.amazon.com/review/create-review/?ie=UTF8&channel=glance-detail&asin=0578818183